Sam

-Want to Hear a Secret?-

by Iain Rob Wright

SalGad Publishing Group

Sam

ISBN-13: 978-1478272960
ISBN-10: 1478272961

Cover art by Stephen Bryant
Edited by Faith Kauwe
Interior design by Iain Rob Wright!

www.iainrobwright.com

Give feedback on the book at:
iain.robert.wright@hotmail.co.uk

Twitter: @iainrobwright

Second Edition

Printed in the U.S.A

To Sally,
My best friend and constant companion.

Want to Hear a Secret?

"Hell is empty and all the devils are here."

— William Shakespeare

"My bed was Shaking, I can't go to sleep."

— Regan MacNeil, The Exorcist (1973), Warner Brothers

Chapter 1

"**H**e's a scam artist!"

Tim Golding faced his accuser. The silver-haired man was tall and wiry like a tree, but Tim wasn't going to be insulted. "Sir," he said flatly, "it was your wife who contacted me. If you'd like me to leave, I shall. I'd rather be watching The X Files, anyway."

The woman pleaded from the back of the room. "No, please. Help us."

Tim could see the trauma on the her face, and after ten years in the business, you could detect the bullshitters. Charcoal bags beneath the woman's eyes were proof enough of her sleepless nights.

"Okay," he said, relenting. "Why don't you tell me what's been happening around here."

The woman's face almost crumbled into sobs, but she forced a weary smile. She led Tim into the plushly carpeted dining room where a set of leather-backed chairs tucked against a polished oak table. Tim slid out a chair and plonked himself down. The silver-haired man sat too, but made no secret of his cynicism, huffing and puffing with every breath.

Okay, asshole, I get it. Thought Tim. You think I'm a fraud, and you're a tough guy that won't get scammed. If only you knew the truth, buddy...

Tim clasped his slender hands together on the table and gave his most reassuring smile. The woman had taken the chair opposite and was staring at him. He started with the obvious question. "When did this all start?"

The lights in the room flickered.

The woman whimpered, but the husband was quick to offer an explanation. "Dodgy wiring. Happens all the time."

Tim nodded and focused on the man's wife. He waited for her to begin her story, and when she did so, she spoke in mousy, timid tones. "It started about a month ago, when our dog, Buster, brought something home."

Tim glanced around the room. No evidence of a dog. No family pictures featuring a pooch. No pet bed in the corner. The room was devoid of anything except the table and chairs.

"You have a dog?" Tim asked.

The woman shook her head and swallowed loudly. "No, not anymore."

"Stupid mutt got himself trapped in our fishpond," the husband added.

Tears welled up in the wife's eyes. "Buster was our little Jack Russell. We were always on at him to stay out of the pond, but he would never listen. He was always taking a dip, like it was his own personal swimming pool, but then, a few weeks ago, I went into the garden one morning and... and I found him dead at the bottom of the pond. His collar caught on a root sticking through the pond's lining. He couldn't get his head back above the water." The woman sobbed. Tim handed her a handkerchief from the breast pocket of his scuffed leather jacket.

"Nice," said the husband. "Is that one of your props?"

Tim ignored him. "So tell me," he asked the wife. "What was it your dog brought home before he... passed?"

"A bone."

Tim raised a coppery eyebrow. "Human?"

"Of course not," the husband snapped. "Don't you think we would have called the police?"

Tim shrugged. "You could have, for all I know. Until your wife called me, I didn't know a thing about you."

The husband scoffed. "I'll bet."

"It was a chicken bone," said the woman. "At least I think. Small and sharp."

Tim rubbed at the stubble on his chin. If it had been a human bone it might have summoned a poltergeist... but a chicken bone...?

Never heard of a malevolent chicken spirit before. Chicken bones were often used in Voodoo rituals, but he'd never seen the practice this side of the Atlantic.

He cleared his throat and got to the meat of the mystery. "So what was the first... occurrence?"

The wife took a breath and shuddered. "It was during the night while we were sleeping. About 3AM."

"What woke you?"

"The light in the bedroom was on. I've never known my husband to turn the light on during the night, but I assumed it must have been an accident. I got up to turn it off, but realised the hallway light was on too. We always turn off the lights before going to bed, so it was strange. Every single light in the house had been switched on—even the lamps."

"Like I said," the husband chimed in. "Dodgy wiring."

Tim nodded, but was weary of the man's abrupt cynicism. An educated guess suggested the man was ex-military and liked being in control.

"Did anything else unusual happen that night?"

The wife shook her head. "I didn't sleep another wink, but it wasn't until the next day I knew something was wrong."

"Go on," said Tim.

"Well, the whole house became like the Arctic Circle for a start. I'm sure you can feel it."

Tim could.

"We have the heat on all the time, but it never does any good. One night I was so freezing that I decided to take a bath to warm up, but when I...." A short sob escaped her lips. "Sorry, just give me a second."

"Daft mare thinks she saw blood coming out the taps," said the husband.

Tim took a deep breath and made mental notes. Then he addressed the husband, staring directly into the man's steely blue eyes. "Did you see it yourself, sir?"

"Nothing but a bath full of water. It was probably just rust from the pipes. It's an old house."

Tim nodded, but disagreed internally. The house didn't look over twenty years old. Still, it wouldn't help to argue. People in need wanted allies not argument. "So how long after that did the dog die?"

"A few days," the wife answered. "Other weird things went on, but nothing like what happened to Buster. We buried him in the garden. That night, I was woken up again. All the lights were on, just like before, but this time there were noises. Buster barking from the garden. It sounds crazy, but I swear it was him. I know his bark. I ran into the garden in my nightie, and when I got there, he was hanging from the tree."

Tim leant forward over the table and paid close attention. "Hanging?" A tear dripped from the tip of the woman's nose. "From the old fern tree next to the pond. Hanging by his collar."

"Sick bloody kids," the husband spat.

Tim wasn't convinced. "This is a nice neighbourhood. Do you usually have a problem with youths?"

The husband shrugged. "There are no nice neighbourhoods anymore. Bloody country."

"Okay," said Tim. "I think I should take a look around. This may be someone's sick idea of a joke, but I won't know more until I conduct some experiments, starting with this room."

"Here we go," said the husband. "The theatrics begin."

Tim once again ignored him. He took off his trainers and climbed up onto the dinner table and pulled a small leather pouch from the back pocket of his jeans.

"What's that?" the husband demanded. "Another prop"

"A set of screwdrivers, all the ghostbusters have them. I'm going to take a gander at your dodgy wiring."

"Oh."

Tim investigated and surmised the original light fixture had been replaced with a modern studio rail containing multiple bulbs. He loosened the fixture until it was hanging by its wiring and then poked a finger inside.

"Be careful," said the wife. "The power's still on."

Tim tapped the green and yellow wire and the lights flickered on and off. "You have a loose switch wire. I'd suggest hiring a local electrician."

The husband frowned as if he'd been expecting a more fanciful explanation; one resulting with Tim charging him money.

Tim reached into his back pocket again and this time pulled out a spool of cotton. Unravelling about ten centimetres, he held it in the air. The tiny thread floated on a breeze, pointing towards the side of the room.

"Thar she blows," Tim muttered.

He knelt beside the skirting board and held his fingers out, feeling for air currents. It didn't take long to spot a hairline crack in the board. Frigid air flowed in from the outside. "You have a crack in the masonry, and it's letting in a draught. A good carpenter will sort it for you."

The husband grunted.

Tim clapped his hands together. "Right, shall we go take a look at that bathtub?"

The husband and wife led Tim upstairs. The light was already on in the bathroom and bled out beneath the closed door.

"Is this the bathroom?" Tim asked.

The couple nodded silently.

Tim grasped the doorknob and let himself in. The room was nicely decorated, with textured tiles with a modern suite. The room was a little sterile for Tim's taste, like a showroom at a DIY centre. It lacked the soapy odours and stray hairs of a well-used washroom. Tim pointed at the L-shaped bathtub. "This is where you say the tap ran with blood?"

The wife pointed. "It was coming out of the hot tap."

Tim leant over the tub and placed his hand on the tap that marked 'H' and turned it clockwise. Water cascaded in a steady torrent, and there was nothing strange about it. "All looks pretty fine to-"

The plumbing began to clank violently, and the hot tap rattled. A viscous stream of brown-red liquid ejected and began filling the tub.

"There," said the wife. "Just like that. It's blood!"

Tim placed his palm beneath the thick stream without hesitation. The mysterious substance mixed with the hot water from the tank and formed a warm syrup. He sniffed at it and then licked it.

The husband grimaced. "My God, man. What are you doing?"

"It's not blood. I don't know what it is, but it's not blood and it's not rust. Tastes kind of sweet."

"What do you suggest?" asked the wife nervously.

"A plumber." Tim washed his hand in the nearby basin. "Let me see where you found Buster."

The woman frowned for a moment, as if confused, but then she nodded. "Yes, okay."

The garden sat at the back of the house, lit by a pair of floodlights attached to the house. The pond sat fifteen-feet from the house. Tim expected to see koi or goldfish beneath the surface of the water, but he found it empty. The fern tree, from where the Jack Russell allegedly hanged, stood behind the pond.

"Buster was hanging from the top of the tree by his neck," the wife said. "The worst thing I've-"

Tim cut the woman off. "Where did you bury him?"

"What?"

Tim looked around the garden. The lawn was short and well kept. "You said you buried Buster in the garden. Could you show me?"

"You leave that dog be," said the husband. "My wife is upset enough."

"I don't want to dig the dog up, sir. I just want to know where you buried him."

The husband and wife stared at each other. It was as though they were trying to communicate without words. The husband eventually answered. "I-I can't remember where I buried him."

Tim smirked. "Really? That's what you're going with?"

"Look here," said the husband.

"No, you look. What are you up to? Why did you hire me? Are you looking to discredit me? Are you writing a book?"

"I don't know what you're talking about," cried the wife. "Why are you being like this?"

Tim turned on her. "And you, my dear, almost had me fooled. Bravo." He clapped his hands. "The loose wiring to make the lights flicker; broken skirting board to cause a draught; and probably food colouring in the water tank—all good stuff. What gave you away was the dog. This lawn is perfect. There's been no digging or burying in this garden. I don't even think this is your house; there's not a single photo of the two of you, or any toiletries in the bathroom. Your acting is good, but I think you failed in the setup. The age difference between you two is a little hard to buy as well. So, I ask you again: what are you two playing at?"

A carnivorous smirk crept across the husband's lips and he seemed to rise up another six inches.

Tim looked around the quiet garden and started to worry. Had his confrontation been a little brash, considering he was alone with two people who'd brought him there under false pretences? He was still yet to find out what those pretences were.

He had a feeling he was about to find out.

The husband pulled a phone from his jacket and dialled. After a few seconds, he spoke into the receiver. "What do you want me to do with him?"

Chapter 2

Angela Murs stared into the bottom of her whisky glass and felt her head spin. At forty years of age, she wondered if the time had come to spend her evenings some place other than grimy hangouts in the city.

Wolverhampton was a University town and its bars were packed most every night. Easy to disappear, easy to be alone amongst strangers. The bars were also student-prices-cheap and crammed full of eye candy. In fact, a slender young thing propped up the bar now. The brunette's legs stretched all the way to Heaven, beginning at a pair of pretty manicured feet in open heels. A tattoo of a rose punctuated the girl's left ankle and got Angela's juices flowing.

The girl was unlikely to be gay, but that didn't mean Angela couldn't appreciate the view. Most senior students knew Angela, and would direct any newly experimenting girls her way. As a result, she got more than her fair share of dalliances for a middle-aged ex-priest.

Amen.

Angela hadn't left the clergy because of her sexuality, although it had played a part. It had been to do with the Church itself. Years at the pulpit had shown her that the Church of England was a business run by hypocrites and bureaucrats. Its religious leaders couldn't even decide what they believed themselves most the time, let alone what doctrine everyone else should be following. Some priests supported homosexuality while others derided it. Some were kind, decent people who enjoyed a fag and a beer, while others were judgmental pricks who derided the slightest hint of being human. Over time, Angela had decided her fellow priests followed a path God would not condone. Three years ago now, she had quit to follow the Lord in her own way. Things hadn't turned out as she'd planned.

Even if God condoned homosexuality, Angela knew he didn't support her drunken debauchery. She wore Sin around her shoulders like a comfortable old cloak and had started to feel cold without it.

The slender brunette noticed Angela staring. She smiled politely, but awkwardness tainted her thin red lips. No doubt, she was wondering why a woman twice her age was eyeing her up.

"You from the University?" Angela asked.

The girl nodded. "I'm studying Creative Writing."

"You plan on being a writer?"

"I guess."

"Nice way to make a living, and you've already started drinking, so that's a good start. You made many friends yet?"

The girl's awkwardness grew and grew. Her bare shoulders narrowed. "A few. I should get back to them."

Angela watched the girl walk away without even ordering a drink. Had she become so creepy that strangers fled from her now?

Wow, that's good for my self-esteem.

Angela glanced around the bar and noted she was the oldest by far—a full two decades on some. A pathetic sight she must be, propping up the bar alone amongst a horde of horny teenagers. It was time to go home.

To a cold and empty bed.

Angela slid off her barstool and checked to make sure her feet were steady. She was drunk but capable, and her tolerance for whisky would put most wrestlers to shame. In fact, it was a rarity she ever got truly rat-arsed.

On her way to the pub's exit, she nodded to a group of lads she knew as regular. The grins on their faces might be from them commenting about how pathetic she was. Angela sighed and headed past them. Your degrees won't help you. The world is a cold and bitter place for everyone, no matter how many pieces of paper you have with your name on.

Outside, the frigid air hit her cheeks. April could go either way; sunny and dry or wet and damp. This evening was dry, but with a sharp chill. Angela headed towards Civic Hall to catch a taxi, which took her past St Peter's House. The looming cathedral towered over her as she strolled in the moonlight. She had the streets entirely to herself.

Wolverhampton lacked much in the way of greenery, but in the shadows of the evening, the modern red-bricked buildings were pleasant.

Angela took a set of steps downward, and in doing so noticed that someone walked behind her. Their footsteps echoed off the pavements. Their movement was hurried as if they sought to catch up with Angela.

Angela picked up pace.

The speed of the strangers' footsteps increased too.

Civic Hall was not far, and with it would be concert goers and taxis. Safety!

But Angela realised she wouldn't get there in time. The stranger would be upon her any second.

The footsteps quickened.

Angela bolted left into a side-street and broke into a run. Her thickset body was intolerant of exertion, so she huffed and puffed immediately. Knowing she couldn't win a straight pursuit, she slid into the alcoved entrance of a printing firm, hoping she'd done so quickly enough to lose her tail.

If they're even following me, thought Angela. I'm being paranoid.

Then why did they speed up when I did?

Angela remained where she was, panting in the alcove. The footsteps stopped. Were they trying to figure out where she went? Had she lost them?

Angela took a deep breath and held it before letting it out slowly. It was unlike her to get so rattled, but a bad feeling had descended over her at once and placed all of her senses on high alert. Was it just the booze messing with her head? Why on Earth would anybody be following her?

I'm nobody; just another drunk in a city full of them.

It was a full five minutes later when Angela's breathing returned to normal. Steeling her nerve, she stepped out of the alcove and back into the street. She was ready to head for the taxi rank and put the whole thing behind her. Instead she found herself face-to-face with two large men, who blocked her path and seemed ready to grab her at the first sign of her running.

"W-what the hell do you want?" she demanded. She could smell the acrid odour of their cologne. It stung the back of her throat.

"We'd like you to come with us, Reverend Murs. We need your help."

Chapter 3

Defying every ounce of sense she possessed, Angela allowed herself to be led to a black saloon parked in a nearby side street. The night was too dark, and her car knowledge too slim, to recognise the model, but it appeared expensive. The seats were soft leather. The dashboard was sleek with chrome.

"Will somebody tell me what this is about?" Angela demanded, feeling closed in as the car doors shut around her.

"We mean you no harm, Reverend," said the man in the front passenger seat. Young with dark hair.

"Let's stick to Angela, shall we? I'm not a vicar anymore."

"My apologies. To answer your question: I have no information to offer you, other than that my employer wishes to speak with you."

"Enough of the James Bond bollocks," Angela said, enjoying the flicker of surprise on the man's face. People were always shocked to hear a priest—excommunicated or otherwise—swear.

Like we're not human beings.

The front passenger twisted more to face her and nodded. "Look, Angela. We don't know why our boss wants to see you, but I believe it has something to do with certain skills you may have."

"What skills?"

"Exorcism."

"Let me the fuck out of here." Angela grabbed at the door handle but it was locked. "Let me out NOW!"

"Calm down, Angela. My employer just wants to speak with you."

"Your boss? Who?"

The driver was the one who spoke. He was older and his answers were snippier. "We can't tell you. Because of the nature of her business. She is a public figure and can't afford to have news of her personal affairs getting out. She is willing to pay you for your time whether you help her or not."

Angela closed her eyes and sighed. I'm not a priest anymore, but if somebody needs my help, can I really say no? I could use the money.

"Start the engine," she said.

The man in the passenger seat nodded happily. "Sure thing, Reverend."

"I already told you not to call me that. How long will this journey take, anyway?"

"We're heading to Warwickshire. Just over an hour."

"Then I hope you don't mind if I get a little shut eye and sober up."

"Be my guest."

Angela closed her eyes.

* * *

She awoke after what seemed like only a few minutes, but the driver informed her that she'd slept the entire way, snoring like a fluey goat. The saloon was currently zipping through country lanes, typical of Warwickshire's rural landscape. It had probably been the unevenness of the roads that stirred her from sleep. She'd spent time in Warwickshire before, covering a parish in Studley—a busy little hamlet with pubs galore. She'd enjoyed her time there.

"We're almost there, Angela," said the man in the passenger seat.

Angela checked her watch. Past eleven. "What am I going to do afterwards? It's late."

"Depending on what transpires, you can either stay at the house or we'll put you up in a nearby hotel and take you home in the morning."

A night in a hotel. Things are getting better. "Do either of you have any water up front?" she asked. "My mouth is as dry as a camel's arsehole."

The man in the passenger seat laughed while the driver cringed. The passenger opened the glove compartment and retrieved a half-finished bottle of spring water. Angela took it from him and finished it in one eager gulp, releasing a satisfied belch afterwards.

"Some fine manners you've got there," the driver commented.

"Bite me."

There was silence in the car for another ten minutes until the driver pulled onto a gravel driveway cut-in-half by an immense wrought iron fence. The saloon stopped in front of the gates and the driver pressed a button on a key fob hanging from the ignition. The heavy gates drew apart like curtains and allowed them access. The car continued up the drive, tyres crunching on gravel.

About a hundred metres up, the driver parked before a vast Georgian-style mansion. The building was a gargantuan square, with four floors of six windows. It wasn't far off being a palace. "I've stayed in worse, I suppose," said Angela.

The man in the passenger seat chuckled. "It's quite a place, isn't it?"

"If you mean a shrine to affluence and greed, then yes, it certainly is. How many people live here?"

"Just my employer and her son. There were various staff boarded here, but at the moment the place is pretty much empty."

"How the other half live, eh?"

"Indeed. Shall we?"

Angela rubbed at her face to wake herself up as much as possible and nodded. "Ready when you are, Jeeves."

The car door opened and Angela stepped out. The night was still chilly, the air fresh and crisp, cleaner than the industry-clogged air of Staffordshire. Angela found it interesting that the super-rich even got a nicer atmosphere than everybody else.

"We can go in through the main entrance," said her chaperone.

"How about you tell me your name," said Angela. "I've just driven fifty miles with you, after all."

The man smiled and offered his hand. "My name is Mike, but to be honest you won't have much to do with me. Graham and I—Graham's the sweetheart who drove us here—are glorified dogsbodies."

"Well, I'm pleased to meet you, dogsbody Mike. Can't say the same about Graham. The guy's a moody get."

Mike replied with a smile. "He's not that bad once you get to know him. I don't think he likes priests."

She shrugged. "I don't like priests either."

Mike nodded and swept an arm towards the house. "Shall we?"

They walked up the driveway and climbed a small set of stone steps. They led to a thick set of wooden doors. Angela didn't know what variety of wood they were cut from, but they were dark and intricately carved.

Mike pressed a button on an intercom beside the door. A brief burst of static. A voice floated out of the speaker. "Who is it?"

"Hey Frank. It's Mike. I have Rev... Miss Murs with me."

No reply except a buzz from the speaker. Mike turned the handle of one of the gigantic wooden doors and shoved it open with ease. Angela followed him inside and found herself inside a cavernous, marble-floored foyer. It looked more like a five-star hotel than a home.

Someone actually lives here?

A tall, silver-haired man appeared at the top of a wide staircase and started to descend. Dressed in an open white shirt and work trousers, he resembled an off duty police officer. "Thank you, Mike," the man said. "That will be all."

Mike nodded and went back outside. The other man—whom Angela assumed was Frank—took the final steps down and approached her in the foyer. He offered a thick-knuckled hand covered by scars—a fighter's hand.

"Hi," said Angela.

"Pleased to meet you, Miss Murs."

At least he didn't call me Reverend.

"Frank, I assume? Are you the person who wanted to see me?"

"The lady of the house will be down shortly," he said. "She has asked that I make you comfortable. I am Chief of House and I will look after your needs during your stay."

"If I stay."

"Of course. Now, can I get you anything?"

Angela shook her head and felt her vision spin. She wasn't completely sober yet. "Just somewhere to sit, please."

Frank nodded and led her to a small ante-chamber consisting of two plush sofas and little else. Two hours ago she'd been hanging around a student bar in

Wolverhampton; now she was sitting in a mansion about to meet some mysterious 'lady of the house' with more money than sense.

And there was the whole exorcism thing.

Angela had left the Church for many reasons, but deep down she feared being a part of the clergy as much as she disdained it. Afraid of confronting evil and having to tend to its victims.

I don't have the courage. Not anymore.

The blood soaking the walls of Angela's old church had been as much a spiritual death of her faith as it was a literal one for her parishioners. She hoped that one day they would demolish the church and build a goddamn Burger King on top of it.

"Miss Murs, I'm so grateful that you came." A slender woman appeared in front of Angela. "My name is Jessica Bell-Raymeady, wife of the late Joseph Raymeady."

Neither name meant anything to Angela, but she smiled. "Pleased to meet you, Ms Raymeady. I'm sorry for your loss... if it was recent?"

"Please, follow me," the woman said, ignoring the implied question. "We can grab ourselves a drink in the lounge."

Angela was wary of drinking again after sobering up, but if her host was partaking, perhaps there was no harm. She'd expected a toffee-nosed aristocrat to be the owner of the house, but Jessica didn't sound affluent at all—not common exactly, but neither was she posh. Her appearance gave the same casual impression as her speech—tatty jeans and a loose sweatshirt.

Angela followed Jessica into a lounge room hidden behind the main staircase. A piano stage and bar, lay inside, and many tables and chairs. It looked a lot like a cruise ship lounge and Angela wondered if it ever got used to its capacity.

"Take a seat, Angela. Do you mind if I call you Angela?"

"Would hate for you to call me anything else."

Jessica smiled, but it was a weary expression. "I'll fetch us some drinks. What's your tipple?"

"Scotch, if you have it?"

"I have a delightful bottle of Longmorn 16. Will that do?"

"Supermarket whisky is fine by me, but hey, whatever's going."

Jessica let out a sharp yelp of laughter. "To be honest with you, Angela, it all tastes the same to me as well. My husband was a connoisseur, but I'm happy with a bottle of plonk and a pizza. My husband was the one with breeding as I'm sure you can tell."

Angela smiled and wasn't just being polite. The woman was not what she'd expected. The surprise was more pleasant than disappointing. "I'm not exactly a Friesian myself."

Jessica disappeared behind the bar and returned a moment later to join Angela at one of the tables. Angela took a sip from the whisky and was unsurprised that it tasted like any other brand. In fact, she preferred the taste of the two-quid shot she'd downed back at the student bar.

Jessica sipped from a large glass of white wine and seemed lost in thought. The lights flickered for a second and a plink came from the piano in the corner. The lady of the house didn't appear to notice.

Angela tried to get the woman to come back to the conversation. Things had suddenly turned very sullen. "So what is all this about, Jessica?"

"My son, Angela. He's sick."

"Then you should call a doctor, not an alcoholic ex-priest."

Jessica laughed again. The same manic yelp. "Oh, believe me, there have been doctors galore. I've had half the NHS in and out of this house in the last six months. Psychiatrists, Paediatricians, Oncologists, GPs; enough to staff a hospital. None of them have done anything to help. My son keeps getting worse."

The lights flickered again.

Angela looked up at the ornate wall sconces, but kept her focus on the conversation. "What is wrong with your son exactly?"

"If only I knew, Angela. Sammie is such a sweet, energetic little boy, but about nine months ago he awoke in the night screaming and yelling about something being inside of him. My husband and I put it down to a bad dream, as one would of course, but the following morning Sammie became sickly and pale, as if he'd come down with some wretched flu. He's been like it ever since. Barely eats or sleeps."

Angela placed her whisky glass on the table. "I still don't see why that would make you seek me out."

"Because you were an exorcist for the Church of England. You performed over one hundred exorcisms, yes?"

Angela picked up her whisky again and took a large gulp that burned the back of her throat. "More like fifty in truth, but none of them were necessary. The church only conducts exorcisms in rare cases to bring people peace-of-mind, but those seeking the service are usually making excuses for other underlying problems; failing marriages, child abuse, thieving relatives. I've seen it all, believe me. Exorcism is nothing but a way for the Church to take advantage of people in the name of faith. They perform their rituals and flick their holy water, but it's a charade. I was a part of that charade, so I know, and nine times out of ten an exorcism is nothing but theatrics. You'd be better off using your money to find a medical specialist. Your son sounds ill."

Jessica smirked. "You said, 'nine times out of ten'. What about the one in ten that's more than mere theatrics?"

Angela sighed. "Scam artists, schizophrenia, unknown phenomena? Who knows? What are you getting at, Ms Raymeady?"

"I know about Jersey, Miss Murs."

Angela felt a chill.

"I know there's more to what went on than the papers reported. You've dealt with evil before. You know it exists."

Angela rose from her chair. "I'm very sorry, Ms Raymeady, but I made a mistake coming here."

Jessica reached out and grabbed her wrist, almond eyes pleading. "Just listen to what I have to say."

Angela sighed. She never could resist a plea for help—especially from a pretty lady her own age.

Damn it.

Angela sat back down.

The lights flickered again and the piano plinked.

Jessica smiled wearily. "Thank you."

Angela span her empty whisky glass in her hands. "Tell me what you need to so I can go."

Jessica sipped at her wine and got started. "Sammie has been sick since that nightmare—when he yelled about something inside him—but that's not everything. Sometimes it's like... like he's somebody else now; somebody older. He uses words he's never been taught and h-he swears. Such filthy language you wouldn't believe it. Then there are the accidents."

"Accidents?"

Jessica nodded. "There's a reason there's no staff here. The ones still in one piece left. Others were less fortunate. Our Head Chef, Nikolas, slipped carrying a pan of boiling pasta; Esme, the scullery maid, tumbled down the stairs and broke her neck like a twig; our gardener, Tom, lost two fingers to his own shears, and my husband... my husband hanged himself, which is something he would never have done. Joseph wasn't that kind of man."

"I've seen a lot of suicides in my time," said Angela. "Anyone can give up."

"With all due respect, Miss Murs, my late husband was Joseph Raymeady, son of Wesley Raymeady, founder of Black Remedy Corporation, the largest commercial entity in the world. My husband, like his father, was one of the wealthiest and most driven men in the history of our world. Suicide to him was the same as failure, and failure was incomprehensible to my husband."

Angela's eyes widened. "Your husband owned Black Remedy? Then there are a shitload of reasons he would have felt guilty enough to take his own life." Black Remedy had been indicted for everything from child labour to illegal arms dealing. Angela had read that the only reason they still continued to trade was because they bought government officials like other companies bought stationary. Angela realised she was talking to a widower and was horrified. "Wow, Ms Raymeady, please forgive me."

"It's quite all right. Black Remedy is not a company with the best of reputations. But Joseph sought to change all that. His maniacal father was in charge of the company until his welcomed death seven years ago. At the end he was insane, waffling on in his bed about building a company so large it crossed dimensions—or some nonsense or other. He was as egotistical as the Gods, the dreadful man. Since his death, Joseph has been trying to clean up Black Remedy. He donated six-hundred million pounds to charity after taking charge. That's more than the fifty preceding years combined. My husband was a good man, Angela, and he loved his family. He would not have hanged himself. There's just no way."

Angela saw nothing to gain by disputing the fact, even though she knew that suicide was often missed by the closest of friends and family. "I admit that the amount of accidents you've mentioned is unusual, but I don't see what makes you think an exorcism will help."

"I have my reasons." Jessica reached into her pocket and pulled out a small dog-eared notebook. She slid it across the table to Angela. "Open it."

Angela thumbed open the cover and looked inside. The pages were covered by the erratic scrawls of a child; crayoned pictures mostly, with a few pencilled words here and there. Many of the drawings contained symbols she didn't recognise and that in itself was disturbing. Most disturbing, however, was what the pencilled words read. TaInTedsoUL, NO EScaPe, He IS ABysS. SALvaTiOn PLeaSe.

"It's nonsense."

"Keep reading."

Angela's eyes fell across a word in the bottom-right corner of the page. Written in neat capitals so that it stood out amongst the messily scrawled words, was a simple plea: SAVE ME ANGELA MURS.

The lights flickered. The piano plinked.

Chapter 4

Following another sixteen-year-old whisky to calm her nerves, Angela agreed to stay at the manor until morning. The notebook with her name in was surely a fake, but she couldn't know for sure. Real or not, it had left her flustered. Something strange was going on, and it seemingly involved her. If these people are messing with me, I will make them regret it.

Frank came by the lounge at Jessica's request and took Angela up to the second floor, where he presented her a suite the size of a modest bedsit. There he left her to rest. The ancient four-poster bed occupying the centre of the room, mahogany corner struts climbing from floor to ceiling, looked incredibly inviting. Opposite the bed, a long window looked out on night's satin darkness.

Above the bed, hung a magnificent oil painting depicting a heavenly battle— Lucifer's war on God. Cherubim, with gossamer wings outspread, wielded spears brother against brother.

Jessica's late husband had clearly been one rich daddy, and it was oddly unsettling staying in the dead man's ancestral home. How could someone so blessed take their own lives?

Angela headed over to the en suite at the far side of the room where a cavernous antique bath stood. It looked like Heaven. But Angela settled for the faucet.

She stared into the mirror above the sink as she splashed steaming water onto her face. Her eyes were red and sunken; eyes of woman a decade older.

How did I end up like this? My life used to make sense, but now... Jessica wants me to exorcise her ten-year-old son, who is just reacting to the death of his father. I need the money. Booze doesn't buy itself.

There was a knock at the door. Angela left the en suite and crossed the bedroom. "Who is it?"

"Frank."

Angela opened the door to find Jessica's Chief of House standing with a tray full of sandwiches. His grim expression told that room service was not one of his normal duties.

"Ms Raymeady suggested you might be hungry."

Angela took the tray from the man eagerly. She wasn't much of an eater but had to admit the sandwiches looked good. Without further comment, Frank presumed to walk away, but she stopped him. "Can you come in for five minutes, please, Frank? I'd just like to ask you a few questions."

Frank seemed confused. His silver sideburns wrinkled. "I... yes, I suppose so." He marched past Angela and entered the bedroom. For a moment, it looked like he would take a seat on the bed, but he remained standing stiffly. "Questions about what, Miss Murs?"

Angela closed the bedroom door and faced the man. "What's been happening in this house?"

"I wish I knew. Things have been... tense. The accidents seem a few too many to be mere coincidences, but I'm sure that's all they are. Mindless superstition has got the better of everybody. The staff resigned."

"Not you though?"

"I have a duty to Ms Raymeady. Her late husband hired me almost ten years ago to look after his family. He was a good man and I intend to fulfil that role even after his death. Besides, I don't believe in any of what is being claimed. Mike and Graham don't either."

"You don't believe in Evil?"

Frank laughed. "Before I took this job, Miss Murs, I spent twelve years in the Army. I absolutely believe in Evil, but I do not believe in demons and monsters. The very notion of an exorcism is laughable."

"You're an atheist?"

"I believe in flesh and bone and what I can see in front of me; but what I believe is of no consequence. Ms Raymeady is concerned about young Samuel—and I agree that there is sufficient reason to be—so if you being here makes her feel at ease then I implore you to stay."

Angela smiled and decided that was as good a welcome she would get from the man. "Tell me about Jessica's son. Samuel, is it?"

Frank shrugged. "Sammie's a good kid. A little strange, but I'm sure that has more to do with his upbringing than anything else. A child isn't supposed to grow up in a place like this, surrounded by servants and a father away more often than he's home. I can't even remember the last time Samuel got to play with another child. Jessica loves her boy dearly, but sometimes this place is a little detached from reality. Samuel has no idea what real life is like. With his father dying, I'm not surprised he's acting out."

"Acting out?"

Frank shifted uncomfortably as if speaking freely was a betrayal of his employer. "The boy's been swearing a lot which is out of character, and he's suddenly gotten much smarter. I mean a lot smarter—like he's been reading a set of encyclopaedias. Plus, he seems to know all about current events, from politics to pop music, but all I ever see Samuel watching is South Park. Personally, I think he needs therapy more than anything else."

"I thought a psychiatrist had already seen the boy."

Frank nodded. "Several. They provided little help, but such things take time. If Ms Raymeady had been more patient, we may have seen a change."

Angela considered things for a moment. In her experience, claims of demonic possession often resulted in a verdict of mental illness. A psychiatrist was almost always more use than a priest was. But not always.

Once Angela had witnessed an event where all the psychiatrists in the world would not have helped, but it was a memory she put out of her mind whenever it threatened to materialise.

"Look," said Frank. "I have other duties to attend to, so if you don't mind...? If you need anything, dial 904 on the handset beside your bed. Otherwise, I will see you bright and early tomorrow. Ms Raymeady will want you to meet Samuel as soon as possible. If you decide to stay longer, Michael will drive to your home and gather some things for you. Try to sleep, Miss Murs, and don't worry if you hear anything in the night. Young Samuel has taken to causing commotion during the late hours, but it is nothing to worry about."

Angela shot the man a questioning look. "Commotion?"

"Samuel likes to quote the Bible, despite never having read it to my knowledge. He can get quite... animated."

"Could you do me a favour, Frank?"

"Of course."

"Write down the passages he mentions. It would be interesting to see which parts of the Bible he's focusing on."

Frank nodded. "As you wish."

The man exited.

Angela got ready for bed.

Chapter 5

Angela woke at 7AM according to her cheap CASIO. Once again, Frank was at her door again, this time with a tray of toast and orange juice. As usual, he wore the same begrudging expression.

"Hey, Frank. Did you get any sleep yourself last night?"

"Ten minutes here and there. Did you sleep well, Miss Murs?"

"Yes, thank you." She had slept like a log, bed so comfy she hated leaving it. She'd been mindful of listening out for Samuel's religious tirades in the night, but once she'd slid between the sheets, she had been unable to resist slumber.

"Ms Raymeady will meet you in the lounge where you shared a drink last night," said Frank. "Along with a colleague you'll be working with."

"A colleague?"

"A young man named Mr Golding. I'll leave you to find out about him directly. He's... enthusiastic, if little else."

Frank turned and walked back down the hallway.

Angela spent the next five minutes freshening up in the en suite before polishing off the toast and juice. Once ready, she exited the room and stepped into the hallway. The plush burgundy carpet stretched in both directions, turning a corner at each end. Angela couldn't remember which direction she'd come from the prior evening, so randomly went left. The corridor wrapped around and led to the main balcony and staircase from both sides, so if she had gone right she would have ended up in the same place.

Angela headed down, continuing past the first floor until she arrived on the well-lit ground floor. Her footsteps echoed as they fell upon marble. It was like being an ant inside a vast catacomb, doors and hallways leading off to a dozen places. Angela remembered the piano lounge at the rear of the staircase and made her way over to it. Through the door she could see Jessica and Frank sitting at a table together, along with a scruffy-haired ginger in his early twenties. When Angela stepped inside, all eyes fell upon her. Jessica smiled, but the expression was unconvincing.

"Can I get you anything to drink, Miss Murs?" Frank asked.

Angela waved a hand. "I'm fine, thanks. Ready to get started."

Jessica gestured to the scruffy-haired man. "Have you met Tim?"

"Not yet. I'm Angela. Pleased to meet you, Tim." She shook his hand and sat at the table.

He nodded to her, a jerking, bird-like motion. "Pleased to meet you, Angela. Look forward to working together."

"And how exactly will we be working together?"

"Tim here is a debunker," Frank explained. "He'll be using scientific methods to monitor Samuel's condition, while you use more..."

"Spiritual methods," Jessica finished.

"So you're here to regulate my religious mumbo jumbo, Tim? Is that it?"

He held his hands up, revealing his green t-shirt with a large picture of the Incredible Hulk upon it. "I'm just here for a pay cheque. I'll do my thing while you do yours."

Angela wasn't convinced. "And what is your thing?"

He shot her a goofy grin. "Science, baby! I've found that you can disprove ninety-nine per cent of 'phenomena' just by using everyday scientific procedures. People get freaked-out over the slightest thing and stop looking for the simple answers. Fear makes imaginations wild. But there's always a rational explanation. My job is to find it."

"At least we're in agreement there," said Angela. "I'm not here to provide any kind of catharsis or religious endorsement. I intend to be brutally honest about what I find."

Jessica nodded and took a sip from a glass of what looked like vodka. Angela realised the woman was tipsy. Her skittish pupils were a dead giveaway. "That's all I ask of you too, Angela. I just want to know what's wrong with my poor Sammie."

Angela eyed the glass of vodka, then looked away. "Perhaps we should go see the boy without further delay."

"Agreed," said Jessica, necking back her drink. "We'll see Sammie right now."

The group stood from the table and Jessica led them into the foyer. The woman's agitated gait bordered on erratic. Alcohol in her system so early in the morning probably didn't help.

"Are you okay, Miss Raymeady?" Angela asked.

Jessica stopped and faced them. "If you and Tim can't help us, I don't know what I'll do. I don't mean to place any additional pressure on you, but this may be my last chance before I go completely bonkers." She tittered anxiously.

Tim placed a hand on Jessica's shoulder. "We will do whatever we can to help you, Ms Raymeady."

Jessica wiped away a tear spilled down her cheek and laughed. "Christ, look at me. Enough dawdling. And please call me Jessica from now on."

The group climbed the stairs to the first floor and took a left past a full-sized suit of armour. A coat-of-arms adorned the wall beside it, featuring a black hillside with a white wolf howling up at the moon. Above it, something was written in Latin.

Angela recognised the quote from Timothy, verse 18 and spoke it aloud. "The labourer is worthy of his reward."

"You speak Latin?" Frank asked, sounding impressed.

"Some. I know my Bible verses at least."

"The Raymeady family motto," Jessica proclaimed. "My husband lived by those words. Hard work equals reward."

"What does the crest mean?" Tim asked.

"The wolf is an independent soul," Jessica explained. "The moon guides it through the darkness. Our family is blessed with vision and independence."

"Interesting," said Angela. "I think my crest would be a Jack Daniels label."

Tim guffawed.

Jessica pursed her lips.

"Okay," Frank said, unappreciative of the humour. "I hope you're both ready because Samuel's room is just up ahead."

The door at the end of the hall was covered in stickers and hanging notices, reading such things as: YOU KILLED KENNY and DESIGNATED FART ZONE. It was the typical bedroom door of a ten-year-old child, and inside the exquisite Georgian mansion seemed grossly out of place. Either side of the door, stood two magnificent bronze statues of four-winged cherubs firing bows into the air. "These statues are beautiful," she commented, running a finger over their flawless surfaces. "There's a painting above the bed you gave me that also features cherubs. They bring love and protection"

Jessica smiled proudly. "Cherubs are all seeing. The artist told me that to place them outside your door or above your bed is to have them watch over you and protect you."

"Beautiful," Angela said. "I once heard the very same thing."

"Samuel likes to draw during the mornings," Frank cut in, voice somewhat ominous. "Some of his pictures can be a little... disturbing. He may also draw pictures of us, which will be... unflattering. Try not to take offence."

"Don't worry," said Tim. "Nothing a caricature could highlight that I don't know about myself already. Besides, Gingers have no souls."

Frank stepped forward and opened the door. Jessica seemed unable to do so herself and remained at the back of the group as if fearing her own child.

Sammie's bedroom was long and wide, cluttered from wall to wall with assorted toys and discarded clothing. The walls were plastered with pinned-up drawings and dirty handprints. An unmade bed centred the room. The sheets were grimy and wet.

"You'll have to excuse the mess," said a new voice from the back of the room. "I'm afraid housekeeping has diminished since the staff left. My dear mother tries her best, but it simply never seems to get any cleaner in here. Quite bizarre."

Angela peered towards the back of the room and saw a pale, bony skeleton of a topless boy. Samuel sat at a desk facing away from them. The knuckles of his spine bulged through his skin as if it were tissue paper. The smell of sweat permeated the air, a musty fog.

"Samuel, I assume?" said Angela. "It's good to meet you. How are you doing today?"

The boy did not turn around, but spoke, "I've been better, Angela, but one mustn't complain. There are those with burdens far beyond my own."

Angela glanced back at the others, made eye contact with Frank ans whispered. "How does he know my name?"

Frank shrugged. "I never told him."

"Nor did I," said Jessica.

Angela asked the boy directly. "How do you know my name, Samuel?"

The boy twisted his neck to look at her. His black eyes bulged like a rodent's. He tapped a finger against his forehead, and with a knowing smile said, "There's someone in here that knows you."

Angela felt a wave break in her stomach. "Who?"

The boy grinned wider, teeth yellow pegs set into brown gums. "Why don't you all take a seat? I'd relish the company."

"You're sure this kid is just ten?" Tim whispered. "He sounds like Mr Darcy."

"It's one of the changes in him," Frank explained. "The doctors placed his mental age as that of a highly intelligent adult, but they could not explain it."

Angela took several steps forward and, for a fleeting moment, felt a buzzing in her head. It ended with a brief spell of dizziness which soon passed. Afterwards she wondered if she'd imagined the feeling completely.

Samuel had turned away again and was drawing something at his desk. The closer Angela got to the boy, the more she was horrified by his condition. Rapidly, she considered reporting Miss Raymeady for neglect. The child's body was little more than a flesh-strung skeleton, unfed, unwashed. She couldn't let her disgust show, though, until she was away from this place.

"How long has this other person been with you, Samuel?" Angela asked the boy, deciding to play along with whatever game he was playing. The make-believe of a neglected child. "Is it just you and them, or are there more?"

"There's just him," said Sammie, "Who came to visit me a short while ago and has remained since. Funny how one can become so attached to new friends, don't you think?"

"So you and he are friends?" Angela confirmed. "What does he do for you?"

Sammie smiled. "Oh, you know—this and that. He's shown me delights of which I never knew, opened doors once hidden. Shown me a world beyond my previous perception. He is glorious."

Angela raised her eyebrow and seized upon something. "Who is he?"

Sammie stood, so suddenly that Angela flinched. "Don't worry yourself about it, priest," he told her. "I'm sure you have more important things to brood over than the ramblings of a ten-year-old boy. Here, take this. I made it for you. And call me Sammie."

Angela walked up to the boy and took a sheet of paper from him. She turned it over and studied the crayoned image drawn on it.

It was impossible.

"I'm leaving," said Angela.

Chapter 6

Tim was confused by what happened. Whatever Sammie had drawn on the paper, it had freaked Angela out in a big way. She'd fled the room as if a fire licked at her heels. Tim couldn't say he blamed her. Sammie freaked him out, too. There was something very wrong with that kid.

After Angela fled the room, Jessica sent Frank to retrieve her, leaving Tim standing in the room alone with the boy and his mother. Jessica now approached Sammie cautiously, while Tim stayed back and examined the walls, which were plastered with paintings of monsters and scenes of bloody destruction. Tim could make out dragons, gargoyles, wolf-monsters, and other bizarre creatures; also crayoned depictions of human bodies torn asunder and mutilated on spikes. Severed fingers. Dangling eyeballs. It was like standing inside an inmate's cell at some high-security psych-ward, not a child's bedroom.

"You shouldn't be so rude, Jessica." Sammie chastised his mother as if he were the authority figure in the room. "You haven't introduced me to your new friend."

Jessica turned around to peer at Tim and seemed embarrassed. "Y-you're right, of course. Where are my manners? Sweetheart, this is Tim Golding. He's here to help Mommy with some things around the house."

"What things?" Sammie asked. There was a sliver of aggression in his ten-year-old voice.

"Just… things. You needn't worry."

Tim started his investigation and asked his first question. "Sammie, could you tell me what you drew for Angela?"

"I just drew what my friend told me to. He wanted her to remember."

"Remember what?"

"Perhaps you should ask Angela. I would be remiss discussing other people's business. Don't worry, I'm sure I'll find time to draw something for you too."

Tim frowned but then chuckled. "Funny, but that almost sounded like a threat."

"Don't be silly, Mr Golding. I'm just a child. What threat could I possibly be to you?"

That's to be determined, Tim thought as he battled a growing feeling of anxiety. The malodour in the room was like breathing in petrol fumes and made him nauseous. Something was not right about this boy. But there would be some rational explanation; there always was. Tim would find out what it was, like he always did.

Almost always.

"Do you mind if I had a quick word with Angela?" Tim asked Jessica. "Perhaps I can persuade her to stay."

Jessica nodded. "If you could, I would be most grateful."

"I'll try my best." Tim left the woman alone with her son, glad to get out of the cloying room. It had been getting hard to breathe.

He headed back over to the main hall and realised he didn't know where to find Angela. The house was vast and easy to get lost in, but he had a thought that could help. There was an intercom on the wall by the foyer's front doors, and Tim dialled 904 on the keypad. Frank picked up on the other end, no doubt answering from the handheld walkie-talkie Tim had seen clipped to the man's belt. "Hey, Frank. I wanted to talk to Angela. Are you with her…? You are? Great. Where can I find you both…? Okay, I'll see you there."

Tim hurried up the stairs.

According to Frank, Angela was on the second floor in the Friedkin Suite. Tim had no idea where that was, but he was sure he could find it. The house was a labyrinth, but he was gaining his bearings. It was more or less a giant cube with four floors of several rooms. How Jessica could stand to live in such a voluminous place, he did not know, as personally he would have gone crazy knocking around the mansion all by himself, even with a skeleton staff. Maybe she went crazy. She does seem a little on edge.

The Friedkin Suite lay up ahead. Tim rapped his knuckles against the door and saw it opened.

Frank blocked the entryway. "She won't come out of the bathroom,"

"Is she okay?"

He moved aside to allow Tim inside. "I don't know."

"Okay. I'll see if she'll speak to me."

Frank shrugged. "By all means. Ms Raymeady really would prefer it if you both stayed."

Tim walked across the bedroom and stood outside the door to what was most likely an en suite bathroom. He tapped against the wood and tried to speak through it. "Angela? It's Tim. I know we've only just met, but I was hoping we could talk. To be honest, I think there may be something going on in this house that's worth investigating. I'd prefer not having to figure it out on my own. I'd like your help."

Silence.

Tim tried harder. "There's something in your past making you want to run away—I have a past too—but if you leave, you're just letting yourself down. If you run, your past is making a coward out of you. If you stay...well, you'd have my thanks at the very least."

The door opened and Angela stepped out. She'd been crying. "You know nothing about me, or my past. Why are you so sure you want my help?"

"Because Sammie went out of his way to freak you out, and that means you know something about what's going on—whether you realise it or not. I don't even know how a ten-year-old boy can freak out a grown woman he's just met, but I think it means he doesn't want you here—which means that I do. I heard about your name being written in Sammie's diary. There's a conflict happening, because if Sammie summoned you, he certainly didn't act like he wanted you here just now. Whatever is going on involves you somehow, so I think we'll have a better chance of figuring things out if you stay."

"I can't stay."

"Look," said Tim. "I don't know what was in that drawing, but you're not alone. Whatever happens, I'll have your back. Let's figure things out and try to help this family, okay? Besides, Frank told me we will get paid a shitload of money, so what's to even think about?"

Angela looked close to tears again, but she held them at bay. She glanced towards the doorway. "Frank? Could you give us both a minute, please? If I'm going to stay here, then I'd like to know a little more about the man offering to watch my back."

Frank obliged and left the room. Tim stepped over to the four-poster bed and perched on the end of it. Angela pulled up a chair tucked beneath a vanity table and sat opposite.

Angela gave him a hard stare. "Why are you all doing this to me?"

Tim frowned. He hadn't expected the question. "What do you mean? I'm as much in the dark about all this as you are. I assumed I was being hired for a simple job at a married couple's house, but it was all a setup to get me here."

Angela raised an eyebrow. "You were set up?"

"Kind of. I suppose it was more an informal interview. Frank and some woman were posing as a family with 'ghost' problems. They called me in to see whether I could see through their bullshit—to see if I was a hustler. I caught onto their scam in about thirty-seconds, so I passed."

"Okay," Angela said after remaining silent for a few moments. "Maybe you are in the dark as much as I am, but that doesn't mean I trust them. They're up to something, and for some reason they've got their sights set on me."

"What do you mean?"

"I mean that they summoned me here to play games with my head. Sammie's drawing.... They must have looked into my past. I just don't know why."

"What was in that drawing that scared the heck out of you so badly?" Tim was dying to know, but he didn't expect her to trust him enough yet to tell him. Yet, he watched Angela reach into her pocket and pull out the slip of paper with Sammie's drawing on. She handed it over.

Tim examined it. "Is this... is this you, here in the corner?"

Angela nodded and Tim looked a little closer. The childish artwork depicted the interior of a church, complete with altar and oversized crucifix. The walls were soaked in blood, depicted by thick red slashes of crayon, and the floor was carpeted by a crudely drawn sea of stickmen bodies. In the corner of the church was a doodle representing Angela, complete with dog collar. Stood opposite her was a tall man with burning red eyes holding a knife.

"What is this supposed to mean?" Tim asked. "It's horrible. Are these bodies down there at the bottom? What does this have to do with you?"

"This drawing is a snapshot from my life." Angela swallowed thickly. "That picture happened to me for real. I was involved in a church massacre."

"Jesus Christ!"

"Jesus had nothing to do with it," she said. "It was a parishioner named Charles Crippley. I was stationed on the isle of Jersey. A dream position: big house, private island full of rich and generous parishioners. But I had one parishioner who was a bit of a handful."

"Charles Crippley?"

She nodded. "He was a local farmer, a quiet man who kept to himself. Some people said he was mentally slow, a child in a man's body. I have to admit he was strange, but not unintelligent. More odd than stupid."

"Odd how?"

"He spoke to an imaginary friend. Barley, he used to call him."

"Just like Sammie says he has a friend?" Tim ran a hand through his brittle, ginger hair and wriggled his bony butt on the edge of the bed, trying to get comfortable. "That's a coincidence I can't say I like."

Angela agreed. "Exactly. That's why I know this family is messing with me. They know the Church of England ordered me to perform an exorcism to cure Charles Crippley of his delusions. He'd been brutalising the livestock on his farm and publically condemning people he felt were 'sinners'. The congregation complained, so the diocese decided to do something about it. I visited Charles at home every day for over two weeks, but every day he was worse. He took to spitting at me and blaspheming. He became sickly and stopped looking after himself. I performed The Rites on him several times but they only seemed to exacerbate his condition. His friend, Barley, was becoming more and more present, as if I was bringing something vile to the surface, pus from a boil. I kept trying to help the man though, even when Charles said Barley would punish me, along with all who followed me."

Tim leant forward on the bed. "So what happened?"

"Sunday Services happened. Charles wasn't there when I began, which was strange because he was always one of the first to arrive. I gave a sermon about the Good Samaritan, and the importance of helping thy neighbour. I was almost finished when Charles staggered down the aisle, bellowing that we 'were a flock of immoral lizards led by a soulless dyke.' He knew I was a lesbian, despite me never having ever admitted it to anyone. In fact, I'm not sure I even knew myself back then."

"That's weird," Tim said. "Maybe the guy had one of those gaydars or something. I hear you can get them on eBay."

Angela took a deep breath and continued, ignoring his humour. "As soon as Charles came in, I noticed he carried the knife—one of those big, curved blades they use in slaughter houses. He killed nineteen people by the time he was through. I was the only survivor."

"That's horrible," Tim said, feeling sick to his stomach. Looking at the middle-aged ex-priest, he could see the lines of torment etched into the creases of her face. She looks ten years older than she is.

Angela blinked, and a tear fell down her cheek. "Enough," she said, wiping it away. "I'm done with trips down memory lane. My point was only that Jessica and Frank have done their homework. They're using my past to manipulate me. Worst of all, is that they've involved a ten-year-old boy in their schemes. Did you see the shape Sammie was in?"

Tim sighed. "I'm not so sure you're on the right track there, Angela. My bullshit meter is sensitive, and I think Jessica is legitimately worried. You must sense how strung-out the woman is? It's clear as day. As for Sammie, there's no way they could coax a kid his age to behave the way he does. There's something not right here, and that's why we should stay and help figure things out."

"If Sammie is so innocent, then how did he know what happened in Jersey? He must have been briefed."

Tim shrugged. "I don't know, but we can find out the answer together. If I get one whiff we're being played for fools, I'll walk right out the door beside you. Until then, I would rather have your help than not."

Angela gave in. "Okay," she let out a breath and deflated. "I'll stay... for now."

Tim hopped up off the end of the bed and clapped his hands together. "Great! Because I could do with some help setting up my equipment."

Angela frowned. "Equipment?"

He winked at her. "It's time to do some science, my righteous lesbian friend."

Chapter 7

A ngela decided to stay in her room and take a bath before doing anything else, so Tim left her alone to enjoy a soak. He'd since made the trip outside to the Raymeady estate's vast driveway where his transit van lay parked— The DeBunkMobile. Beside Tim's van sat the long black Mercedes Frank had driven him there in two nights earlier. The five-door saloon was as indulgent as the house and its grounds.

A garage block sat at the edge of the pebbled driveway, and beyond it lay a modest pond. The water's surface was devoid of ducks and other wildlife, which seemed strange for that time of year. Tim reached into his pocket and pulled out the key for his van. He disengaged the lock and opened the rear doors. A wide smile stretched across his face as he looked inside. "Hello, my little friends."

The back of the van was Tim's office, stuffed full of his gadgets and gizmos. His investigations always sought to debunk claims of the supernatural or paranormal. Science—along with common sense—was the best remedy for superstition, and his equipment included audio recording equipment, infrared cameras, microscopes, barometers, thermometers, motion detectors, assorted chemicals, and even a toaster—but that was for making Poptarts. Most of the tools helped Tim separate the 'normal' from the 'paranormal', but for now all Tim wanted was his environmental testing kit. It would be best to begin by investigating the grounds and working inwards towards the house.

He rummaged around and picked out a small plastic clip-case, before closing the van's doors. The nearby duck pond was as good a place as any to investigate so he headed there first. Maybe he would find out why the peaceful habitat was devoid of wildlife. Maybe the groundwater is polluted. If it's got into the plumbing, it may have led to Sammie becoming sick.

Tim detected a sharp odour as he approached the water's edge. It was a mild tang, subtle yet faintly eggy, like the fumes from an exhaust pipe. The pond water lay still, undisturbed by the light breeze of the day.

Tim crouched beside the bank and unclipped the plastic clip-case. From within its contents, he plucked a strip of litmus paper and doused it in the pond water, waving it to-and-fro in the air for a few seconds before examining it—it turned a dark red. Acidic. Tim pursed his lips. Factoring in the eggy smell, he suspected sulphur. It may have been used by the gardeners to alter the pH of the soil, especially if there was a high lime content. It could then have seeped through into the pond which would explain why there was no wildlife. Tim looked around but saw no vegetable patches or gardens, just overgrown lawns, so it seemed unlikely a gardener had been by for some time. So what then? How did the pond get so badly contaminated?

Tim headed away from the pond, just a few meters, over to a patch of grass. There, he knelt and plucked a few grains of soil, cupping them in his palm. Next, he produced a slim plastic test tube and dropped the granules inside. Finally, he added litmus flour and pure water from a small flask. Rattling the test tube around, he waited for the solution inside to settle. Just like the pond water, the soil was acidic. The liquid in the test tube turned red.

A noise behind Tim made him turn. A hissing sound. He headed back to the water's edge and saw that the surface of the pond had become unsettled. At first, it merely shimmered, but then it bubbled and popped like soup in a cauldron. The pond boiled. Tim could feel the heat coming off it on his cheeks. The smell of eggs grew to eye-watering levels. What the Hell...

Tim crept closer, staring into the water's murky depths. He got down on his knees, moved his face closer. The pond continued to churn, frothing and bubbling, almost as if it could detect his increasing proximity. He'd never seen anything like it. Even if some gaseous vent heated the pond, there was no way it could have gotten so hot so fast.

The pond hissed.

The water boiled.

The air grew thick with stench.

Then suddenly the pond was airborne.

Several fist-sized drops of boiling water flew toward Tim's unprotected face. He swung an arm around to shield himself but was too slow. Some of the liquid got through his defences and doused his face. The soft flesh of his cheek and forehead cried out in agony. He leapt backwards, crumpling to the ground and holding his face in his hands. He screamed.

"Tim! Tim... are you okay?" It was Angela's voice. Tim felt the woman hit the ground beside him and place her hands on him. She forced him over onto his back and tried to look at him, but he clutched at his face and struggled against her.

"The water. It burned me. It burned me."

"What are you talking about?"

"The pond. The pond is boiling."

"I don't understand." Angela sounded frantic. "The pond is boiling? What do you mean?"

The pain in Tim's face lessened. He removed his hands tentatively. "The pond is boil-" He stopped mid-word as he gazed at the pond. It was no longer boiling. Its surface lay still and serene. It was also full of fish and frogs. Goldfish zipped through the water merrily, flitting back and forth. Frogs lay motionless at the bottom, waiting to strike anything mouth-sized. There was even a family of newts frolicking by the water's edge.

Tim's mouth worked back and forth, but no sound came out. He could not understand it.

"What's wrong?" Angela urged. "I don't understand what's happened."

Tim tried to catch a breath and calm himself down. "I.... Oh, Helsinki, I don't have a clue what just happened. Maybe I'm fucking losing it." His face no longer burned and as he fingered his cheeks, the skin felt normal. Had he imagined the entire thing?

"Can I ask you a question, Angela?"

"Of course."

"What does my face look like?"

Angela looked confused, but she gave him an answer. "Ugly, same as usual."

Tim laughed. "Cheers. No burns, though?"

Angela shook her head. "You want to tell me what happened?"

Tim heaved himself up onto his feet and shook his head. "Nothing happened. At least, it appears that way. Come on, let's go back inside the house."

Angela didn't ask him any more questions, but as they walked away, she stopped and pointed at something on the ground. It was Tim's environmental testing kit. "Do you need that?" she asked him.

"No," Tim replied. "I'm beginning to think my usual methods might not be as effective as I'd hoped."

"Guess you need a Plan B then."

Tim scratched at his fuzzy beard. "To be honest, I don't think I've ever needed a Plan B before."

"I will take that as a bad sign," said Angela.

"Yeah," said Tim, thinking about things a little deeper. "Me too."

Chapter 8

Frank unlocked the door to the security office and shuffled inside. He hadn't slept in twenty-four hours, too mistrustful of the recent houseguests to allow sleep. He would need to aside time soon—his mind was getting cloudy—but right now there was just too much to do.

Jessica is relying on me.

Frank's main priority was the protection of the Raymeadys. With a disgraced priest and a professional ghost hunter in the house, Frank needed his mind fresh and alert, ready for any tricks the two charlatans might pull. While Tim had proven himself to be a man who valued fact over fantasy, Frank still didn't trust the man. And as a servant of God, he didn't trust Angela either. But it was Jessica's prerogative to have them there, yet that didn't mean Frank had to like it. He had no better ideas to help young Sammie, so there was little argument he could give. The boy was heading straight for life in the funny farm the way he was behaving, but he was also Joseph Raymeady's son and the only existing link to a man Frank had spent a decade serving. He would do what he could to protect Sammie, but at this point he had to admit that things were looking hopeless.

He took a seat at his desk and gave a quick glance to each of the CCTV monitors in front of him. The house was in order, for now. Mike and Graham stood in the kitchen, fixing a batch of towering sandwiches to take out to the car. Jessica slouched in the piano lounge with a large glass of wine, staring into space. Frank watched her for a while, his heart aching to ease her burdens. On the next monitor, he saw Tim and Angela strolling around the grounds, already as thick as thieves. Finally, Frank checked on Sammie and spotted the boy in his filthy room, scribbling away at his desk as per usual.

The child had a sick mind—the things he drew a concoction forged by dark thoughts. His sketches were also frighteningly astute. Frank himself had received many a sketch from the boy depicting things no one else could know—things from Frank's Army days. Sammie drew scenes of torture in Sierra Leone one day and dead children in Northern Ireland the next. The one thing the pictures always had in common was that Frank had witnessed them all first-hand. It was as if Sammie were reaching into his nightmares for artistic inspiration and seeing the faces of the dead. Nine men, one woman. I remember them all.

The worst picture Sammie had ever drawn featured a soldier firing cartoon bullets into a pregnant woman. The foetus spilled from her guts along with intestines, slopping on the sandy floor in a sickly pile. Frank knew the soldier in the picture was him. What he didn't know was how Sammie, a ten-year-old boy, could know his darkest secret. A secret from that day he had led a squad into a quiet little village in the Muthanna Province in Iraq. It had seemed safe, a good place to rest up, but it had been an ambush. Frank's bad decision-making had cost lives, and a pregnant woman her baby.

One of the CCTV television screens flickered.

Frank gave the monitor a tap, but it only made things worse. The picture scrambled with static. Frank hit the monitor again, harder.

The picture snapped back into focus.

Frank flinched in his seat.

Sammie was no longer sitting at his desk. He was standing in front of the camera lens, staring up at it and grinning. His eyes were dark orbs in his skull. His teeth jutted out from swollen, brown gums. He seemed to watch Frank as Frank watched him.

Does he know I can see him?

Frank leant closer to the screen, trying to work out what the boy was doing. Sammie inched closer and closer to the camera, little by little, but the lens was fixed eight feet off the ground. It was almost as if the boy was levitating. His pale face getting closer and closer....

Crack!

The monitor's screen split from corner to corner. Frank leapt back in his swivel chair, his momentum and the wheels taking him away from the desk.

The screen shattered, struck by some invisible hammer.

Frank sat in silence, twiddling his thumbs and trying to control his breathing as he processed what just happened. From the way things were going it might be another twenty-four hours before he got any sleep.

Chapter 9

Angela was still freaked out by the picture Sammie had drawn for her, and the incident with Tim at the pond had done nothing to calm her nerves, yet she was determined to take charge of the situation, unwilling to be manipulated or frightened. The look on Tim's face when she had found him on the lawn was enough to convince her he was as much a pawn in this game as she was. The two of them were now back inside the manor, standing in the cavernous foyer. There was no one else around.

Tim put his fingers in his mouth and whistled. "Hello?" He turned to Angela and shook his head. "It's a bloody nightmare trying to find people in this place, you know?"

Angela nodded. "I'm not surprised Jessica's on edge. Empty houses have a way of making people skittish–especially old empty houses."

"You think that's what's going on? Simple paranoia?"

"I hope so, because what're the alternatives?"

Frank appeared, his polished work shoes clicking on the marble. "Miss Murs, Mr Golding. I was wondering where you two had gotten to."

"Yeah, sorry about that," said Tim. "We're ready to see Sammie again now."

Frank nodded. "You may be wasting your time. The boy likes to watch South Park during the afternoons. He can be quite unresponsive."

Tim frowned. "You let him watch that cartoon?"

"You can try stopping him."

Tim shrugged his shoulders. "Hey, I'm not here to raise the kid. Just to take a stool sample or two."

Frank led them to Sammie's room again, and even before they got there, Angela could hear the television blaring. She'd never watched South Park herself, but she knew the show was new and popular like most things kids enjoyed nowadays. She also knew it wasn't suitable for ten-year-old boys. "Why do you let him watch the program? Isn't it meant for adults?"

"It is, yes, but he gets violent if you turn it off. He tends to fixate. Before South Park, it was Power Rangers, and before that it was Beavis and Butthead."

Tim scoffed. "Can't you control him, a big man like you?"

Frank's expression was impassive. "Samuel is stronger and more aggressive than he looks. The only way I could restrain him is by hurting him, and that is not something I am permitted or inclined to do." He turned around and unlocked Sammie's door. "I'll leave you 'experts' to do your job."

"Thank you," said Angela, stepping through into the bedroom. Tim followed her as Frank left. The door snapped shut behind them. Angela felt that muggy stench close in around her again, the room humid and tropical like a Florida storm. She loosened the cuffs on her shirt.

Sammie lay in his bed, wrapped up to his neck in a sweat-stained bedsheet. A dusty old television sat on a wall bracket and flashed in front of him. Poorly animated cartoon characters frolicked on-screen.

Angela waved a hand. "Hello, Sammie. How are you feeling?"

The boy said nothing. His gaze transfixed on the television, eyes unblinking. Angela could not be sure, but he seemed to mutter to himself quietly.

Tim stepped forward and perched on the end of the Sammie's bed. "Hey, little man. So you dig South Park, huh? Who's your favourite character? I like that fat kid, Cartman. Respect my authoritaar."

Sammie said nothing. There was movement beneath his sheets.

Tim continued his attempts to get through to the boy by talking on his level. "Have they killed Kenny yet? Is this the one where Cartman has an Anal probe shoot out of his ass? Huh? Sammie, are you listening to me?"

The movement beneath the bed sheets got faster.

Angela frowned. What is he doing? He's in some kind of trance.

Suddenly, she realised what the boy was doing. A wave of disgust washed over her. "Tim," she said, horrified. "I think he's…"

Tim leapt away from the bed as he reached the same conclusion. "Sammie, you stop that right now. That's really rude. And totally gross!"

Angela couldn't believe the young boy was masturbating in front of them. The sheets leapt up and down, Sammie's small hand pumping away like a piston.

"Turn off the television," said Angela. "He's in a trance."

Tim looked around. "I don't see a remote."

Angela couldn't see one either. She went over to the television and rose on tiptoes, reaching for the power button. She jabbed it with her index finger and South Park disappeared. 'Screw you guys, I'm going-'

Click!

"Look out," Tim shouted at her.

Angela spun around. Sammie was standing on the bed, naked body taut and flexing. He wore only a pair of grimy underpants, which did nothing to hide his virulent erection. Sammie glared at Angela, growling like a hungry wolf. The noise was guttural, unnatural for a child, or anything human.

Angela raised her hands in front of her. "Sammie, maybe you should just get back into bed and we'll talk."

Sammie leapt at her, seeming to hang in the air as he covered the ten feet between them in a single bound. His bony fingers closed around her throat and he deafened her with a high-pitched shriek. Angela's back hit the wall, and for a moment she worried that the mounted television would rock loose and fall on her head.

Tim rushed over to help. Together, they struggled to remove Sammie's clawed fingers from around her throat. The boy was trying to snap her windpipe. Angela tried to cry out, but strong hands restricted her larynx. Her eyes felt like they were going to pop loose from her skull.

He's going to kill me.

Tim grabbed Sammie's left arm, but failed to gain enough leverage to pull it away. Angela felt the blood vessels in her face overload as the pressure increased in her skull. Frantically, she prayed for an idea.

Then she had one.

She stopped struggling with Sammie and pointed her left hand at the television above her head. She made eye contact with Tim and tried to make him understand what she was thinking.

After what seemed like an eternity, with Angela's life choking away with every second, Tim finally understood. He leapt up and bashed the television's power button with his palm.

"Hidey Hooooo, children!"

The television flashed back on.

Sammie released his grip.

Tim placed a hand against the boy's shoulder and eased him back towards the bed. Angela slumped against the wall, clutching at her throat and hacking up phlegm. Her throat felt like sandpaper. Another couple of seconds and she would've been unconscious for sure. Or dead.

Tim got Sammie tucked back into bed and then came to check on Angela. He helped her stand up by putting an arm around her. "Helsinki, are you okay?"

"I'll live," she said, wondering if it were true. "I think so, anyway. What the hell was that?"

"I don't know, but he's the strongest ten-year-old I know. If he hadn't let go, I don't know what I would have done. We need to be more careful from now on. He's dangerous."

"No shit," said Angela, fingering her bruised throat. Her mouth had filled with coppery saliva.

"Come on." Tim moved her away from Sammie's bed. "Let's go get you checked out."

"I'm fine," she said, but quickly reconsidered. "Although, I could use a drink."

Tim looked at his watch. "It's one in the afternoon!" He grinned wide. "What took you so long?"

Angela let out a laugh and wasn't surprised to find that it hurt a lot.

Chapter 10

Angela and Tim were surprised to find Jessica sitting alone in the piano lounge. The lady of the house nursed a half-finished bottle of chardonnay in front of her and stared at an empty glass as if contemplating whether to pour another. Angela took a seat beside Jessica while Tim went behind the bar to get drinks. They'd agreed to have just one, considering the early hour.

"Are you okay, Jessica?" Angela asked.

Jessica replied with a grim smile. "Just ruminating. There was a time I was able to do my thinking without alcohol, but it's hard to concentrate in this place since my husband passed. Joseph was always the man about the house, keeping everyone busy. It's lonely without him."

Angela nodded. "Have you considered living somewhere else?"

"I have, but this was Joseph's home. It wouldn't feel right to bring Samuel up outside of it."

Tim sat with the drinks—a whisky for Angela and a beer for him. He said, "We went to see Sammie again earlier."

Jessica sighed. "I hope you didn't turn off his program."

"We did," Tim said. "Won't make that mistake again."

"I'm sorry if either of you were hurt. I'll tell Frank he needs to pay closer attention to the both of you."

"Don't worry about it," said Angela, rubbing her sore neck. I only nearly died. "What was more concerning, Jessica, was what he was doing while he was watching television."

Jessica sighed, and the shame was abundant in her eyes. "He started touching himself a few weeks ago. The first time he did it, the maids were still around. He ejaculated into his hand and threw it into Margaret's face. That was the last we saw of her, of course."

"Don't worry, I'm sure it wasn't her first time," said Tim, and then seemed embarrassed by what he had said. "Sorry. Bad joke."

"Indeed," said Jessica. "None of this is funny to me, Mr Golding. The only reason you're here is because of the previous success you've had with finding rational explanations behind several high-profile cases. You were not, however, brought here for your wit. Have you formed any opinion about my son yet? Can you help?"

Tim shook his head and let out a sigh. "I don't know yet, but I will try my best to find an answer. Safe to say, something strange is going on. I for one would like to know what."

"Me too," said Angela. "I'm determined to get to the bottom of this."

Jessica seemed to lighten at the sound of that. "So you'll perform the exorcism?"

"I didn't say that," Angela said. "I'm not about to admit that Evil has anything to do with this."

Jessica grunted, began filling up her wine glass. "Then what help are you going to provide?"

"I've experience with sick people behaving in bizarre ways, and I'm certain my observations will tell me more about your son's condition. I won't need a Bible to help you."

"And I'll run tests," said Tim. "Try to find out if there're any environmental factors to blame."

Jessica let loose a breath. It whistled between her teeth. "Thank you, both. Now, if you'll excuse me, I'm going for a lie down. Please contact Frank if you need anything."

"Will do," said Tim, waving goodbye. Once the lady of the house departed, he turned to Angela with a sad look on his face. "Poor lady. She's at breaking point."

Angela agreed. "Can't say I blame her. This whole thing is very strange."

"You ever seen anything like it before?"

"I've seen a lot of messed up shit in my time, none of which I wish to speak of now."

Tim looked her in the eye. "Do you believe in Evil, Angela? Have you witnessed it?"

"I... yes, I believe so. Once."

"Charles Crippley?"

"Yes. Have you ever encountered a genuine case of–what do you call it–the 'paranormal'?"

"I've seen a few things, here and there, which I can't explain. Most of the time it's just hoaxes and superstition. There was one time..."

Angela leant forward. "Go on."

Tim shrugged and seemed to change his mind about wanting to talk about it. He sighed. "I used to be a conman, just like Frank thought. I screwed people over left-right-and-centre, playing off their grief to steal their money. A reprehensible piece of shit, I was, no denying it. But one night in a hotel changed my entire outlook on life. Now I try to help people. I try to find rational explanations for the things that are scaring them. Nine times out of ten, I do that. The other one per cent keeps me awake at night."

Angela pulled a face and seemed thoughtful. "Ironic, but I feel like I used to be a conman too, back when I worked for the church. I played off of people's grief too and gave them the same line of bullshit you probably did—only wrapped with a different bow."

"Guess, we'll make good partners then, huh?"

Angela shrugged her shoulders and felt a twinge in her injured neck muscles. "Think the jury is still out on that."

"So what's the plan? You have any ideas how to tackle this?"

Angela shrugged. "I plan on spending more time around Sammie, to see what I can observe. When I worked as an exorcist, I took an interest in psychology to supplement my skills. In most cases, a person's mind is more likely to be damaged than their soul. I want to find out what is going on in Sammie's head. What about you, Tim? What tests are you going to perform?"

Tim smiled as if excited. "I will confront Ms Raymeady's assumptions head-on. If she believes a demon is at work, I will first seek to disprove that."

"How?"

"Best way to get a bear's attention is to poke it."

Angela didn't like the sound of that.

Chapter 11

Angela waited patiently in an antique chair while Tim hefted his equipment to the first floor, amassing it in a cluttered circle outside of Sammie's bedroom. Frank agreed to help with the experiments and was currently setting up an infrared camera and several microphones. Tim would record the data and video feeds onto his bulky laptop twenty-four hours a day. It all seemed like Atari video games to Angela—boys and their toys—but she was determined to show Tim and his methods the proper respect. They were colleagues now.

Tim came up the stairs, on his fourth equipment run. This time, he carried what looked like a doctor's saddle bag. "That's everything," he said, wiping sweat from his forehead with his free hand.

Angela nodded to the satchel he carried. "What's in the bag?"

"Medical supplies. I want to see if Sammie is healthy before we begin anything else."

"Are you qualified to perform medical tests?"

"Nope, but I haven't been sued yet. Besides, it's not as hard as it looks."

Frank opened the door to Sammie's room and stepped outside to join them. "Your equipment is set up. What's all the rest of this junk you've left out here?"

"Oh, you know, just an Ecto Containment Unit, proton packs, the usual."

Frank stared at him blankly.

Tim shook his head and sniffed. "That was a joke. The small machine that looks like a coffee maker is a blood analyser. The larger machine on the right is an ultrasound machine and heart rate monitor. All hooked up to my laptop running Windows 98 baby. Latest and greatest."

"Where did you get all this stuff?" Angela asked.

"Various places. Auctions mostly, but some stuff I got cheap from China. They don't give a shit who they're selling to over there and it's cheap as chips. China's going to be the new Taiwan, you mark my words."

Angela stood beside one of the cherub statues outside Sammie's door. "Let's get started."

Frank flanked them as they entered Sammie's bedroom. Tim set his doctor's satchel down on a nearby dresser and opened the clasp at the top. He pulled the two sides apart and pulled out a syringe.

"What do you plan on doing with that?" Frank demanded, eyes wide beneath fuzzy, grey eyebrows.

"I thought I would use it to play darts. What do you think I'm going to do with it? I'm going to draw blood."

"Samuel's already been poked and prodded enough."

"Well," said Tim. "If you don't mind, I would like to take a small amount of blood, anyway."

"You're most welcome," came Sammie's reply from the far side of the room. The boy was staring out of the large bay window behind his crayon-covered desk. Thankfully, Sammie wore clothes this afternoon.

Frank rubbed at his eyes and shrugged. The man seemed tired. "I suppose if Sammie doesn't mind...."

Tim nodded and headed over to the boy who had already rolled up one of his shirtsleeves to offer out a veiny arm. A knowing smile on his face made Angela uncomfortable.

"Okay, Sammie," Tim said soothingly. "Just feel a little pinch."

"It's okay. Pain doesn't bother me, Mr Golding. Take your blood."

Angela watched in anticipation while Tim rubbed Sammie's arm with a disposable alcohol swab. Next, he uncapped the syringe and placed the nib against the boy's flesh. Angela stepped closer, to get a better look at Tim's medical skills, but also to be nearby if Sammie had another bout of aggression. She needed to watch Tim's back the same way he had watched hers.

Tim prodded the needle against Sammie's flesh, but there seemed to be resistance. He moved the needle and repositioned it.

Sammie smiled politely. "Is there a problem, Mr Golding?"

"I... I'm finding it hard to break the skin."

"Perhaps you should push harder."

Tim nodded and tried again.

The needle plunged in.

Deep.

A torrent of blood arced high into the air, a dark-red arterial spray drenching Tim's face in a hot shower. He stumbled backwards, spluttering and spitting, and his thigh hit against Sammie's desk and sent him tumbling to his knees. Angela dashed forward to help him, but realised it was Sammie who needed the help. The boy bled monstrously, his bodily fluids jetting into the air and forming glistening puddles on the floorboards.

"Jesus Christ!" Frank shouted as he rushed across the room. "What the hell have you done? Oh God!"

Sammie spat foul black fluid in Frank's face. "Blasphemer! Speak not the name of the great charlatan."

Angela stood in shock.

Then the bleeding stopped as suddenly as it had started. The arc of blood ceased like someone turning off a tap. Sammie turned to face the window and seemed almost to slither towards it. He sat in his chair and began sketching furiously with his crayons, bare feet dangly innocently.

"What the fuck just happened?" Frank shouted at the top of his lungs.

"I have no idea," Tim spluttered. "A syringe can't open up an artery like that. And bleeding that heavy doesn't just stop either."

Angela bent over. The tang of fresh blood had taken her mind to a place of nightmares and misery. She felt dizzy. "I think I'm going to be sick."

Tim came and put an arm around her. "Come on. Let's get out of here until we can think this through."

"Yes," said Sammie, hunched over his desk. "Why don't you all GET THE FUCK OUT OF HERE AND LEAVE ME ALONE?"

Angela stumbled. "Maybe we should go get a doctor."

Tim pulled her towards the door. "He's fine. Look at him. It's like nothing ever happened. Let's go, I got what I needed."

"What was that?"

"Sammie's blood," said Tim. "It's all over me."

Chapter 12

"Y ou need to get those amateurs out of this house," Frank informed Jessica as firmly as his position allowed. The lady of the house was lying in bed, attempting to sleep off her most recent hangover. "They almost killed Sammie just now. There was blood everywhere."

Jessica sat bolt upright, sobriety returning to her at the news of her son being in danger. "Sammie? Is he okay? Frank, tell me!"

Frank ran a hand over his throbbing forehead. No, that boy is definitely not okay. "He's fine. I don't understand what happened, but I know it started when that clown stuck a needle in your son's arm."

"Where is everybody now?"

"Sammie is drawing at his desk. Angela and Tim are somewhere in the house planning their next performance."

Jessica patted the bed beside her. Frank sat down reluctantly. Jessica rubbed his shoulders.

"Frank, you promised me you would give this a try. Angela and Tim are the only hope we have left. I know you don't agree with their methods, but let's see what they come up with. I fear for my little boy."

"He's in more danger since those two arrived, but..." He moaned as Jessica pressed a knot above his scapula. "If that's what you want, Jessica."

"Thank you, Frank." She kissed the nape of his neck and stroked his chest inside his shirt.

Frank stood quickly, not because he was averse to her touch, but because he knew he couldn't deal with the distraction right now. *She is my weakness.* "I need to get back downstairs," he said. "Keep an eye on things."

"When was the last time you slept, Frank? You're not usually this rattled."

Maybe if you stayed sober, I wouldn't need to be so alert all the time. "I'm fine," he said. "I just want the situation dealt with so things can return to normal."

"Me too, Frank. I appreciate your loyalty this last year. I couldn't have coped without you."

You aren't coping. "It's been my pleasure, Ms Raymeady. I take it you will be joining us this evening?" *Or will you still be dealing with your hangover?*

Jessica must have caught the disapproving look in his eyes because her reply was short and clipped. "I will be down shortly."

"Very good, ma'am." Frank opened the door and departed.

The uppermost floor of the house was lavish. Frank hated it. It represented the dirty money of Black Remedy and the wealth of its late owner. Joseph might have been a better man than his father, but the opulence he inherited still bore stains of blood and corruption. Now that Joseph was dead, the Black Remedy Corporation would no doubt become an even bigger cesspit of immoral greed. Jessica would inherit half of the company, but she was weak. Her late husband's business partner, Vincent Black, would run rings around her until he was in complete control of the company. By the time little Sammie grew up, he would inherit zero control.

Frank would do his best to protect Jessica and Sammie for now. Whatever happened, he would deal with as best he was able. For now there were more pressing matters to attend to than thoughts of the future.

Frank headed into Joseph Raymeady's former office at the east end of the floor and unlocked it with his master key. Frank knew what he was looking for, so didn't hesitate approaching the wall-safe behind the broad, walnut desk that took up half the room. After keying in the combination and swinging open the hatch, Frank fumbled between the various papers and wads of cash until he placed his hand around a wooden handle. He held the police-issue Glock 17 handgun and checked it was loaded, then slipped the weapon into his waistband, He pulled his suit jacket over the top to keep the weapon hidden.

I don't know what those two clowns are planning, but I'll make sure they think twice before trying to take advantage of Jessica. Any more of Sammie's blood hits the floor and I'll make them sorry.

Frank locked the safe and sat down in Joseph's high-backed leather chair. He pressed a button on his ex-boss's computer and waited while the hard drive whizzed to life, loading the operating system. Frank felt small sitting at the grand desk, surrounded by shelves full of books he could never hope to understand. He wasn't a big enough man to fill his ex employer's shoes, and he wondered what Joseph Raymeady would have made of the feelings he held towards his wife. Joseph had been a fair man, but loyalty had been important to him. Jessica might be a widow, but Frank still felt like he was betraying her late husband.

You're not doing anything wrong. You're protecting the man's family. Joseph would have wanted that.

The computer monitor lit up and Joseph's desktop appeared. Why the computer wasn't password protected, Frank would never understand, but it had made it much easier for him to look into his late boss's activities.

In the months prior to his death, Joseph had been increasingly unnerved about something, and Frank needed to find out why. Was it something presenting a danger to Jessica and her son? Already he had checked through Black Remedy's financial records and found nothing. Profits were down, but that was due to Joseph's efforts to clean up the company and start doing things ethically. Overall, Black Remedy still had its fingers in hundreds of extremely lucrative pies. From banking and finance to a chain of successful bakeries, there was nary an industry the company didn't have at least some influence in. The company even owned cruise liners for and upcoming tourism arm that was due to join its already vast shipping fleet. But, as always, the jewel in Black Remedy's crown was pharmaceuticals. Whether a common cold or full-blown AIDS, every time someone in the western world popped a pill there was a sixty per cent chance it came from one of Black Remedy's processing plants. The company possessed such power that it could regulate people's health on a whim.

Frank had reached the conclusion that whatever had been worrying Joseph was not a financial issue. The concern must have been personal. Frank clicked on a folder marked 'Personal Files' and was met with a list of several hundred documents. Organisation had not been one of Joseph's strongpoints. Computers were relatively new, and more the domain of the next generation.

Frank searched through randomly named files: Car Insurance, holiday booking confirmation—March 1996, Receipt—Television for lounge, Tax summary—1995, Letter to Thom Brady (Real Estate) January 1998, Job applicants—Gardeners. Invoice—George Farley, Corporate Researcher. Most of the files Frank saw were things he understood. That last file, though—George Farley, Corporate Researcher—referenced someone Frank had never heard of. He double-clicked the file.

A document flashed up on screen that looked like a typical corporate invoice. The letterhead read FARLEY DOSSIER SERVICES: Corporate Fact Finding.

"What the hell is Corporate Fact Finding?" Frank asked himself out loud. He scanned the document and saw a chargeable item listed as: Asset Investigation - £13,500. The next item read: Personnel Background and Surveillance - £24,000.

Frank took a slow steady breath. What the hell was Joseph paying almost forty grand for? He looked over the document until he located an email address in the small print of the footer. He opened the email manager and pasted in the address. Then he began typing:

Dear George Farley:

I am an employee of the late Joseph Raymeady, CEO of Black Remedy Corporation. I currently reside at his former home and am charged with the protection of his widow and orphan. My believe is that, prior to my employer's death, he was under a great deal of stress. Something was concerning him, and I believe that something could pose a threat to his surviving family. Please disregard the typical etiquette of confidentiality and divulge to me the nature of the work you undertook for Joseph.

Yours faithfully,

Frank Senz, Household Coordinator, Raymeady Estate.

Chapter 13

"Who was that?" Graham asked.

"Frank," Mike replied, putting down the car phone. "He was just checking in."

Graham took a sip from his coffee flask and dropped it into the dashboard's drinks holder. The man's expression was always one of irritation. "How's everything inside the house?"

"Tense, by the sound of things. I don't think Frank trusts Jessica's guests. There was an incident with Sammie, apparently, and now he wants them gone."

"I don't blame him."

Mike sighed. "They're okay. Angela seemed pretty normal."

Graham laughed. "You know she's a dyke, right?"

"What's your point?"

"Nothing. Just saying. No point wasting your time on a rug muncher."

Mike rolled his eyes. He wasn't interested in Angela, but meeting new people was a rarity in this current line of work. The woman seemed like fun. If she and Tim were asked to leave, Mike's job would get that little bit more boring again. I expected more than this when I signed on.

Graham switched on the radio and flicked through the stations. After finding nothing he liked, he gave up and rested back in his seat. "Did Frank give us anything to do? I'm going crazy stuck in this bloody car."

Mike exhaled and shook his head. "Me too, but he wants us to stay put. I think he needs us here as back-up."

Graham scoffed. "Back-up? Against a weedy loser and a dyke ex-priest?"

"Like I said, Frank doesn't trust them. He's worried about Sammie."

"Why? It ain't his kid. If I were that guy, I would get a job working for some other rich idiot, instead of babysitting a drunk woman and her freak kid."

"Don't talk about Sammie like that," Mike admonished, jutting out his stubbled chin. "Sammie will be our boss one day. He's going to inherit all of his father's power and influence. Greatness is that kid's birth right."

Graham waved a hand dismissively. "Yeah, yeah, I know. Until then, he's just a weird little brat."

"Perhaps, but there're reasons for that."

Graham sipped his coffee. "You think those two will figure out what's wrong with him?"

"Who knows?"

They both saw Angela ahead, wandering out of the house and onto the driveway.

"Speak of the devil," Mike said, getting out of the car. When he saw there was blood on her shirt, he swore. "Are you okay?"

Angela looked down at herself and realised why he was worried. "It's Sammie's blood."

"Sammie's?"

"He's fine," she quickly assured him. "He just had a little accident. I came out for some fresh air. I'm feeling a bit sick."

"Can I get you anything?"

Angela chuckled glumly. "You know what, I think it's about time you went and got me a change of clothes."

"Yeah, no problem. Graham and I would be glad to have something to do. We'll get going right after I clear it with Frank."

Angela reached into her pocket and pulled out some keys. "My house keys. There's something else I need too."

Mike nodded. "Of course, what is it?"

"In my bedroom closet there's an old black duffel bag. Bring it back with you."

Mike nodded. "What's inside?"

"My exorcism kit."

"Oh," said Mike, stepping to one side as the woman vomited onto the driveway.

Chapter 14

Tim prepared to run a blood test for the third time. After extracting a sample of Sammie's blood from his shirt, Tim had run it through his portable analyser. The results it gave were bizarre. Impossible really.

According to the printout, Sammie's blood bore no recognisable type and was neither Rhesus positive nor Rhesus negative. In fact, the analyser spat out nothing but errors. It was as though Tim had loaded the centrifuge with motor oil instead of blood. It made no sense. He was considering running his own blood just to make sure the machine wasn't faulty.

"Where's Angela?" Frank asked as he strode down the corridor.

"She went out to get some fresh air," Tim answered. "Not feeling too good after all the blood."

"About that," Frank barked. "What the hell happened?"

"Hell if I know. One minute the kid's skin is like concrete, the next he's opening up like a cantaloupe. That's the green one with the seeds and the red flesh, right?"

"No," said Frank. "That is a watermelon."

"Oh."

"You had no right to take his blood," Frank snapped. "You're not qualified."

Tim stood in front of the larger man and looked him in the eye. "Hey, you gave me the go ahead. You could have stopped me if you'd wanted to. Besides, I did everything by the book. I didn't cause that bleeding."

"Then what did?"

"I don't know, but according to my tests it wasn't even real blood, which leads me to ask myself if I'm the butt of some big joke again, like last time."

Frank bristled. "You think this is a trick? Look, Mr Golding. I would love nothing more than for you to leave, so trust me when I say the last thing I want to do is play games with you."

"I'm just telling you that something doesn't add up."

"Then it's your job to do the math. I suggest you gather up your colleague and get back to work."

Tim saluted. "Yes, Mein Fuhrer."

Frank's eyes narrowed, but he said nothing as he departed down the hallway.

Tim shook his head, muttering under his breath. "Jackass. I never asked for you to bring me here."

Angela climbed the staircase and Tim smiled at her as she approached, glad to see a friendly face after Frank's frosty hostility. "Everything okay?"

"Mike's gone to get my things, but it looks like I'll have to put up with being caked in blood and vomit until then."

"If it even is blood. I'm not so sure."

Angela looked confused. "What do you mean?"

"I mean all the tests I've run on Sammie's blood have come up inconclusive. I can't get a blood type, mineral traces, or anything you would normally find. It's weird."

"This whole house is weird."

"So what should we do next?"

Angela pointed at his machines. "Don't tell me you're all out of science experiments?"

"Not even close, but I think it may be best if I switched to observation mode for the rest of the day. I think I'd like to know more before I jump back into the fire."

"Good idea," Angela agreed. "Has anyone told you what Sammie will be doing for the evening?"

"No, but whatever he gets up to, we'll have a front row seat." Tim patted the lid of the laptop sitting amongst his equipment. "How bout we set this up in the lounge and help ourselves to more overpriced booze?"

Angela glanced at her watch—a little after five. "Yeah, why not? My nerves could do with a tipple."

Tim nodded. "Let's get our tipple on then."

* * *

After drinking together for an hour, Tim discovered Angela was as much of a drifter as he was. She listened to his stories about how he'd been free and single for several years now, floating from one town to the next while living out of his van, and that most of his work was gained through a gaudy website he accessed through local libraries. His professional notoriety came from a high profile case in '94 when he'd debunked a poltergeist claim for someone loosely connected to the Royals. Turned out that one of the staff was having fun by rigging parts of the house with practical jokes and false hauntings. Several national newspapers had picked up the story afterwards and Tim's business had skyrocketed. Angela laughed when he showed her the photograph they printed of him kept in his wallet.

Placed on the table between them sat Tim's laptop. It was expensive, like most of his equipment was, and he enjoyed how Angela looked at it with awe. On the screen, several windows streamed footage of Sammie's room—cutting edge stuff. One feed was from an infrared heat camera while another was from a standard lens. Dials and readouts cluttered the bottom of the display—temperature, air pressure, sound frequencies, and a bunch of other scientific garble.

Angela pointed to Sammie. "How long has he been sitting there at his desk?"

"Since we started the feed, which was more than an hour ago. I wonder what he's thinking about."

Angela seemed to consider the answer. "I don't know, but I don't imagine it's anything a normal ten-year-old would think about."

"Tomorrow we'll start trying to make some sense out of everything. Until then, bottoms up." Tim raised his glass and Angela finished off her whisky. She quickly poured another from the bottle on the table. She poured Tim another too. Then she shivered.

"Cold?" he asked her. He was getting a little chilly himself.

Angela rubbed at her shoulders. "Yeah, it's getting frigid."

"I imagine it's difficult to heat a place this size."

The patter of rain started against the windows and Tim looked across the room to the French doors. Pebble-sized splashes appeared on the panes as the downpour beat harder against the glass. "Well, I wouldn't bank on it getting any warmer. Looks like we're in for a dreary evening."

The lights in the room went out. The moon shone in on their darkness.

"Oh, great," said Angela. "If I wasn't cold before, I'll definitely freeze with the power off."

"I'm sure it will come back on in a minute. Maybe there's a storm coming."

"As if tonight couldn't get any more cliché. A dark, stormy night at an old English manor and the power just went out. Are you kidding me?"

"All we need now is an axe-wielding maniac."

The doors to the lounge burst open making them both scream.

It was Mike and Graham.

"Mind if we join you?" Mike asked. "It's a little nippy to sit around in the car. I brought your things, Angela, and placed them in your room."

"Fantastic. And, yes, you are welcome to join us. More the merrier, I say."

"Yeah," said Tim. "Take a load off." Might be interesting seeing where you stand in all this. Are you just drivers, or are you both up to something more?

"Thanks," Mike said and took a seat at the table. Graham said nothing and headed behind the shadowy bar.

"I see Graham is as sociable as ever," Angela commented.

"What was that?" Graham grunted from behind the bar, a glass of gin already in his hand.

"Nothing," said Angela. "It's just delightful to have such charming company."

"Let me tell you something, lady." He marched over to the table and thudded his glass down on the table. "You're just a guest here. I've been around for two years, so maybe you should show a little respect."

"Of course," said Angela. "My apologies. I didn't realise that the respect of a stranger was so important to you."

Graham swigged his gin. "You'll end up walking home after this is over if you're not careful."

"I don't think Jessica would appreciate you speaking to us like that," said Tim.

Graham tittered. "Woman's a mess. Doesn't have a clue what's going on half the time."

"Yet, alas, here I am now listening to you speak." Jessica appeared in the doorway, dressed smartly in trousers and an ivory blouse. She looked more in control of her wits than the previous times Tim had seen her.

Is she sober?

No, not quite. But nearly.

Graham leapt up from his seat, gin splashing out of his glass and wetting the table "J-Jessica! I mean, Ms Raymeady. How are you doing this evening?"

"I'm good, Graham. Thank you for asking. I would feel safer, however, if I knew you were outside in the car."

"But it's freezing out there."

"Then I suggest you turn on the engine."

Graham stomped off in a huff. Mike got up to go after him.

"No, no," said Jessica. "Stay, Michael."

Mike sat back down again. "Thank you, Ms Raymeady. Will you be joining us?"

Jessica shook her head. "Perhaps later. I think I should keep a clear head for now. I hear Sammie had an accident today?"

"Yes," Tim admitted. "We're not quite sure what happened. I'm sorry it happened."

"That's alright," said Jessica, "but let me assure you, I won't tolerate my son being hurt again. Next time, there will be consequences. Do you understand?"

"Yes," said Tim, feeling about five years old—yet with a glass of booze in his hand.

"Good," said Jessica. "I will be with Sammie if anyone needs me."

Everyone at the table nodded, but remained quiet. Jessica had gotten a hold of herself in a big way. Tim could now see her as the wealthy and powerful woman she was. Jessica must have given herself a reality check. Either that or the woman's close to a breakdown. The calm before the storm.

Tim snapped shut the lid on his laptop. "So much for my equipment. Not much use with the power off."

"Frank will look into the power," said Mike. "Power's been going off a lot lately."

"Doesn't your laptop run off a battery?" Angela asked Tim.

"Yeah, but not the cameras. All the feeds have gone down."

"What feeds?" Mike asked.

Angela poured herself another drink and explained. "Tim has video cameras set up in Sammie's room. We were going to observe him this evening and try to figure out what's going on with him."

Mike chuckled. "Yeah, good luck with that. Jessica has had half the medical community through here the last few months. No one could figure it out. Most of them ran screaming from the building."

Tim frowned. "What do you mean?"

Mike rubbed his hands in front of him to warm them up. "Sure you've seen by now, but Sammie has a temper. There was a psychiatrist here a few weeks ago who tried some behavioural adjustments—one of which was trying to take away Sammie's crayons until he promised only to draw nice things. Next thing you know, Sammie attacks the guy. Bites one of his ears clean off. The doctor crawled around on his hands and knees, squealing, looking for his missing appendage for ten whole minutes before we realise Sammie swallowed the thing whole."

Tim's face scrunched up with disgust. "Helsinki."

"Tell me about it. Jessica had to write the guy a fat cheque to keep him quiet about the whole thing."

Angela finished her whisky in a single gulp and poured herself another. Tim raised an eyebrow and wondered whether to be impressed or worried by her constitution for alcohol. "How come you've hung around though all this, Mike?" she asked. "Frank told me everybody left."

"Me and Graham work outside. We have no contact with Sammie. I guess we feel safe enough."

"So you think Sammie is dangerous?"

"I know he is. Whatever the reason for that, I can't say, but you wouldn't catch me alone in a room with him."

"He's just a ten-year-old boy," said Angela.

Mike shrugged. "Maybe. Maybe not."

"What do you mean?"

"I mean, maybe you being here is exactly what is needed. Your exorcism kit is in your room. You might want to think about using it."

"So, you're going to perform an exorcism?" Tim asked. "Can you still do that as an ex-priest?"

"Guess we'll find out. Unless anyone has any objections?"

"Not me," said Mike. "I'm not much of a believer in God, but I'd like to see what happens. Every other option has been exhausted, so there's there's nothing to lose."

Tim sighed. "I still believe there's a rational explanation for all this, but I'd like to dispel any notions of 'possession' as soon as possible, so I would like to see it done."

"I'm not sure I even remember what to do anymore," Angela admitted.

"It will come back to you," said Mike.

Angela huffed. "Like riding a bike... backwards... over water."

They all shared a laugh and sipped at their drinks. After a few moments passed, Tim looked at Mike. "Tell me about Jessica."

"What's to tell? She's lived most of her life in the papers and most of what they've written is true. She met Joseph Raymeady at University. I'm not sure what she was studying, but she never finished. Joseph asked her to marry him right after he graduated and joined his father's company. Eventually, both she and Joseph took a place on the Board of Directors." Mike motioned to the surrounding room. "You've already witnessed the fruits of their labour. Jessica is one of the richest women in the world, but I don't think she knows what to do with it all without her husband. Things have been hard on her."

"How long has she been drinking?" Tim asked.

"Not long, to be honest. The woman you saw earlier is more the real Jessica Raymeady. She's a kind soul, but very much in control of herself . The drinking and depression has been out of character, but who can blame her? In fact, I was pleased to see the way she just dealt with Graham. Perhaps she's on the mend. I think she feels better with the two of you here. Let's hope you can help Sammie."

"We'll do our best," said Tim. "I don't plan on leaving until we get to the bottom of-"

The laptop on the table vibrated. The speakers emitted static.

Angela thrust her chin at the computer. "What's happening?"

"I don't know." Tim put his hands on the laptop and slid it in front of him. Slowly, he raised the lid.

His breath caught in his throat.

"What is it?" Angela asked.

Tim spun the laptop around so she and Mike could see it. "The feeds are back up," he explained. "I don't know how."

Angela looked at the screen and squinted.

Mike did the same.

Tim had a bad feeling.

Sammie's room was dark except for a single candle burning beside his bed. Sammie lay tucked beneath his sheets with Jessica sitting beside him. She was reading a paperback novel while her son slept. Keeping a vigil, Tim thought.

Besides the standard video feed, there was also a second feed displayed. The infrared camera showed several multi-coloured blotches on-screen. Heat signatures. Jessica's body glowed beside the prone form of her son beneath the covers, but Sammie's heat signature seemed in constant flux—reds and yellows pulsing and changing constantly.

They all continued watching the screen, eyes glued as Jessica placed down her paperback and turned to her son.

"What's she doing?" Mike asked.

Tim shook his head. "I don't know. She's going over to Sammie's bed, I think. She's... oh, Helsinki."

They watched in horror as Jessica pulled a pillow from beneath Sammie's sleeping head and pressed it down over his face.

Chapter 15

A ngela galloped through the hallways of the house, trying to navigate her way to Sammic's room as quickly as she could. With every corner, she shouted out Jessica's name at the top of her lungs. The woman had lost her sanity and was trying to eliminate the cause of all her stress–her ten-year-old son. Angela knew it was a defence mechanism for a shattered mind, and that Jessica's action were a temporary madness brought on by trauma. If she were to succeed, the act would terrorise her for the rest of her life. Angela had to stop the mother before it was too late.

Sammie's room was up ahead. Mike and Tim were right behind her. Even in the dark, she could see the posters and signs adorning the boy's bedroom door. Angela wasted no time barging inside.

It was like entering a nightmare.

Dark pervaded the bedroom. Shadows shifted and swirled. The stench of sweat and faeces lingered. In the depths of the shadows, the single burning candle Jessica had been reading by. The flickering cone of light surrounded it, but was incapable of illuminating anything beyond a few inches.

"Jessica!" Angela called out. "Whatever you are doing, you need to stop."

No answer.

Angela stepped forward into the darkness. Sammie's bed lay ahead of her. The boy rested beneath the covers–silhouette grey and unmoving.

"Sammie? Are you okay?" Angela smelt the sweat coming off the bedsheets. "Sammie, answer me!"

Tim and Mike slunk in the shadows behind her, but Angela felt alone. It was just her and the bed and the grisly secrets it held. She another step and reached out her hand, dreading what they were about to find. Were her fingers about to connect with the soft flesh of a dead child? She stretched forward, inch by inch, reaching on her tiptoes.

Something wrapped around Angela's wrist.

She tried to leap back, but whatever had her would not let go. She cried out for help and struggled to break free. Tim and Mike rushed up behind her and grabbed her around the waist, pulling her back.

The power came on with an audible click! Light flooded the bedroom and Angela blinked as her retinas responded with pain. Sammie lay on the bed before her, staring through narrow black slits. It must have been his hand wrapped around her wrist. But how could it have been with him lay in bed beneath the covers?

"What are you doing, Angela? I was sleeping."

Angela found it hard to speak. Her lungs had seized up as if an invisible python had roped itself around her chest. "Sammie, w-where is your mother? Where is Jessica?"

"Oh, I think she went up to her room to get some air. She was feeling rather unwell."

"Sammie? Has something happened? Did you mother do something to you with a pillow?"

Sammie giggled. "I don't know what you're talking about. As I explained, I was sleeping soundly until you awoke me. Maybe you should go check on my mother. I would hate for anything to happen to her."

Angela leant closer to the boy. "What does that mean, Sammie?"

"Erm... Angela?" It was Tim's voice, coming from behind her. "I think you should take a look at this."

Angela stepped away from Sammie and turned around. What she saw on the walls was impossible. More of the boy's crayoned drawings had appeared, attached to the plaster with pushpins so densely that they overlapped one another like horrid wallpaper—hundreds of them. They depicted the house, rain outside and no power, the windows shaded black to show the lack of light. More disturbing, were the depictions of Angela, Tim, and Mike. The drawing showed them sitting in the piano lounge huddling around a table with a laptop between them. Sammie had drawn them watching him. There was no way he could have known how they were sitting or what they were doing—it had been only minutes ago. He could never have drawn it in time. Not a hundred times over.

Tim placed a hand on Angela's shoulder and turned her to her right. He pointed at one. "Look."

Angela stared at the drawing and felt a boulder roll through her guts. Scrawled in harsh black pencil was a picture of Jessica. Hanging by the neck from a rain-drenched balcony.

Chapter 16

When Angela and the others reached the top floor, they heard Frank shouting. He was crying out for help in a way that made it clear something terrible had happened.

Mike led the way and motioned to a doorway at the end of the wide hallway. He told them it was Jessica's bedroom, and Frank's voice came from inside.

Angela grabbed the door handle and yanked, but it was locked. She rattled it back and forth, then bashed a fist against the wood. "Frank? Frank, let us in. What's happening?"

"I can't," came Frank's muffled voice. "I can't let go. Please, help me. I can't hold her much longer."

Angela glanced at Tim and Mike, saw they were as confused as she was. At least Mike seemed to have an idea. He shrugged his shoulders and took a step backwards, leaping forward and aiming a heavy kick at the door.

Bamph! The wood cracked.

Mike kicked again.

The door swung open.

Angela rushed into Jessica's bedroom, dragging Tim along with her. She searched for Frank, but the room lay empty. "Frank! Frank, where are you?"

"Out here, on the balcony."

Angela peered across the lavish bedroom and saw a pair of French doors at the far side, hanging open. Wind and rain buffeted the room. Frank leant over an iron railing, struggling with something unseen. The shirt on his back was sodden from rain and sweat. He strained to turn his head and look at them. "Help me!"

Angela hurried over. Tim and Mike did the same. Angela gasped to find Jessica's limp body hanging over the balcony from Frank's grasp, four stories above ground. She was unconscious, with a thick noose cutting into her throat. The rope was secured at the other end to one of the balcony's iron railings.

"Holy mama!" Tim cried out.

Angela threw her upper body over the railing and grabbed a hold of Jessica. Frank held the woman under the armpits, but she was slipping from his grasp. Angela reached over and grabbed a handful of the woman's shirt and almost ended up tumbling over the balcony herself. Mike wrapped both his arms around her hips and anchored her before she went plummeting to her death. With Mike securing her, she got both hands on Jessica's clothing and pulled with all her strength. She and Frank worked together, and slowly they hoisted Jessica back towards the balcony. Once they had her near the top, Mike and Tim helped out and they managed topple the lady of the house back over the railing to safety. Her limp body collapsed to the floor.

Frank dropped to his knees beside Jessica and clawed at the ligature around her neck. He was frantic, sobbing. This was not the stone-faced man Angela knew.

"Frank?" Angela placed a hand on his shoulder. "What happened?"

He managed to loosen the rope around Jessica's neck and slumped back on his heels when she coughed, spluttered, and resumed breathing. "Thank God!"

"Frank? What happened?"

"I-I got here just as she was about to jump. I caught her but her weight dragged me over the side. I think... I think she'll be okay. She wasn't hanging by her neck for more than a minute."

Angela studied Jessica and saw that, at least physically, she was okay. Her breathing was steady as she lay on the rain drenched balcony.

"We need to call an ambulance," said Tim.

Frank shook his head firmly. "No!"

Angela thought the man was in shock. "She just tried to kill herself, Frank!"

Frank shook his head again. "If word gets out about this, she'll be removed from the Board of Directors. All of Joseph's work will be undone and his business partner will take over."

"What are you talking about?" Tim butted in. "Who gives a shit about business? She needs help."

Frank was still adamant and shaking his head. "We'll keep her safe. She'll be okay. No one can know about this. Mike, get Graham. You can take turns keeping an eye on her until she's better."

Mike nodded in agreement but from the look on his face he was disturbed by the situation.

"This is insane," Tim said, pulling at a clump of ginger hair as if he were mad. "Why did she even do this? She seemed perfectly fine earlier."

"No," said Angela. "She wasn't. People who commit suicide often seem fine right before they try to end it all. Killing yourself takes courage and a certain amount of inner peace. The reason Jessica seemed stronger and more in control earlier was because she wanted to die with the dignity of being herself. When people lose control of their lives, sometimes the only thing they have any power over is whether they live or die. It comes as a relief, and all the stress and misery melts away."

"I wish we'd known what she was planning," said Tim. "I wish we could have, you know..."

"It's not your fault," Angela told him.

"Like hell it isn't," Frank said. "You people and your games are what sent her over the edge."

Mike put a hand on Frank's shoulder. "Come on, Frank. That's not true and you know it. Things haven't been right around here since even before Joseph died. Angela and Tim are just trying to help."

Frank's shoulders drooped. "Just help me get her over to the bed. She needs rest."

Mike and Frank hoisted Jessica up off the floor and carried her over to the bed. Tim pulled back the covers for them. Angela remained where she was. Focusing on the caress of rain against her bare arms. Things are a mess. But I can't turn my back on Jessica now. She needs help more than ever. I became a priest, not because of my belief in God, but because I wanted to devote my life to helping others. I don't have to be part of the Church to uphold that vow.

I'm here for a reason.

A rumble of thunder jilted Angela away from her musings and prompted her back inside. She closed the French doors, shutting off the room from the wind and rain.

Jessica was now tucked up in bed, awake and staring up at the ceiling. "I'll stay with her for now," Mike said. "I'll let Graham know what's happened in the morning."

"Thank you," said Frank. "I will keep an eye on Sammie while she recovers."

"What would you like us to do?" Angela asked.

Frank glared at her for a moment, and she expected another one of his verbal tirades, but he just let out a sigh and said, "Get some sleep. We'll figure things out in the morning."

Angela didn't argue. In all honesty, her bedroom seemed like the safest place to be right now. She left Jessica's bedroom without complaint, not even bothering to say good night. Too much had happened for niceties to count for very much.

When she reached the Freidkin suite a few minutes later, Angela noticed that her suitcase had been placed on the bed. It reminded her she still wore bloodstained clothing. I'm beginning to feel like I might never feel clean again.

Beside her suitcase lay another bag. The old leather satchel sill carried a layer of dust, despite its recent travels. Angela hadn't faced its contents in a long time. She wasn't about to deal with them tonight either, so she placed both her suitcase and the satchel onto the floor, then headed into the en suite.

Inside, she reached into the bathroom's shower cubicle. She turned the brass valve and a cold stream of water gushed from the showerhead. It began to heat up slowly, and while she waited she stripped off her dirty clothes and let them fall to the floor in a heap. Come morning, she would ask Mike to dispose of them, as no amount of washing could save them now.

The mirror above the sink showed Angela a reflection of her naked upper body. She cringed, not because her own flesh disgusted her, but because her chest was stained with Sammie's blood where it had seeped through her shirt. The crusted blood against her flesh made her think about Charles Crippley.

Will that man ever stop haunting me?

She ran a hand beneath the shower stream to test the temperature, then stepped beneath the hot waterfall. She shuddered beneath the heat and watched dried blood flake and peel from her body. It was like being reborn, shedding an unwanted skin. It wasn't long before the blood was gone, but she still felt stained.

She took a nearby bar of soap to lather herself up and finally wash the horrors of the day away. Her strength ebbed back, even as the hot water softened sinews.

She thought about Jessica and what could have made the woman want to kill herself. She thought about the images on Tim's laptop, of Jessica smothering her son. *But there's no way that could have happened. We got there too quickly. And Sammie had been asleep. It was almost like we were sent on a wild goose chase to keep us from finding out what Jessica was really up to. Thank God Frank was there.*

Why was Frank there?

Something still didn't add up. Jessica could not have been in two places at once, so what exactly had Angela seen on Tim's video feed? Sammie's drawings had predicted the rain, the darkness, and everyone being huddled together in the piano lounge. They had also shown Jessica hanging from the balcony. Sammie had known what would happen.

He knew.

Angela thought about Charles Crippley again. That man had also possessed a certain talent for clairvoyance. He had known Angela was a lesbian before she'd even known it herself and had also known many of the sins of her parishioners— he'd yelled them out in church as he butchered each one of them.

Fornicator, swindler, wife-beater...

And on it went.

Was that what was happening now? Was Crippley inside the boy? Sammie had known Angela when they'd first met—known her because of his 'friend' the boy had said. *Was his friend Crippley?*

Don't be ridiculous, Angela. Whatever's going on here, there's no reason to think there's something–or someone–inside of Sammie.

Angela turned off the shower and let the water drain from her skin. Steam rose from her flesh, and for a moment she felt light-headed. Stepping out onto the cold tiles of the bathroom soon brought back her senses.

Careful not to slip, she padded across the bathroom tiles and back towards the plush carpet of the bedroom. She planned to go to bed and reassess things in the morning—too tired to figure anything out tonight—but as she reached the bedroom door, something stopped her dead in her tracks.

Angela turned towards the mirror hanging above the sink where she had noticed something in the corner of her eye. Written in the condensation on the glass, by unseen fingertips, were two simple words: SAVE ME.

* * *

Angela dared not look at her watch for fear it would show a time closer to dawn than midnight. Sleep deprivation was one of her common dreads, and it felt like she'd lain awake for hours. If she checked her watch and saw it was nearly time to rise, it would depress her and destroy any slim chance of catching any rest at all.

I hate this house.

Angela could be a bad sleeper at the best of times, but tonight there were several causes. Questions filled her head, the main one being—Who had entered the en suite while she showered and wrote that message on the mirror? If it was a joke, she didn't find it funny. Tomorrow, she would get to the bottom of things, but something else demanded her attention first—the main reason she could not sleep.

Sammie's voice was an endless babble of noise. It was muffled by the floors between them, but was still loud and bellowing. Angela struggled to believe the boy's voice could travel so far. The words he spoke, however, were indecipherable at such a distance, but Angela could guess what Sammie was babbling about. Frank had already told her. Sammie liked to quote the Bible during the small hours. But which parts of the Bible?

As Angela tossed and turned beneath the fine Egyptian sheets, something occurred to her. When Frank had first told her about Sammie's nightly activities, she had asked him to record the verses the boy quoted. Whether Frank had done so and forgotten, or just not done so at all, was unclear, but so far he had not even mentioned her request. It was something she needed to remember to ask him about tomorrow. The Bible verses could point to a message that Sammie's subconscious sought to communicate. It could provide vital clues about how to help the boy.

Angela gave in and checked her watch. A little past 3AM—not as bad as she'd thought. She felt more hopeful about getting a modicum of sleep, but it was still likely a losing battle.

The lights flickered on for a split-second, then fizzled out. The alarm clock on the bedside table went black. Rain beat at the windows, and the pitch-blackness of the unfamiliar room sent shivers through Angela's skin. She shook her head and cursed. "I really hate this house."

Chapter 17

Tim awoke well-rested in his van at 10AM. Frank had offered him a room inside the house, but the van was his home. He saw no reason to obligate himself to anybody else. Sleeping in his vehicle also gave him the option of a midnight getaway if things got hairy. Running was one way Tim survived.

Although he intended to see this job through, he was fully prepared to scarper at the first sign of real danger. Just because I dig the X-Files doesn't mean I want to live it.

Not again.

Rain still fell from the ashen sky, leaving the vast grounds waterlogged and glistening. Fat crows stalked the gardens, looking for plump worms. Tim rummaged in the clothes hamper he kept in the back of his van and pulled on a pair of jeans, along with a bright orange ATARI t-shirt that matched his hair. He knew he looked like a massive nerd, but that was just his protection—his camouflage. Anyway, he was sure Nerds would be the new Cool one day. Growing his bright ginger hair out into a shaggy mess, not shaving, and wearing teenager's clothes was a penance of sorts. He deserved nobody's respect, so he ensured that he received none. With nobody respecting him, there was no reason for him to confront his past, or for anybody to expect anything from him.

Nobody wants anything from a loser.

Tim hopped out of the van and into the morning, worn trainers crunching in the wet gravel of the driveway. The large Mercedes again sat nearby, but neither Mike nor Graham sat inside. They were on suicide watch. Poor Jessica. She must have been through hell to reach such desperation. Tim remembered a quote he read once: One needs more courage to live than to kill himself.

True dat!

When he reached the front door of the house, Tim realised he was locked out, but when he pressed the buzzer it didn't take long for Frank to arrive and let him in out of the rain.

The Chief of House looked exhausted, sunken eyes as grey as his hair. New wrinkles had appeared all over his face. If Tim knew any better, he would say Frank hadn't slept in days.

"Everything okay, man?"

Frank tilted his head as if he was too tired to hold it up. "As well as can be expected. Sammie is in his room and Ms Raymeady is sleeping. I trust there will be no disruptions today?"

Tim shrugged. "No intentional disruptions, but they seem to be an unavoidable habit around here."

Frank said nothing.

"Is Angela awake yet?"

"I believe not. I am yet to see her this morning. Perhaps you should call on her."

"I'll do that."

"No need." Angela came down the staircase. She looked exhausted too, but at least she had a clean set of clothes on—a thin blue sweater with black trousers—and she was carrying a satchel.

"How'd you sleep?" Tim asked her.

"I didn't."

"That sucks. You going to be okay?"

Angela nodded. "Don't worry about me. Frank, did you record the things Sammie was saying in the night? You said you would."

Frank shook his head dismissively, but it was clear by the brief flicker in his expression that he'd forgotten. "I'm afraid I haven't gotten around to it."

Angela exhaled. "Frank, you brought us here to help. How can we do that if you're not helping us?"

Frank seemed insulted by her chastisement and stiffened up defiantly. "I don't see what knowledge it would provide you, anyway. Seems like a fool's errand to me."

"That's your opinion. Now I have to wait another night to find out what Sammie's been saying."

"No you don't," Tim said. "When the power came back on, so did the video feeds I set up. I'll have audio recordings of everything Sammie said."

Angela grinned, but her expression quickly turned to a frown. "The power went off again during the night."

Tim shrugged. Having slept outside, he hadn't been aware of any power cut, but as he looked around he saw the electricity was still yet to return. "Okay, then I'll have recordings up until that point. May still be helpful."

"You're right," said Angela, patting him on the back like a buddy. "Good work."

"My laptop is still in the piano lounge. Shall we take a look now?"

Angela was in favour of the suggestion, so they got going. Before they left the foyer, though, Frank had one last thing to say to them. "Let me know if you intend on seeing Sammie. No one sees him today without informing me first."

"Sure thing," said Tim, actually preferring Frank to be there if they went to see the boy again. *Maybe he can keep the kid from attacking like a wild animal.*

In the lounge, Tim's laptop was still on the table where he'd left it. The lid was closed, so he pushed it open and took a seat. The screen was black for a few seconds while the computer came out of sleep mode, but then several images popped up on-screen.

The video and audio feeds were no longer running. An error log reported an interruption, which must have been when the power went off. Tim checked the video cache and found several hours of recordings. With any luck, there would be plenty of footage Angela could work with.

Tim clicked on the backup file.

A video popped up on screen. He moved the laptop so that Angela could see it.

"What time is this from?" she asked him.

"It's from... half-past-twelve."

"Can you fast forward it? To about 2AM?"

"Yeah, sure. Did something happen then?"

Angela nodded. "I was awake. Sammie was rambling."

Tim clicked on the video's timeline to find the approximate section. "Okay... here, let's see what we've got."

The video stuttered briefly, then ran smoothly. Sammie paced his room like a caged lion, sticking close to the walls on all sides, never encroaching on the centre. The boy shouted and was gesticulating wildly. "Behold, I am coming soon! My reward is with me, and I will give to everyone according to what he has done."

"What does that mean?" asked Tim as he listened to the boy's guttural expulsions.

"It's from Revelations," Angela explained. "It's about being judged for our sins when the end comes."

"The end?"

"Yeah, you know. The whole Four Horsemen of the Apocalypse shebang."

Tim pulled a face. "That's comforting."

"Be not overcome of evil, but overcome evil with good. A brave man is a man who dares to look the Devil in the face and tell him he is a Devil. Be ever engaged, so that whenever the Devil calls he may find you occupied."

"What's he quoting now?"

Angela shook her head. "Various chapters, but they all seem to be about the Devil or having evil tempt us."

"Isn't that all a bit cliché? I mean, we're here to maybe perform an exorcism and Sammie's quoting verses about the Devil. Next, he'll be puking mushy peas and doing the crab walk."

Angela sniffed. "Could be mental illness. Religious mania tends to focus on the Devil. An excuse for the afflicted to explain their actions—to pass the burden of responsibility onto some intangible force."

"Are we still thinking the kid is just a regular-flavoured whacko then?"

"I don't know," Angela admitted. "If it were not for the past two days, then I wouldn't hesitate in saying that, but with all the strangeness that has been going on, I think I'm ready to take this to the next step."

Tim thought about his experience at the duck pond and knew what she was talking about when she spoke about strangeness. "So what is the next step?" he enquired.

Angela looked at him and sighed. "I'm going to conduct an exorcism. I will do what Jessica brought me here to do."

Despite his years in the 'ghost business' Tim had never witnessed an exorcism. The prospect made him more than a little anxious. He wasn't willing to show that though. "Can I be of any help?"

Angela nodded. "I'm sure you can. For moral support if nothing else."

The laptop's video feed went blank.

"Must have been when the power cut off," said Tim. "Hmm, that's interesting. It went off at 3AM exactly."

"Yeah," Angela said. "I checked my watch. It was about that time."

"The witching hour," Tim said. "Jesus was crucified at 3PM, but 3AM is said to belong to the Devil. Between midnight and 3AM is when the veil between our world and the next is at its thinnest."

"Are you shitting me?" Angela said while laughing. "I thought I was the Christian here."

"I'm not saying I believe it.In fact, it's yet another cliché to add to the list. We're well ensconced in Horror Movie 101."

"Perhaps they only became clichés because they're true," Angela suggested. "Are you trying to say you still think this is a set up?"

Tim cleared his throat and sat up straight in his chair. "I don't know. There's definitely a mystery afoot, but let's just say, hypothetically at least, that Sammie is possessed—why him? It's not like there's a long list of people possessed by demons. It's a rarity, if it even exists at all, so what is so special about Sammie that it happened to him?"

Angela thought about it. "I don't know. Some schools of thought say only the devout are at risk of an evil entity invading their soul. Others claim repetition of a specific sin attracts the Devil's minions—excessive masturbation or swearing, for example. Some say it's a random occurrence while others say that for a demon to inhabit your soul you must consciously invite it."

"And what do you think?"

"I think evil takes advantage. I think it plays the human race like chess pieces on a board. If a demon were to possess a person, it would do so for a specific reason— to further the cause of evil. I read a Judaic theory once that several demons cast out from Mary Magdalene inhabited Judas, Emperor Nero, Adolf Hitler, and many other powerful men. I think what attracts the Devil is power. Power to do harm."

"And you think a ten-year-old boy is powerful?"

"A ten-year-old boy who stands to inherit a fortune one day and a place on the board of the world's most powerful company? Yeah, I think little Sammie is more powerful than we realise. Hitler influenced millions towards evil, but the Black Remedy Corporation has the influence to affect billions."

"So you think if there's a demon inside Sammie, it's a power-hungry entrepreneur?" Tim laughed at his own joke. "Sorry, I do get your point. Sammie has boundless potential for power, but that would mean this hypothetical demon is in it for the long haul."

"Hypothetical is the word," said Angela. "I'm still not willing to accept a demon is the cause of all this."

The laptop flashed back on.

Tim jolted back in his chair. "What the...?"

The footage on-screen was of Angela's room. It showed her lying in bed, tossing and turning in the moonlight.

"How... What... I never placed a camera in your room. I'm not a Peeping Tom."

"What time is this?" Angela asked, apparently not about to accuse him.

Tim checked the time stamp. "5AM, but I swear I haven't set up any cameras in your room. I don't know where this footage came from."

"Someone was in my room last night," Angela said. "I got out of the shower and someone had written a message on my mirror. Maybe they left a camera in my room at the same time."

"Who, though? Frank?"

The laptop flashed again. The feed changed back to Sammie's room. The boy was no longer pacing the room or quoting Bible passages. He was in bed asleep, a normal ten-year-old boy.

Tim tried to jog the video backwards, to re-examine the footage from Angela's room, but when he tried to rewind...

"This makes zero sense," he said.

Angela frowned. "What doesn't?"

"The footage of your room is gone. Look..." He moved the video's timeline back and forth slowly for her. The images showed only Sammie in his room. "The video from your room is gone—like it deleted itself."

Angela stared at the laptop's screen. "Or maybe it was never there."

Chapter 18

Mike sat on a chair opposite Graham. Jessica lay on the bed between them. The lady of the house rested fitfully, eyes flickering like loose marbles beneath closed eyelids.

"Are you okay to take over?" Mike asked Graham. "I need to crash or I'll pass out on my feet."

Graham's face was as grumpy as ever, and he shrugged. "Don't have much choice, do I? Why did she do something so bloody stupid. Daft mare."

Mike sighed. "You know there's more to it than that, Graham. I'll be back later. Call Frank if she wakes up."

Mike left and headed down to the second floor. Most rooms there had belonged to the live-in staff, but were all vacant now. He picked a room at random and headed inside. An ottoman-style bed met him, a welcome sight. Opportunity for imminent sleep made his body limp with anticipation.

Things were in motion, Mike could feel it. Destiny was at work. Jessica would not be the last person injured before all this was through. Sammie was just getting started.

Mike stood in front of the room's full-length mirror and took off his shirt. The runic symbols carved into his chest were still red and swollen, thick, pink scars bringing memories of agony and suffering. A price he had been willing to pay. The symbols would keep him safe.

Not just a chauffeur, Mike's role was far greater than anyone in the house knew. His employers–his true employers–were counting on him to make sure things went as planned.

Sliding beneath the bedsheets, Mike prepared to sleep all day. The night was more his time.

Chapter 19

Angela had spent the last hour praying and confessing her sins.

To perform an exorcism, one must first humble themselves before the Lord. To invoke the power of Christ, one must not withhold any part of themselves. Angela reconnected with Heaven again after a long absence.

To her surprise, she had found her old cassock and dog collar packed in her suitcase. Mike must have found it. Wearing it now, after so long, felt oddly comforting, as if she'd donned another layer of skin to protect her from injury. She didn't feel so worthless anymore.

She felt like herself.

Picking up her exorcism kit, Angela exited the room. Tim and Frank arranged to meet her outside Sammie's room, and that was where she headed. Both men acted impatiently by the time she got there.

"Beginning to think you weren't going to show," said Tim. The sound of his voice wasn't just impatient, but anxious also.

"Sorry. I needed to prepare."

"Are you ready now?"

"Almost. I need to run through a few things with you both first."

"Such as what?" Frank asked.

"If—and I mean if—it turns out that Sammie has been infiltrated by a demon, there are several rules you need to abide by at all times. Number one: Do not converse with the demon—leave the talking to me. Number two: Do not challenge the demon in any way. Remember that it can hurt Sammie. Number three: Control your emotions. Any sign of anger, fear, or even empathy, the demon will use it to control you. Number four: Do not touch Sammie once I have begun and do not hand him anything. Finally, and most importantly: Do not interfere. Once this process starts, Sammie will appear to get worse as the demon is brought forth. No matter what, you must let me finish. Do you both understand?"

Tim nodded. Frank grunted.

"Okay, then let's go see Sammie."

Frank opened the door, and they entered. As soon as they did so, the familiar stench of stale sweat washed over them. Sammie was at his desk as usual, half-naked and sketching away. Repetition of tasks were not uncommon with mental illness, but nor were they uncommon with genuine possession.

"Do we need him lying down in the bed?" Tim asked.

Angela shook her head. "That's just the movies. As long as Sammie can hear me."

"Should we at least make a circle of protection? Sprinkle salt around or something? Just feels like we should be-"

Angela hushed Tim with a finger. "The Lord will protect us, Tim. You can keep your circles of salt for Halloween parties. Stop babbling."

Sammie moved out of his chair and faced them. The movement was sudden and quick, but he stared at them serenely. "How lovely to see you again, Ms Murs—and in your Christian armour, no less."

"Jesus Christ is my armour, Sammie. Do you know who Jesus Christ is?"

A thin smile crept onto Sammie's face. "A childish fairytale, as I understand it. A creation of mankind to lend credence to your own importance. Fiction, Miss Murs. You are wasting your life on fiction."

"Not fiction, Sammie. Jesus Christ is here with us now. He sees you. He sees all."

"I fear you are misguided," Sammie told her, but the anxious twitch of his cheek spoke of something else.

Angela took a step closer. "Jesus Christ loves you, Sammie. He wants you to come to him and join him in the light."

Sammie sniggered, a bitter, animalistic sound. He gave no other reply.

Angela took another step closer. Scratch marks covered Sammie's skinny arms, as if he'd been clawing at his own flesh and trying to escape his own body. "When did you last eat, Sammie?"

"I have all the nourishment I need, Ms Murs."

"Do you get it from your friend?" Tim butted in, trying to be helpful.

Angela shot a glare at Tim to remind him of his promise to stay quiet. He averted his eyes immediately and stared down at the floor, chastised.

Sammie's smile grew wider. "Naughty Tim. Angela is in charge here. You're just here to observe." He winked at Angela. "Am I correct, Ms Murs?"

"Yes, Sammie. I am in charge here. I am an adult and you need to answer my questions. Okay?"

"I wouldn't dream of obstructing your investigation. Although, you must forgive my confusion. What precisely are you investigating?"

"You," said Angela. "You're not well, Sammie, and I want to help you get better."

"Seems like a poor use of your time, Ms Murs, seeing as how I've never felt better. Perhaps it is you who is sick." Sammie empathised the word 'sick,' almost spat it at her.

Angela ignored his attempt to sow doubt. "This is about you, Sammie. Tell me about your friend."

Sammie looked up at the ceiling and sighed as though he were imagining a beautiful day at the beach. "At first we were not friends at all. In fact, he disapproved of me. Came to me in order to change who I was. We didn't see eye-to-eye on many things when first we met."

Angela frowned. "And now?"

"Now my friend prefers to take a back seat and be quiet. He offers only whispers."

Angela asked the important question. "What is your friend's name?"

Sammie wagged his finger at Angela. "I'm afraid it would be a betrayal to impart such information. Names have power and I wouldn't like to compromise someone so dear to me."

Angela took two steps forward, almost to within arm's reach of the boy. "Let's be honest with one another. I'm not talking to Sammie now, am I? Who are you? By the authority of Jesus Christ, I demand you name yourself!"

"Your words mean nothing, priest. Leave!"

"No," said Angela, reaching into her pocket and bringing out her silver crucifix.

She held it in front of Sammie's face. "Be gone, demon. Leave this boy and never return." She looked up at the ceiling. "I ask you, Jesus Christ, to cleanse this unclean spirit. I banish you, demon. Return to hell and never come here again."

Sammie clambered backwards, falling across his desk in a bundle of skinny arms and legs. He thrashed and kicked, screamed and whined. His crayons and drawings scattered onto the carpet. He was in pain. The Rites were working.

Angela thrust her crucifix before her like a sword. "Leave here, minion. Return to your master to burn in hell. The power of Christ compels you. Be gone!"

Sammie fell from the desk onto the floor, rocking side-to-side on his hands and knees and choking. He retched, whole body wracked with seizures as his diaphragm spasmed. His screeches were like a wounded cat.

"Be gone, demon!"

Sammie screamed, a strained keening, but slowly...

Sammie's screams transformed to laughter. He bellowed so hard his entire chest heaved. He stood before them and pointed his finger. "You're theatrics are wonderful, priest."

Angela stumbled backwards. "W-what?"

"Bravo," Sammie said, clapping his hands slowly. "Quite the little scene we had there. I enjoyed the part about Christ compelling me. Classic stuff. Please do tell me you have planned next?"

"Why are you here?" she asked him, angry and wavering at once.

Sammie looked at her, seemed to study her. "Why are any of us here, priest? We have our parts to play, and we play them whether we choose to or not."

Angela had lost control over the situation. She didn't understand what had gone wrong. "And what part do I have to play?" she asked. Don't ask questions, Angela. You're playing into his hands.

Sammie's eyebrows lowered and a look of grim amusement seemed to settle over him. "You, Ms Murs, are here to play the Martyr."

Chapter 20

"What does he mean, you're a martyr?" Tim asked Angela as they stood in the piano lounge. Tim kept on tapping the piano's keys nervously, and the constant plinking sound was beginning to set Angela's teeth on edge. She bit her lower lip until it bled.

"I don't know what it means," she snapped. "I think Sammie expects me to die for my beliefs, which is strange seeing as I'm not even sure what I believe. It doesn't even matter though; a demon will say whatever it takes to get a reaction. I'd say it won that round."

Tim raised his eyebrows. "You think we're dealing with Evil?"

Angela slumped forward so that her forehead rested against the cold, polished wood of the piano. Her temples throbbed with pressure. "Jesus, I don't know. I would have expected something more than we got, but my words were powerless. I invoked the Lord and nothing happened."

"How could that be?" Tim asked, still plinking at the piano. "Why would it not work? Is there a success rate you have to work with?"

Angela pushed away from the bar and shook her head. "Evil is Evil and God is God—there are no variables. An exorcism performed by a priest should be an unstoppable force in the presence of Evil. I am convinced of that Evil, but perhaps

God is no longer with me. An exorcist must be devout, connected to Heaven… I've been following the wrong path for years now. I shied away from God and now I'm a charlatan speaking His name." She pulled the dog collar from her neck and let it fall to the floor. "I'm a blasphemer."

"Sounds like Sammie got what he wanted," said Tim, running his finger down the piano keys and playing a scale. "He's got you running scared, doubting yourself. Isn't that what you warned us about."

"Will you stop messing with that bloody piano! It's giving me headache."

Tim leapt back from the piano like it was a smoking gun. "Yikes, sorry!"

Angela rubbed at her temples. "No, I'm the one who's sorry. You're right. I lost my confidence as a Christian a long time ago and Sammie played with that weakness."

"But that's a good thing," said Tim.

"What? How is that a good thing?"

Tim walked over to the bar and hopped up onto it, almost banging his head on the overhanging glasses shelf. He grinned sheepishly at his own clumsiness, but then went on to explain what he meant. "In the army they break down cadets, right? Rip their self-esteem to shreds and leave them swimming in their own tears."

Angela shrugged. "Bunch of macho bullshit."

"But then they rebuild them into warriors," Tim went on. "Ass-kicking, gun-toting, heroes of the free world. Or, you know… self-serving fascists, depending on the country."

"What's your point?"

Tim shook his head as if she were an idiot. "My point is you've hit rock-bottom, so you've got nothing to lose. There's nothing left for Sammie to use against you. Now you have the advantage. Time to rebuild yourself as a warrior, so come on Christian Soldier."

"You're full of shit, you know that?"

"Yeah," said Tim. "But now and then I'm right on the money."

"And now would be one of those times?"

"Who knows? I'm just a ghost-hunter who lives in his van."

Angela smiled. "Maybe that's why it worries me so much that I trust you."

"Perhaps it's time to trust yourself. You're not so bad as far as bible-bashers go."

A voice came from over by the door. It was Graham. "Sorry to interrupt your Hallmark moment," he said, "but I was looking for Frank."

Tim scratched his beard with his middle finger, but the other man didn't seem to notice he was being flipped off. "He was in Sammie's room last we saw him, dude. Aren't you supposed to be watching Jessica?"

"Not that it's any of your business what my movements are, but yes I am supposed to be watching her. Frank told me to come and get him if she woke up."

"She's awake?" Angela asked.

"She's been awake for ten minutes."

"Is she okay?"

Graham looked a little squeamish. "Not exactly," he said. "There's something wrong with her."

"What?" Tim asked, sliding down off the bar.

Graham cleared his throat and said, "She's gone blind."

* * *

The afternoon gave way to evening. The light inside the house wound down gradually, but it wouldn't be long before shadows enveloped the hallways. From the top floor, closest to the manor's slanted roof, the rainfall sounded like a million tiny drums. The weather was angry.

Jessica still lay in bed, and Frank moved immediately to her side. "Jessica. Jessica, what's wrong? Are you okay?"

Jessica gazed around the room—except that she didn't. Milky cataracts covered her eyes. She reached out a hand to locate Frank's face. "Frank," she said, voice thick with approaching sobs. "I-I can't see anything, Frank. I can't see!"

Frank embraced her tightly. "I'm here. We will get this sorted out." He turned his head and made eye contact with Graham, leant up against the doorway. "Call a doctor."

Ashen-faced, Graham left to make the call.

Angela padded across the plush carpet and sat herself down on a clothes hamper at the foot of the bed. "Jessica? It's Angela. Do you know what happened?"

Jessica turned her head toward her voice, but could only gaze into nothingness. "I-I don't know. I don't remember."

"Do you remember trying to jump off the balcony?"

"What?" She sounded even more distressed at hearing that. "No, no, no. I don't know what you're talking about. Frank, what is she talking about?"

Frank held her. "It's nothing, Jessica. Don't worry."

Tim turned to Angela and whispered. "She doesn't remember trying to kill herself? Makes me wonder if she even knew what she was doing when it was happening."

"What do you mean?" Angela whispered back. "That she was sleepwalking or something?"

"Or in a trance. People can manipulated by hypnotic suggestion, can't they?"

Tim shrugged. "Maybe. You think what we're dealing with is the great Sammie-Mundo?"

There was a thick gurgling sound.

Angela saw Jessica and knew what was about to happen. The lady of the house hitched forward in bed and vomited on the sheets. The mixture was revolting: blood mixed with bile mixed with semi-digested food. A foul odour filled the room.

Angela fought her body's own reactive urge to vomit by smiling—an old trick she'd learned during her visits to various hospices on behalf of the church. For some reason, it worked.

Frank leapt aside, narrowly avoiding the stream of steaming puke. Jessica continued vomiting until all that could have been left was her internal organs. Then she slumped backwards into bed as if shoved by an invisible hand. She wept uncontrollably, but between sobs she choked out a garbled statement. "I... I... I'm being punished for.... for betraying Joseph. God is punishing me for betraying my husband. Please, please... please forgive me."

Jessica passed out, so suddenly it was like someone had flicked a switch in her brain.

"She's sleeping again? After that?" Tim's expression was stricken.

Frank placed a hand against Jessica's clammy forehead. "Give her some privacy, please."

"Of course," said Angela. "Just let us know if we can help."

Angela and Tim left and walked down the hallway in silence. There was nothing to say that would make any sense. Jessica's sudden malady, her complete blindness and unholy sickness, appeared medically impossible. What sickness could seize a person so? Was it poison?

On the next floor down, they met with Graham. The man seemed flummoxed.

"Are you okay, Graham?" Angela asked.

"The phones aren't working. Don't know if it's the weather."

Tim seemed surprised. "Really? The rain isn't that bad, is it?"

"What do you want me to say?" said Graham. "The phone lines aren't working. I don't know why."

"Okay, okay. Let me take a look at them. I might be able to figure it out."

"Be my guest," said Graham, barging past them to the stairs and heading upwards.

"I'm starving," said Angela, realising she hadn't eaten all day. It was now early evening. It felt wrong thinking about her belly when Jessica was in need of a doctor, but she knew herself well enough to know she'd be little help to anyone if she was hungry.

"Me too," Tim said, "but I better go take a look at the phone lines first. Why don't you find the kitchen and rustle up some grub? I'll find you."

It was a good idea, so Angela watched Tim head out the front door into the rain outside, and then headed off to find the kitchen.

She found it at the end of a long corridor in the east wing, its presence forecast by the double aluminium doors marking its entrance. Inside, the grandness was as expected. A double range cooker occupied one wall beneath a large, metal extractor fan. An American-style fridge sat beside a deep chest freezer, and the other equipment, along with the preparation area, was fit to feed a small army. But it was obvious the facilities hadn't been used anywhere near capacity in some time. Dust covered most surfaces.

Angela headed for the fridge and opened it. The stench of rotten meat slapped her in the face and made her gag. If only she'd had time to smile. When she examined the contents on the various shelves, she found a mould-covered chicken carcass. Cringing, she grabbed the plate of spoiled poultry and flung it into a nearby bin, plate and all. The smell lingered. Angela located two bottles of offensive milk where the white substance had curdled into a malignant paste. She threw those in the bin too. Her appetite being ruined, she gave up on the fridge and rooted around the cupboards. Finally, she found a large box of mini cookies and some still-in-date crisps. It wasn't a feast, by any means, but it would do. She laid her finds out on the stainless steel centre island and pulled up a stool. The slightly stale cookies tasted heavenly, and her stomach gurgled as it was being filled. She would need to be careful not to eat them all and save some for Tim. Guy was so skinny, he could do with some junk food.

The fleshy stench of rotten chicken wafting out of the bin stirred memories in her. Images of Charles Crippley hacking into innocent people with his bloody butcher knife. The scene played back in her mind like a grainy VHS videotape. That day...

When Crippley had walked down the aisle that fateful Sunday morning, Angela knew right away that the man's fractured mind had finally splintered. Her attempts to help him over the previous few weeks had resulted only in worsening him. The expression on Charles's face as he stalked down the centre of the church was bestial, more animal than human. He tore apart those in his path like a lion ripping apart gazelles. Before long, the small church was a carpet of pink flesh and leaking brown fluids. At the end, Angela was the only one left. A lone woman facing down a mountainous beast.

Out of instinct, Angela performed The Rites from the Rituale Romanum. She renounced the Devil and implored Jesus Christ to protect her from Evil. Charles snarled and growled at her, but seemed unable to approach further. He kept his distance as if held back by some invisible force. I'll burn your flesh in hell, you pussy-licking cunt, he screamed at her. I will tear your soul apart.

Angela continued with The Rites, shutting out the vile curses of the madman before her and the sight of her mutilated flock. She closed her eyes to the bodies of her former friends and parishioners and instead concentrated on Christ's love and the power of the Lord. Even when Charles finally took a step forward, plunging his knife into Angela's chest, she had continued undeterred. There was no pain inhibiting her, for she was protected. She felt the Lord's presence in every part of her being.

Her words brought Charles Crippley to his knees. The bloody knife fell from his hands and cluttered against the flagstones. Frantically, he clutched at his chest as the strength of Angela's beliefs stopped his heart. It was then Angela knew, with absolute certainty, that God existed. What she could not understand, was why He'd allowed over a dozen people to die on the floor of His church.

God was mysterious.

God was great.

But God was not Good.

Charles had stared up at Angela, eyes bulging as the pressure rose inside of him. A voice spoke through him that was not his own. "YOU HAVE WON NOTHING, PRIEST. YOUR TIME OF AGONY WILL COME. YOUR DEATH WILL LAST AN ETERNITY. YOU WILL DIE A LONELY MATRYR IN A WAR ALREADY LOST."

Then Charles Crippley died at her feet.

"Yuck! It stinks like my ass in here."

Angela was yanked from her memories by Tim entering the kitchen. She was glad of his presence and almost felt like he had rescued her. Her memories would not let go.

"Great," Tim said. "Are those chocolate chip?"

Angela pushed the box of cookies across the table towards him. "Did you fix the phones?"

"Afraid not. The lines are totally dead. I can't figure it out. Frank is heading out to get help."

Angela frowned. "Didn't he want to send Graham or Mike?"

Tim threw a cookie in his mouth and spoke while he chewed. "I think he wanted to make sure it got done quickly. That guy is one totally freaked-out mamajama."

"I get the impression there's more to his relationship with Jessica than meets the eye."

"Yeah, I'm getting that. You know what sucks about this whole thing?"

Angela popped a crisp into her mouth and munched. "What?"

Tim picked out a cookie and examined it before he ate it. "While Frank is gone, Graham is in charge."

"Ouch," said Angela. "The Devil really is at work in this house."

Chapter 21

The rain beat against the windows like the march of an approaching army. Thunder clashed. Mike hadn't slept for more than a few hours, but he could survive on less. It was early evening. They would need to light candles if the lights didn't come back on.

A few moments ago, Graham had woken Mike with a sudden clap of his hands, and given him five minutes to get ready and join him in Jessica's room. Graham hadn't explained what was going on, but Mike assumed from his colleague's rattled manner that some crisis had occurred.

So he left the bedroom and went to join his colleague. The door to Jessica's room was ajar. Graham stood inside.

"Hey," said Mike. "So what's been going on?"

"I need you to watch Ms Raymeady until Frank gets back. He's left me in charge and I need to keep an eye on the house guests."

"Okay," said Mike, not quite understanding. He noticed the putrid stains on Jessica's bedsheets and motioned towards her with a thrust of his chin. "She okay?"

Graham shrugged. "She's gone blind."

Mike spluttered. "Blind?"

"As a bat. Frank's already left for the hospital to get help. The phones aren't working, so we couldn't call."

"That's weird. Okay, you do what you need to do. I'll keep an eye on everything here."

"Thanks, Mike." Graham put a hand on his shoulder and looked him in the eye. "I'll be happy when those two are out of the house and we can get back to doing an honest day's work, instead of hanging around babysitting. This shit is no good for my heart."

Mike smiled at his colleague and patted the hand that was on his shoulder. "Don't worry, buddy. Things will be over soon enough."

"I hope so. This family has suffered enough."

Mike watched Graham walk away, then took a seat beside Jessica's bed and examined her. He couldn't see her eyes, since she was sleeping, but all colour had drained from her skin, leaving her flesh looking like porcelain—a sleeping doll. Her silent beauty was a stark contrast to the ghastliness of the vomit-stained sheets, and Mike wondered why nobody had bothered to change them.

He got up and wandered out into the corridor, opened one of the linen closets that housed spare bedding, and selected a fresh bed sheet from the neatly ordered pile. He headed back inside Jessica's room and stripped away her dirty bedclothes.

She stirred as he covered her with a fresh blanket. "Frank?"

"No, Jessica. It's Michael. How are you feeling?"

"I... I can't see. No, wait... I-I can. I can see." She sat bolt upright in the bed like a spring triggered in her spine. Mike tried to ease her back down, but she pushed him away. "I'm fine. I need to get up. I..." She tried to out of bed but her strength failed her. She fell back down onto her elbows, out of breath.

"You need to rest!"

"W-what is wrong with me? I... I want Frank. I need to see Sammie."

"Sammie is fine. Frank has gone to get you a doctor."

"I'm fine." She tried to get up once more. Again she failed.

"You're not fine, Jessica. You need checking over. Maybe you've just caught a nasty bug or something, but it's better to be safe than sorry. I'm sure Frank won't be long."

Jessica was confused, lack of understanding carved into her face. The poor woman really must not remember a thing. "What's happening?" she asked meekly.

"You tried to kill yourself," Mike explained.

"You're lying. Where's Frank?"

"I told you, Jessica. He'll be back soon."

"This is all because of this wicked house. It's cursed, Mike. It took Joseph and now it's trying to take me. I can't stand it anymore."

Jessica pushed herself up in the bed and this time swung her legs round onto the floor. Mike reached out to grab her, but she was up on her feet too quickly and he lost her. Unsteady, she stumbled away from the bed.

Mike rushed after her.

She headed to the wardrobes. "I need to get dressed. Please leave me."

"I can't do that," Mike explained. "I'm here to keep you safe. You need to remain here."

"I'm going, Michael. I'm taking Sammie out of this house before anything else happens." She sorted through the clothes racks, looking for something to wear. The woman had a hundred things to wear.

From behind, Mike wrapped his arm around her neck and squeezed hard, imagining he was trying to pop her head right off her shoulders. He felt her windpipe against his wrist.

Jessica faded quickly, already weak from sickness. The pressure on her carotid artery sapped her brain of oxygen, and unconsciousness bore down on her fast. Mike felt her go limp in his arms. He dragged her back over to the bed and laid her down. With her current state of mind, she'd most likely remember nothing at all of this, but even if she did he would just deny it, make her think she was going crazy. It would be easy considering recent events.

Jessica and Sammie would stay in this house whether they liked it or not. It was his job to keep them there, and that's what he would do.

No matter what.

Chapter 22

Tim sat outside Sammie's room and calibrated his equipment. He was past the point where he felt any of it would do any good, but it was still important to maintain it. This would not be his last job.

Although it's starting to feel like it.

The urge to flee—to just get the hell out of there—rose in him again. An atmosphere cloaked the house. Foreboding, for want of a better cliché. It felt as if danger lurked around every corner. And the epicentre—the reason for it all—was the ten-year-old boy in the next room.

Tim's primary intention whenever he was on a job was to disprove claims of ghosts and monsters, but he was beyond that now. Little doubt that an unnatural presence resided in the house. Others might not admit it, but Tim knew better.

Tim had met true Evil before. At a hotel in Basingstoke: The Grey Gardens Hotel. Tim and his brother had been called to the hotel to investigate any environmental factors that might have caused a recent spate of deaths. The hotel had been forced to close its doors until an explanation was found.

At this point in his life, Tim had possessed zero belief in the paranormal, and he and his brother were simple conmen—dazzling their marks with expensive gadgets and pointless tests. The money was good, and the work was easy. In the Seventies, nobody understood technology so a couple of blinking lights was all you needed to convince people that you knew something they didn't.

Tim's easy life had changed the evening he and his brother slept at The Grey Gardens.

A beeping sound brought him back to the present. He glanced at his equipment and tried to locate the source. His electronic barometer had lit up and was chirping. It warned that the air pressure had dropped. A chance it was due to the stormy weather, but even if it was... Tim hadn't switched the barometer on. In fact, he could see it was unplugged.

Here we go again, Tim thought to himself. Nothing in this house surprised him anymore, but he wasn't about to throw himself onto the fire. He would sit right here. That way, nothing bad could happen. Other people could take the risks and he would observe and take notes.

Tim's heart rate monitor began to sing, the rhythmic tune of a steady pulse. It, too, was unplugged.

Tim was a coward, and he was well aware of the fact. He even embraced it mostly. For being a coward was a valid method of survival—the flight to a braver man's fight. Both instincts were human, and there was no shame in being human. Tim's brother had always been the reckless one and look where that had got him.

I could have done something.

I should have done something.

Tim decided. There was some bad mojo targeting him, and he wasn't about to sit around and see what happened while his equipment went haywire. He needed to find someone. Safer with company. Safer from what exactly, he didn't know.

More of his machines beeped, and he took it as his cue to leave. Rising from his seat, he hurried down the hall towards the staircase. The lights flickered back on briefly overhead as thunder rocked the house, but the power remained off. Like walking through a horror movie, Tim thought to himself as he battled to stay calm.

Reaching the piano lounge behind the staircase, Tim detected the mellow tones of Beethoven's Moonlight Sonata.

This house even has a horror movie soundtrack!

Tim pushed through the doors to the lounge and stepped inside. He found Angela sitting at the back of the room, playing Beethoven's tune quite expertly on the ivory keys. "I didn't know you played," he said. "Glad it's not playing itself."

She looked at him and continued playing, all the more impressive now she wasn't even looking at the keys. "Six years of convent school. You learn a few things."

"You play beautifully. Do you know anything a little more upbeat though?"

"Yeah, I think I can play something." She broke into a jaunty rendition of When I'm Sixty-Four.

Tim slid behind the bar. "That's better. You fancy a drink?"

"My liver says no, but my heart says yes."

Tim poured her a healthy measure of whisky before pouring himself a much smaller one. Tim liked a drink, but he had the constitution of a poodle. Angela could easily out-drink him. He placed her large whiskey on the top of the piano and took a sip from his smaller one. "Just been through some more freaky-deaky shenanigans upstairs," he told her.

Angela stopped playing and looked at him. "What do you mean?"

"Oh, you know, usual stuff: my equipment turned on despite the fact none of it was plugged in and there's no power. I can't help thinking this place is building up to something."

"Please, don't you wig out on me, Tim. So far you've been the only one to keep a clear head."

Tim took another sip of whisky. The liquid burned his throat. "I can take strange, I can even take frightening, but what I can't take is dangerous. Not my thing."

"You've had my back, Tim. I promise to have yours if anything happens."

"Thanks, but all the same I figure I'll be off in the morning. This whole thing is getting a little too far out of my comfort zone."

Angela sighed, picked up her whisky. "I plan on seeing this through, but it's your decision."

"I just think, with what happened to Jessica, it would be better to get a team of doctors in here rather than a guy like me."

Angela stood up and closed the piano's lid. She took her drink over to one of the tables and sat down. "What do you think happened to Jessica? Spontaneous blindness?"

"I've never heard of such a thing, but again that's why I think a doctor should be here."

"Frank will reach the hospital soon. We'll know more then. Perhaps you should postpone your decision."

"Maybe," Tim said. "But perhaps the whole thing was just to get Frank out of the way."

Angela frowned at him. "I don't understand."

Tim sat at the table beside her. "I'm just saying that the last 'man of the house' is dead. Frank seems to be trying to fill Joseph Raymeady's shoes. With him gone, everyone is left rudderless. What are we even doing here anymore?"

"Trying to help," was Angela's answer, but she let out a sigh. "Whatever that means. Maybe when Frank gets back, things will be a little clearer."

"If he comes back."

"Will you stop?" said Angela. "You're such a pessimist, Tim."

"After a couple days in this house, I've learned that expecting the worst to happen is the way to go."

Angela finished her drink and went to get another. "We'll see," she said. "Let's relax for now. I don't plan on leaving this room while Graham is in charge. I can't believe I actually miss Frank."

"Yeah," Tim agreed. "Me either."

Chapter 23

Frank kept his foot on the accelerator, despite the wet on the roads. The rain fell in thick sheets, impossible to see more than a dozen yards ahead, but Frank couldn't afford to slow down. Jessica needed him. Whatever virus could send a person blind overnight was serious—meningitis or some other malady affecting the brain. For all he knew, Jessica could be dying.

Please, no more death. I've had my fill.

Frank had to brake as a bend came out of nowhere. The tyres slipped sideways on the wet surface, but he got the car back under control. He'd driven in worse conditions. Iraq, for one example. Once, he'd driven a 3-tonne truck through a sandstorm so thick he couldn't see beyond the windscreen. He'd survived that and he would survive this. When Jessica is well, things are going to change. I'm taking her and Sammie out of the wretched house. We can be happy somewhere else.

The A429 was coming up on his right. Frank slowed down and took it. The highway would take him to Warwick Hospital. He had no plan for when he got there, too desperate to form one, but at the very least he could get an ambulance to follow him back.

The road was lit, but the heavy rain obscured the street lamp's glow. Frank had no choice but to shave ten miles off his speed. Acres of farmland must have been flying by either side of him, but in the darkness he might have been driving through space for all he saw. He leant forward against the steering wheel, trying to get as close to the road as possible.

"What are you doing, Frank? Why aren't you at the house looking after my family?"

Frank jolted when he heard the sound of Joseph Raymeady's voice. He looked in the rear view mirror and saw his the man's face staring back at him.

The next thing Frank knew, the world was spinning.

Frank lost control of the wheel as it fought against his grip. The tyres slid across the wet tarmac. Gravity threw him against the car's interior.

Then, suddenly, he was upside down.

Frank floated, his body weightless. His vision filled with stars. Then gravity returned and knocked the life out of him and crushed the car's interior flat.

"Now that was careless," said Joseph Raymeady in the back seat. "What am I even paying you for, Frances?"

Rain water pooled around Frank's head as he blinked away his dizziness. Once again, he saw Joseph Raymeady's face in the now-cracked rear view mirror.

"What... what do you want?"

"I want to make sure you're doing your job. How is my family?" Frank struggled with his seatbelt, trying to get himself free of the wreck. Joseph's voice rose in volume. "I asked you a question, Frank. How is my fucking family?"

"They're... they're okay."

"YOU'RE LYING!"

"No," said Frank. "I will keep them safe. They will be okay."

"Then why aren't you with them now?"

"Because Jessica needs a doctor."

"A doctor? A DOCTOR! What have you done, Frank? Why does my darling, sweet Jessica need a doctor?"

Frank made eye-contact with Joseph through the mirror. What he was seeing was impossible. His employer was dead. Frank had been the one to find the body. "You're not real. I've had an accident and you're a hallucination."

"You're the hallucination, Frank. You think you can take my place? I was a great man, a man of principal. You are nothing. A killer of men and children. You deserve to be dead, not me. Your job was to protect me and my family. You let me die."

Frank squirmed, wanting more than anything to get out of the upturned

Mercedes. "You took your own life."

Joseph laughed maliciously, mockingly. "Did I?"

"Go away, Joseph. You're dead."

"Yes. And soon, you will be too. We're all here waiting for you, Frank. All the people you killed in Sierra Leone, the Gulf, Northern Island... so many, Frank. So much death at your hands. And now you want to add my little Sammie and Jessica to your list of sins."

"No!"

Some part of the car ignited. Frank could not see the flames because his neck was jammed up against the car's roof, but he could smell the burning and hear the distinctive crackling. The car was burning. If he didn't escape he would cook to death.

But as much as he tried, Frank could not get himself free.

"We'll be waiting for you, Frank." Joseph Raymeady cackled, a sound unlike anything he had ever made in life. "We are here."

Chapter 24

The lights were still out, and now that the evening was late, they had needed to light candles throughout the house.

Angela sat with Tim on the building's rear porch. A large camisole kept them dry. A lit candle flickered on a small, round table between them, fighting against the breeze. Something about being outside made Angela feel safer. With the heavy rain and the approaching storm, she could feel God's presence. Inside the house, she felt something different.

"You think we should have heard from Frank by now?" Tim asked her.

"The phones are still out."

Tim shook his head. "I mean, shouldn't he have gotten back by now? He's been gone two hours."

"I don't know how far the hospital is, but I bet this rain is slowing him down."

"It's really pouring now, isn't it? Why exactly are we sitting outside?"

"Helps me think," Angela answered. "I like the weather being like this. Makes me feel connected."

"To God?"

"It's more than that. It makes me feel connected to life. Everything begins and ends with the rain. Without it nothing could live."

Tim looked confused. "Has it helped you think any clearer?"

Angela stole a glance at the candle flame. Its healthy glow made her think of Hell and demons that sprawled its infernal hallways. "There's something inside Sammie. The drawing he gave me, the things he knows, and what's happened to Jessica. There's Evil at work in this house for sure, and Sammie is the root of it."

"I wish I could disagree."

Angela ran a hand through her hair and loosed a few knots. "So my question is: what is inside Sammie? If there's a demon inside the boy, then why didn't it respond to my attempts to banish it? Why did the exorcism fail? The Rites have never failed me before."

Tim looked at her. "Is it an exact science? Is there no way for a demon to resist attempts to exorcise it?"

"I don't know. Demons often try to mess with your mind, to prevent you from even going through with the procedure, but Sammie was happy to let me speak freely. At the end it was obvious he found the whole thing ridiculous. A demon should quake at the sound of Christ's name. They should cower at the power of the Lord. They cannot resist God's command."

"Can't say I saw any cowering," said Tim.

"That's my point. What went wrong? What did I misjudge?"

"Maybe it's not a demon. Maybe there could be something else inside of him: a ghost or spirit, perhaps?"

Angela shook her head. "It would make no difference. They should react the same way as a demon. Anything that does not belong on Earth can be compelled by the power of Christ to return to its proper realm—be it Heaven, Hell, or betwixt."

"What about Charles Crippley?"

Angela shuddered. "What about him?"

"Sammie seemed to know you. Perhaps it's Charles Crippley inside of him."

Angela rubbed at herself, feeling the cold. "The thought has crossed my mind but, again, an evil spirit would be as susceptible to exorcism as any demon. There's something I'm not seeing. I need to go back to my books. I just wish I could get the name of Sammie's 'friend.'"

"Why don't you go straight to the source?"

Angela frowned. "What do you mean?"

A sudden gust of wind caused the candle to flicker out, but the flame hung on and came back to life a few seconds later.

God's light does not die.

Tim looked at her earnestly, and expression that looked odd on his scruffily-kept face. "Sammie won't tell us the name of his friend, right? So why don't we ask his friend to name himself? We could use a Ouija board."

Angela huffed. "I have absolutely no experience of those toys. You know they were invented by Hasbro, right?"

"I do," said Tim. "They started out as toys, but they tap into something, I've seen it. To be honest with you, the last time I used one I promised never to use one ever again, but I think now might be the time to break that promise."

"They really work?"

"Yes," Tim said, but said nothing more.

"Okay, when do you want to do it?"

Tim smiled. "No time like the present. I have everything I need in my van. We'll do it there."

"In your van? Seriously?"

"Worst thing that could happen is we get interrupted. My van is perfect for it—nice and private. Plus, I have all the Poptarts we can eat."

Angela chuckled. "Doing a Ouija board in the back of some guy's van. I'm in college all over again."

"You're not wrong," said Tim. "Tonight you might just get an education. I don't think you're going to like it."

* * *

Tim's van was cramped but clean. Obvious that he lived there and treated it like his home as soft cushions covered the piny-fresh interior. Not a thing lay out of place. The rain on the vehicle's metal roof sounded like a drum roll—perhaps in anticipation of what they were about to do.

Tim reached up and pulled an antique-looking box from a storage net lining one side of the van's interior. He set the box on the floor between them and unhooked a brass catch on the side. Inside sat a flat board, finely painted with calligraphic letters and numbers. YES and NO were printed in opposite corners either side of the word GOODBYE. One side of the board lifted up to reveal a hollow. A carved heart-shaped planchette sat inside.

Angela was cynical. She held no stock in things such as voodoo and witchcraft—nothing but primitive superstition. "So how does this go?" she asked Tim.

"Much like you'd expect. We light a few candles—sandalwood works well—sprinkle some copal shavings into a flame and then try our best to concentrate. Afterwards, we make out. Just kidding!"

"What on Earth is copal?"

"It's a resin imported from Mexico, a bit like amber. The Mayans used it to contact the underworld—and that's pretty much what we'll be trying to do. Simple sage works just as well, but I'm always tempted to cook with it."

Angela tried her best to suspend her disbelief and waited patiently while Tim rummaged around the van. From various compartments, he procured a candle and a small plastic baggie filled with golden flecks. Finally, he produced a pair of necklaces. They comprised of simple string loops threaded through the centre of an acorn.

"Wear this," he said, handing her one of the necklaces.

Angela took the looped acorn and examined it questioningly. "Why?"

"Druids used acorns for protection. I never perform a spell without one around my neck. Place it under your shirt against your skin."

Angela did as he asked her, but felt ridiculous. In fact, she felt more than ridiculous—she felt blasphemous. The Church had taught her to forsake anything even bordering on witchcraft.

But I stopped caring about what the Church said a long time ago, didn't I?

Tim lit the candle and sprinkled some of the golden flecks on the flame. He sat crossed-legged opposite Angela and positioned the Ouija board between them. He shuffled forward a little so that their knees were touching. Finally, he reached up and switched off the van's interior light leaving them in darkness aside from the flickering glow of the candle.

"You ready?" Tim asked.

"As ready as I'm going to be."

"Okay then, here we go." Tim placed his index and middle fingers on the board's planchette and motioned for her to do the same. Once she did, he closed his eyes and raised his chin to the roof. "Spirits of old, evil and wicked, I forbid you from doing harm. You are permitted to communicate through us and do no more. I command you to remain in your own plane. We are not portals. If you circle the planchette, we will withdraw and you may be trapped between worlds."

Angela grunted. "Circle the planchette?"

Tim scowled at her. "It signifies a spirit trying to force itself into our world. This won't work if you're against it. You need to be quiet and open your mind."

"I'm sorry. Please continue."

"We wish to speak to the one who claims to be the friend of Samuel Raymeady. We wish to speak with the one who has descended upon this domicile. Come to us, explain yourself. Name yourself."

Nothing happened. Tim sat with his eyes closed. Angela watched him and tried to remain serious. The whole thing was ludicrous, and she felt ashamed of herself for even allowing herself to take part in such a cha-

The planchette twitched.

A jolt of adrenaline prickled Angela's nerve endings. Her muscles stiffened. Tim opened his eyes and grinned. She saw then that there had been no doubt in his mind that this would work. Tim had faith in voodoo as much as she did in God.

The planchette moved an entire inch, hovering between C and D, before finally hopping left and resting on C.

"It's trying to spell out a word," Angela noted.

Tim spoke the letters as they came, one after another, the planchette settling on each one. First had come the C, but afterwards came, "H... A... M... U... E... L..."

The planchette stopped.

Angela thought hard about the spelled-out word. "Chamuel?" she said out loud. "Why does that word ring a bell?"

Tim shrugged, being sure to keep his fingertips on the planchette. "Doesn't mean a thing to me. You know it?"

She frowned, tried to think. "I can't quite remember, but it's there somewhere. I've heard that word before."

Tim cleared his throat and spoke into the empty air. "Hello, Chamuel. Can you tell me why you're here? What do you want?"

This time Angela spoke out the letters as they came up. "D... E... A... T... H..."

Tim let out a breath in a short huff. "That's jovial."

"We want you to leave," Angela commanded. "Leave Sammie alone."

N... O... The planchette moved quicker. N-O... E-S-C-A-P-E... F-R-O-M... D-A-R-K-N-E-S-S...

Tim frowned. "Is that a threat, Chamuel?"

The planchette did not move.

"I said is that a threat? Are we in danger?"

Y-E-S.

"Are you going to hurt Sammie?" Angela asked.

The planchette did not move. Angela made eye contact with Tim who had gone a little pale. There was resolve in her colleague's eyes, however, and she knew he would continue on with the séance for at least a while longer.

The planchette moved again, quicker than before—frantic.

Y-O-U... W-I-L-L... D-I-E...

H-E-L-L... W-I-L-L... T-A-K-E... Y-O-U...

R-U-N...

O-U-T-S-I-D-E... W-E... C-O-M-E...

Something struck the back of the van, rocking it on its wheels.

Chapter 25

"What is that?" Angela shifted towards the front of the van, away from the rear doors. The thud had been so forceful that the steel buckled inwards.

"Felt like we were just hit by a goddamn rhino. Oh, er sorry."

Angela wasn't concerned about the blasphemy. "Should we open the doors?"

"I don't know. Maybe you should check it out while I wait here."

The darkness inside the van was cut only by the light of the single lit candle, which miraculously remained in its brass holder.

No more impacts struck the van. All was still. All was quiet. Except the rain.

"I'll open the doors," said Angela, inching towards the back of the van.

"Be careful," said Tim. "If you get eaten by something I'm not cleaning up the mess. In fact, I'm out of here at the first sign of anything bitey."

Angela placed a hand against the door's release-trigger. She took a breath, held it, then opened the door.

Darkness met her.

The house and its grounds were obscured by the silvery sheets of relentless rain. A gust of wind blew in and filled the van with its cold touch. They were alone. Isolated in an abyss.

"There's nothing out there," Angela said, sliding a leg out of the van and towards the pebbled driveway. She shivered as the temperature outside extinguished the warmth in her blood.

Something leapt out of the shadows.

Reached for her.

Angela screamed.

"Oh, what a relief," came a disembodied voice. "I thought I'd been abandoned."

Angela leapt back into the van, pulling her feet up as if she'd seen a mouse. Sammie stood in front of her, wearing nothing but his underpants. He seemed unaffected by the icy rain glistening on his pale skin. He shone in the darkness like a spectre.

"S-Sammie, what are you doing out here?"

"I was wondering where everybody was. I've been alone in my room for hours without a single visitor. To tell you the truth, I was getting a little stir crazy."

Angela's flesh crawled, buzzing as though it were covered by ravenous ants. "L-Let's get you back inside, Sammie, before you freeze to death."

The boy looked at her, tilted his head. "Oh, the cold doesn't bother me, Angela, but your concern is heartening all the same. Is Frank back yet?"

Tim slid out of the van behind Angela and asked his own question. "How did you know he was gone, Sammie? You said no one had visited you for hours."

"I heard him leave in the car. Sounded like he was in a hurry. I do hope he doesn't have an accident. That man has become like a father. He feels guilty about my father's death."

"Do you feel guilty about it?" Angela asked.

Sammie wore a look of confusion. "Me? Why would I feel guilty about it? Unless you're trying to imply I was responsible. That's very unkind of you, Angela."

"You're right. I'm sorry. Let's go inside."

Tim locked up the van, then he and Angela ushered Sammie back towards the house. They kept a distance of a few feet from the boy who walked barefoot across sharp pebbles. He did not flinch.

Angela whispered to Tim. "Where the hell is Graham? He was supposed to be keeping an eye on things."

"With that guy, who knows? I get the impression he doesn't take his responsibilities very seriously."

Angela opened the front door and the three of them entered the house. The foyer was a dark cave; power still off, weather still bad. The grand marble-floored space seemed smaller without light. Angela wanted to be back outside in the open air, but with the rain that would make her a mad woman. She needed to be inside the house. She needed to take control of the situation.

"Are you okay to take yourself back to bed, Sammie? We'll find out where everyone is and get someone to stop by with dinner." Angela checked her watch. It was almost midnight. Dinner was a long time ago. "Well, perhaps it would be more of a supper."

"I'll go watch television," said Sammie.

Sammie headed towards the stairs, but Tim asked a question first. "Why do you like that program so much, Sammie?"

Sammie turned back around and smiled. "Are you referring to South Park? I suppose I enjoy the irony," he explained and then left.

"Irony? Wonder what he meant by that?"

Angela shrugged. "Who knows? We need to find out where Graham got to. I'm not comfortable with Sammie wandering around un-chaperoned."

"Think he'll end up getting hurt?"

"No," Angela said. "I'm more worried about him hurting someone else."

"So where should we start? This place is huge."

"If I know Graham, there's only one place he'd be."

Tim nodded. "Drinking in the lounge."

They headed behind the stairs and could hear the piano playing. Someone was playing Mozart's arrangement for Twinkle Twinkle Little Star (or 'Ah! Vous Dirai-je, Maman' if her Music Theory lessons served her correctly).

"Is Graham playing that?" Tim asked. "He's even better than you."

Angela frowned and pushed open the door.

The music stopped.

No one was in the lounge.

"Hello?" Tim shouted.

"Save it," Angela said. "There's no one here."

"Then who was Bach-ing it up on the piano?"

"Mozart."

Tim frowned at her. "What?"

"It was Mozart, not Bach."

"Well, whoever it was, they're either invisible or fast as greased lightning. Where did they go?"

Angela shook her head. "There was never anyone here. It's just more games." She crossed the room, slinking between the tables and chairs. Her destination was the piano and as she got there, the hairs on the back of her neck stood up. She spoke a single word "Blood."

Tim remained on the other side of the room. "What's that now?"

"Blood. The piano keys are covered in it."

"Of course," Tim said. "Why not?"

Where there would usually have been several dozen fingers of ivory, there was now a congealed river of thick blood. The plasma filled the gaps between the keys and splashed the wooden frame of the piano. It looked like a pig had been butchered.

Tim moved up beside her. "Helsinki. What on Earth happened here?"

"I don't know," said Angela, "but I think now would be a good time to do a head count."

Chapter 26

Commotion downstairs. Mike left Jessica's bedside and headed out into the hallway. Looking left and right, he saw only darkness. The sound of people screaming did not frighten him—for he'd been taught to expect it—and he knew it would only continue through the night. When the screaming was finally through, a new future would be set forever in motion.

Mike found Angela and Tim on the second floor. Both guests were racing through the hallways and shouting out at the top of their lungs.

"Hey, hey, hey," Mike said, holding up a hand to stop them. "What's wrong?"

Angela almost clattered in to him, and only just stopped in time. "Mike! Thank God, you're okay."

"I'm fine. Why wouldn't I be?"

"There's a shitload of blood in the piano lounge," Tim said, panting. "Someone's hurt."

Mike frowned. "What? Are you sure?"

"I know blood when I see it!" Angela said firmly. "Have you seen Graham? He was supposed to be looking after things, but we found Sammie wandering around in the pouring rain."

Mike was surprised to hear that. "Sammie left the house? That's unlike him."

"Never mind that now. We need to find out whose blood is downstairs. Where's Graham? What about Jessica? Is she okay?"

"Jessica is fine. She's sleeping."

"Then it must be Graham's blood," Tim surmised. "Guy finally had his period."

They both groaned at Tim.

"You don't know Graham is hurt," Mike argued.

"Nothing is certain until we find him," said Angela. "So let's find him."

"I'll check the ground floor," Tim said.

Angela nodded. "I'll check the first floor."

"I've just come from the top," Mike explained, "so I'll check the second."

The three of them set off to their own separate floors, agreeing to meet back later in the piano lounge. Mike would only search half-heartedly, however, for he knew, with total confidence, that Graham would turn up, eventually. In how many pieces would remain to be seen.

* * *

Angela had taken the first floor for a reason. Sammie's room was located there, and she wanted to keep a close eye on him. The only way she could be sure of him not wandering around the house was if she remained close.

The first floor also contained a modern lounge, incongruent with the antique furnishings of the rest of the house. A large LCD television adorned one wall while a plush green sofa took up the one opposite. Aside from the furniture, the room lay empty. Angela moved on.

The next room she checked featured a low-beamed ceiling with a full-sized snooker table. Decorated with horse brasses and a dado rail, the billiard room was like something from a Sir Arthur Conan Doyle novel—a fitting place for a Victorian murder mystery. At this moment it sat empty. Angela moved on.

Angela checked another half-dozen rooms and found them all empty too. A mixture of bedrooms and living space, the entire floor lay abandoned. All except Sammie's room.

She placed a hand on Sammie's doorknob and was sure she could feel subtle vibrations coming from it. The door creaked as she opened it, despite having not done so on previous occasions.

Welcome to my parlour, dear.

Sammie lay in bed, staring at a blank television screen. A chunky stack of South Park videos peeked out from the open drawer of a candle-lit dresser, but without power they were useless.

"Sammie," she said. "Sammie, will you talk with me for a moment?"

The boy ignored her.

"Sammie, have you seen Graham?"

No answer.

"Sammie? Is your friend's name Chamuel?"

Sammie continued to ignore her, but this time there was a brief flicker of his dark eyelashes. A physical response to her question. Sammie could definitely hear her. But maybe he isn't the one in control. Maybe he wants to answer me but can't. He's a prisoner, gagged and bound. A child.

"Chamuel." Angela said sternly. "Are you here with us now? Speak!"

"I don't know what you're talking about," said Sammie. "I'm trying to watch my program and you're interrupting me. Please leave."

"I will, Sammie, but first I want to know who Chamuel is? What does he want?"

Sammie turned and looked at Angela, then shook his head. His expression was one of anger—more anger than a ten-year-old boy should be able to display. "Chamuel wants to kill me, Angela. Does that make you happy?"

"No," Angela said. "No, of course not. I'm not happy at all. Why does Chamuel want to kill you, Sammie? Talk to me."

"I wouldn't be what he wanted me to be, so he wants me gone. He's a nasty bully."

Angela took a step towards Sammie's bed, almost close enough to touch the boy. "What did Chamuel want you to be, Sammie?"

Sammie cleared his throat, and it sounded full of phlegm. "He... wants me to become something I am not. Wants to change me. He never stops trying to get his own way. Angela, I'm getting so tired of fighting him."

Angela looked at the little boy in front of her and felt her heart beat faster. She could not fail this child who needed her. "I am going to help you, Sammie. I want to make Chamuel leave."

Sammie stared at her, dark eyes swirling with a mixture of emotions she couldn't work out. "Please..." he muttered tearfully. "Please make Chamuel stop."

Angela placed a hand on Sammie's naked shoulder and knew she was meeting the boy for the first time. "It's good to finally meet you, Sammie. My name is Angela and I will help you if it's the last thing I do."

I just hope it isn't.

The door swung open and Angela span around. Tim ran inside, his beard ragged, hair dishevelled. "It's Graham," he said. "We found him."

Chapter 27

Angela hurried after Tim, struggling to keep up with his rocket-like pace. He'd not yet told her what happened, just said to follow him and follow fast. They took one flight of stairs up to the second floor where Mike had been searching and stopped at a door midway down the hallway. It was open and Mike waited inside for them.

Angela started grinning, doing all that she could not to vomit at what she saw in front of her... when she saw Graham.

"Why are you smiling?" Mike asked, a look of disgust on his face.

"So I don't puke."

Nobody asked to expand, so she opened her eyes wide and took in the scene fully. The room was some kind of spa. A sauna cubicle stood against the far wall and a small steam lay room next to it. In the centre of the room was a large hot tub, and hanging out of that hot tub, upside down, was Graham.

Dead.

His head and shoulders crumpled against the carpet while his legs pointed upwards, still inside the bubbling hot tub. His arms stretched at right angles from his body, and from where Angela was standing, the man's body resembled a cross.

Or, more accurately, an inverted crucifix.

The calling card of the Devil and his minions.

Angela repeated a prayer in her head, which seemed to make the scene before her more bearable. God would see her through this. She felt him for the first time in ages. Evil had sent him away from her, and now Evil had brought him back again.

Saint Michael the Archangel,

defend us in battle;

be our protection against the wickedness and snares of the devil.

May God rebuke him, we humbly pray:

and do thou, O Prince of the heavenly host,

by the power of God,

thrust into hell Satan and all the evil spirits

who prowl about the world seeking the ruin of souls.

Amen.

Angela's eyes picked up more details, but she had to turn away and leave the room. The sight and smell of fresh blood was too much for her to bare—an instigator of nightmares and memories. Graham's naked body had been plastered with gore, but Angela hadn't looked long enough to figure out where it came from.

Mike had followed her into the hallway which was surprising, as she would have expected Tim to be the one to go check on her. "You okay?" he asked her.

She slumped against the wall and rubbed at her eyes, like lead bearings inside her skull. She cleared her throat and took a second. "I'll be fine. I just don't like the sight of blood."

Mike clamped a hand on her shoulder and gave it a friendly squeeze. "I don't think anybody does."

"What the hell happened to him, Mike?"

Mike shook his head and looked down at his shoes. When he looked back up again he was chewing his bottom lip. "From what I can tell, he bled to death from a gash in his genitals just beneath his scrotum. There's a broken whisky glass in the hot tub and a near-empty bottle on the floor. I think he had some kind of freak accident."

Angela shook her head. "Bullshit! He was murdered. He didn't accidentally sever his ball sack, or whatever it is you're suggesting made him bleed to death. This was murder, Mike, anyone can see that. Just look how he's been positioned."

Mike frowned. "What do you mean?"

"He's in an inverted cross. Feet submerged in water like a reverse baptism. The slicing of his genitals is an act against God, a condemnation of procreation and the spreading of the Lord's creation."

Mike huffed. "Who are you? Perry Mason's religious sister? The forensics act is all very impressive, but if you're suggesting Graham was murdered, then who the hell are you accusing?"

Angela ran the possibilities through her mind. "Tim has been with me all night, Ms Raymeady is asleep, and Frank is gone, which just leaves Sammie—a ten-year-old boy--and you."

Mike laughed, but there was an edge to the sound—a hint of aggression. "You think I killed Graham? That's rich! I've worked with the guy for a whole year. It's you and Tim who are the new faces around here."

"I had nothing to do with it and neither did Angela." Tim joined them out in the hallway. His face was pale, but he seemed in control of himself. "But Graham was definitely murdered, and I can prove it."

"How?" Mike asked.

Tim held his arm out between them and opened up his palm, displaying two long slivers of metal. "Iron nails," he explained. "I found them embedded in Graham's feet. No way he did this himself. He's been crucified."

"Fuck this shit," said Angela. "I'm going to the police. Someone in this house is a goddamn psychopath! Tim, will you drive me the fuck out of here, please?"

"With pleasure. I was already out of this madhouse before someone sliced Graham's ball bag like a joint of ham."

They took the stairs at a gallop, and quickly made it down to the foyer. Mike was right behind them, shouting protests and insisting they shouldn't leave. "You're needed here," he kept saying.

Angela headed for the front door.

It didn't budge when she tried to open it.

She fumbled with the deadbolt and rattled the handle.

It wouldn't budge.

"Mike! Open this goddamn door, right now."

"It isn't locked," he said behind her. "Turn the deadbolt."

"I just did!" Angela thumped her hand against the thick wood defiantly. "It won't open."

Tim stepped up to the door to help. He fiddled with the locks and rattled at the handle. Eventually he threw a fit and started kicking and hammering at the door. Once he was out of breath, he looked at Angela with an expression of dread. "It's stuck."

"What are you trying to pull?" Angela demanded of Mike.

"Nothing. I haven't touched the bloody door. I swear!"

Angela examined Mike's expression. The guy seemed to be telling the truth, but something else was going on—something he wasn't telling her.

"Come on, Tim," she said. "We'll try the patio door in the piano lounge."

They hurried across the marble floor and into the candle-lit room behind the stairs. The French doors at the back led to the gardens, and as Angela headed past the piano, she smelt the metallic tang of blood again. It was still a mystery where it had come from, seeing how Graham had bled to death two floors above them.

Tim rattled the handles on both French doors. "Damn it! These are locked too. I'm going to freak out. I'm literally going to freak out."

Angela grabbed a nearby chair. She glanced at Mike and snarled.

"Angela, don't..."

"Send me the bill!"

She threw the chair at the French doors. It hit the glass panes with a resounding clatter and broke into a dozen pieces. The glass panes remained intact.

"What the hell, man?" Tim was tugging at his hair, making it stand up in bright orange bunches. Angela picked up another chair, and this time swung it like a bat towards. Again it broke into pieces and the glass remained intact.

"This is impossible," Angela said.

"We're trapped," cried Tim. "Stuck in a box with a ball-slicing maniac."

"Calm down," said Mike, moving up beside them. "It's time to take a breath and stop panicking."

Angela glared at him. "If you're behind this, Mike. I'll leave you in worse shape than Graham, I swear it."

"I'm telling you, I had nothing to do with any of this!"

"Then who did?" Tim asked. "Who would want to keep us in this house so bad?"

Mike shrugged. "I guess we'll find out soon enough."

Chapter 28

Tim didn't like this at all. Locked inside a house with no power, no lights, and no escape. Once upon a time, he'd been in a similar situation. It had not ended well.

When Tim and his brother, Steve, had agreed to stay the night at the vacant Grey Gardens Hotel, both of them expected to find some rational explanation for the five deaths which had occurred there, each one after midnight. In a previous investigation of a similar hotel, Tim and his brother had found a slow gas leak in the kitchen. It had been making the staff light-headed and accident prone, which led to rumours of the place being cursed. That wasn't the case, but Tim and his brother spun the owners a tall tale, all the same. Tim fixed the broken gas main while his brother performed a dramatic séance. After 'speaking' to a malevolent spirit called Lloyd, who didn't actually exist, Tim and his brother declared the building cleansed.

The pay had been decent, and the owners were happy. So on to the next job. Grey Gardens Hotel. Despite the worrying number of deaths, Tim expected to enact the exact same routine, and get paid jus the same.

But things hadn't gone as planned.

With no one in the building other than Tim and Steve, there was no need to perform a fake séance—they could tell the owner they'd done one and that the building was cleansed. Footloose, they drank and made good use of the hotel's many amenities. A cushy gig.

The first warning sign had occurred while they were sipping from a bottle of the hotel's best champagne. They were sat naked in the bridal suite's giant Jacuzzi, and very gradually, to the point that they hadn't even noticed it at first, the water heated up. The thermostat was set to a cosy 40-degrees-C, but when Tim began sweating and glanced at it again, it was over 50! By the time he and Steve leapt out of the tub, the thermostat was reading 68C. They looked like lobsters as they flung themselves onto the cold granite tiles and lay there, squealing.

But they didn't learn their lesson. They continued their drinking, playing pool on the tables in the downstairs bar. Steve was thrice the player Tim was, with his additional five years on Earth being spent hustling at various pubs and clubs. Tim still enjoyed the game, though, despite losing. It was time with his big brother. The guy who all but raised him.

When the eight-ball left a long streak of blood behind it on the baize, they thought it odd, but still they did not let it bother them. They were obscenely drunk, and the supernatural was a job to them, not a reality. They ignored what they were seeing, like a pair of fools. Tim wished he could go back in time and shake some sense into himself and his brother.

Once the evening got late, they retired to one of the hotel's twin rooms. Their drinking had slowed, and they were feeling drowsy. Tim plopped down on one of the two beds and closed his eyes. Steve went to take a bath. It was a peaceful ending to a wild night, and in the morning they would get paid.

Tim must have fallen right to sleep, because when he next checked his watch, it was almost 4AM. Steve was still in the bathroom. The lights were off, but sounds of trickling water crept out from the en suite.

Tim dragged himself off the bed and moaned in agony as a fat elephant ran loose inside his head. His mouth was as dry as an overfilled ashtray. His bare feet took him across the room where the sounds of water grew louder. "Hey, Steve? You fall asleep in there?"

The bathroom door was ajar. Tim pushed it open all the way. He had to strain his eyes to see, but a small glow brought everything gradually into sight.

What Tim saw changed his life forever.

The monsters he invented to scam money out of innocent people were real. One stood before him now.

And it feasted on his brother.

The old lady's ancient face was a withered mass of flaking skin. Her black, sunken eyes seemed to drip crude oil. Kneeling in the bath tub at the old hag's feet was Steve. He was half-conscious and shaking with hypothermia, while a pair of talon-like hands wrapped around his skull and held him in place. The old woman's crooked, brown teeth formed a smile as she saw Tim standing in the doorway.

"S-Steve?"

The old hag hissed. She yanked Steve up by his skull and lifted him into the air, offering him to Tim like a rag doll. "Taaaaake him iffff youuuu daaaare..."

Tim looked at his brother's dangling legs and saw the pleading terror in his eyes. He was still aware, could see his brother standing there.

Standing there and doing nothing to help.

The old hag squeezed Steve's skull and Tim still did nothing. Even as blood ran down Steve's temples from where the bony fingers piercing his temples. His eyes bulged. Tim still did nothing.

He stood in fear as he watched his brother die.

The old hag cracked Steve's skull like a chocolate egg and let his body flop into the bathtub. She turned to Tim and stretched wide a maw of rotting fangs.

Tim's legs finally obeyed, and he bolted out of the en suite. He lumbered across the bedroom like a wounded gazelle, terror and alcohol making his movements clumsy, and collided with the door. He got a grip on the handle but found that it wouldn't budge.

Oh shit!

Tim spun around. The old hag drifted across the room towards him, arms reaching towards him. Shadows parted before her, extinguished by a sickly green glow. Death's putrid stench preceded her.

"Please." Tim begged.

Spiteful, hate-filled cackling was her only reply.

Tim slumped to the floor and closed his eyes.

Please!

More cackling, louder... closer. Hot, fetid breath against his face.

"Please...."

Tim's Casio watch beeped—the changing of the hour.

He squeezed himself into a ball as tight as he could and waited for the slithering hands of death to seize him.

Nothing happened.

Tim opened his eyes. The old hag was gone.

She had gone.

His watch flashed 4.01. An hour gone by in an instant.

The hotel owners found Tim at dawn, still cowering in that same corner by the door. A brief police investigation determined Steve had been heavily inebriated, causing him to slip in the bathtub and smash his skull. Tim knew the truth. The only reason he was still alive was thanks to nothing more than timing. The old woman had disappeared at 4AM exactly—his watch had beeped to tell him so—which was when the witching hour ended. Tim would never forget his inaction in preventing his brother's death. He had done nothing to save Steve. Tim was a coward.

Two months later, after one hell of a drinking binge, Tim went back to the Grey Gardens Hotel and torched the place to the ground. No one else would ever die there. The old hag could go to Hell. The owners would be glad of the insurance money. The business had been forever tarnished.

But Tim had never stopped being afraid—especially of locked doors and dark rooms—which was why he was kicking himself now. He'd placed himself in a bad situation all over again, and this time, instead of Steve, the victim had been Graham.

At least this time I'm not responsible.

I've been trying to help...

"Stay with me, Tim?" Angela ordered. "You look like you're about to hit the floor."

Tim shook away bad memories and tried to smile for her. "I don't like being trapped. Sends me into a panic."

"We're going to be okay. Long as we watch out for one another, we'll get out of this house infernal."

"God, please don't start using horror speak." He took a seat on the bottom step of the grand staircase and winced. "This sucks."

Angela paced the moonlit foyer, clasping and unclasping her meaty fists. Mike attempted to get the front door open. It was still unclear whose side the guy was one. Someone had killed Graham, that much was obvious, but the only person Tim knew was innocent was Angela—because she had been with him. That left few remaining suspects. It didn't look good for Mike, but it was still far from conclusive. For all they knew, there could be a nutcase in a hockey mask roaming the gardens.

"I don't know what's going on," Mike admitted. "The door won't open no matter what I try."

Angela huffed. "Don't act like you're surprised."

Mike ignored her. He'd stopped defending himself a while ago. Tim didn't blame the bloke for not wanting to waste his breath, but he still had Angela's back before he had Mike's.

"Do you think we should try the phones again?" Tim asked. "We really need to get a hold of the Old Bill."

"Try them again," said Mike. "Be my guest."

"No," said Angela. "Nobody is splitting up. We'll go together. Where is the nearest phone, Mike?"

"In the antechamber." He took them over to the small side room with a couch. A phone sat in a cradle on the wall. Mike went to pick up the receiver.

"No, let me," Angela said. She snatched the receiver from the wall and placed it to her ear. From the way she slammed the handset back down, Tim knew the lines were still dead.

"So what now? What do we do?" Tim heard the anxiety in his voice and took deep breaths to keep from panicking. "We can't just stand around all night waiting to be hacked up."

Angela stopped pacing and folded her arms. "We group together somewhere and wait for Frank. We need to have Sammie and Jessica with us as well."

Tim blanched at that. "For all we know, Sammie is the threat."

Angela shook her head. "I don't think so. I got through to him earlier. He's just a scared little boy."

"What about Chamuel?"

"Who?" Mike asked, looking confused.

Angela explained. "Chamuel is the name of the presence inside of Sammie. And to answer your question, Tim, I don't know. I don't know if Chamuel is a split-personality or if we're dealing with something supernatural, but Sammie said the thing inside of him wants him dead. I don't think we should leave him alone. Even if I'm deluded, he's still a child in danger. We came here to help him."

Tim let out a long, whistling sigh. God, how he wished he could run the Hell away from there. "Okay, okay," he said finally. "Let's hole up in the kid's room and sing Kumbaya until the power comes back."

"Then we're agreed," Angela said. "Let's go see Sammie."

But when they entered Sammie's room, the boy wasn't there.

Chapter 29

"We need to find him," Angela said. "Right now."

Tim looked around Sammie's room and wondered where the boy could have got to. A candle burned by the window, illuminating the drawing desk. Even from several feet away, Tim could see the drawings arranged on top of its cluttered surface. One drawing was perched on top of all the others, seeming to take pride of place. Tim picked it up and examined it.

Holy shitballs!

The picture should have chilled Tim to his core, but he only felt numb. Maybe he was approaching a mental breakdown? The old hag's charcoal eyes leapt right off the page. The crude stick figure clutched a severed head that Tim knew belonged to his brother.

How does Sammie know? It's impossible.

He crumpled the drawing and threw on the floor. The urge to flee rattled him again, but he glumly remembered there was no way out. His bladder yearned to void itself, yet mixed with that urge to flee was a tiny ember of a fire--the desire to fight. Anger flowered in the pit of Tim's stomach and he found a tiny sliver of resolve. He'd had enough of being messed with by the forces of Hell's arsehole.

Angela stepped up beside Tim and placed a hand on his shoulder. "What was the drawing?"

"Something only I know about."

"Yeah, I got one of those too, remember?"

Tim remembered how freaked out Angela had been upon receiving her own tailored sketch. "How do you think he does it?" he asked her. "How can he see things from our pasts that only we know about?"

"I don't think it's Sammie. Whatever possessed Charles Crippley is the same entity inside Sammie, I'm sure of it. Chamuel. That's how he knows about my past. And maybe yours too."

Tim wondered if this Chamuel was the same malevolent spirit that had crushed Steve's skull. If it was, then it was a chance to get even. A chance to not run away. "Do you have any theories about who Chamuel is yet?"

"I'm working on it. The name is familiar, but I still can't place my finger on it. I can't figure out why my attempts to exorcise a demon were such a failure, but I want to try again. As for Graham, I can't see how a ten-year old boy could do that to a grown man, which means there's something else at play here we're not seeing. Right now, we just need to worry about finding Sammie."

"Maybe he went to see his mother," Mike chimed in from behind them. "We should go check on Jessica."

It was a reasonable suggestion, so Tim didn't object. Nor did Angela. They headed out of Sammie's room and into the hallway to take the staircase to the third floor. Angela carried a candle she took from a windowsill in Sammie's room.

Jessica's door was open when they got there. Light from her own bedside candles flooded weakly out into the hallway.

"I can see Jessica sleeping." Mike stated the obvious. "Sammie's not here."

"Then we keep looking," Angela said.

Tim wasn't so sure. "Do you think it's safe to leave Jessica alone?"

"I'll stay with her," Mike offered.

Angela shook her head. "No way. We stick together."

"Let's search the rest of this floor," Tim said. "If we don't find Sammie we'll come back and wake Jessica up."

Everyone agreed.

The first room they came to after leaving Jessica's bedroom was a large office with an antique desk. On top of the desk sat a computer. Somehow, it was still on--the only thing in the house that still had power.

"How is there electricity in here?" Angela asked.

"There's not," Mike answered. "That was Joseph Raymeady's personal computer. He used it for his work at Black Remedy. It's installed with a backup power supply to protect against the constant power cuts out here in the countryside. The battery charges off the house's supply when it's on and kicks in if the electricity cuts off. It'll switch off eventually."

"Mind if I take a look," Tim asked. He didn't know what he expected to find but he couldn't see how it could hurt either. There might even be a way to contact the police.

"Go ahead," Mike said. "I don't think Joseph's in a position to complain."

Tim sat himself down in the high-backed leather chair and stared at the chunky monitor. The Black Remedy Corporation logo bounced around the screen, skipping from corner to corner. Tim shoved the mouse and the desktop appeared. It was neatly organised with just a few folders and a recycle bin icon. Tim also noticed that the email manager was blinking on the bottom taskbar. An unread email. Tim clicked on it.

The email application flashed up on screen and a message appeared with the subject line: WORK UNDERTAKEN, JOSEPH RAYMEADY. Tim read the email that followed:

Dear Frank,

I trust you will keep our communication confidential as it is of a sensitive nature. You are correct that, prior to his death, Joseph Raymeady was unsettled. He believed the company he owned was working against him from within, and that his life was in danger.

When Joseph's father died and his controlling interest of Black Remedy passed on to Joseph, Joseph involved himself in all aspects of the company. He became aware that great portions of Black Remedy's funds were unaccounted for. When he sought to investigate these discrepancies, the other members of the board were not forthcoming. In fact, they were actively hostile.

That is when Joseph sought my services.

Through a series of investigations, which unfortunately I cannot go into, I found evidence that Black Remedy Corporation was involved in acts of corporate espionage, government bribery, extortion, arms dealing, insider trading, and attempting to buy-off the Monopolies Commission. Even more bizarre, the company spent several million in undisclosed capital acquiring the deeds to several religious buildings, only to close them down and destroy them. The Acquisitions Board also purchased a group of historically significant artefacts which were unearthed at the Golgotha site in Jerusalem (where Jesus was allegedly crucified). I can't imagine what the purposes of such acquisitions are, but the company certainly seems to have religious interests as of late.

There was also a list of large payments made to several unnamed persons, leading me to believe Black Remedy has a personnel of 'freelance' employees to perform tasks 'off the books.' It was upon learning this that Joseph became most anxious. He held the opinion that the company employed hitmen and mercenaries to deal with obstacles. He believed this even more when my investigations discovered the untimely deaths of several of the company's adversaries (such as French politician, Frank Gerome, who sought to shed light on Black Remedy's exploitation of the current African AIDS epidemic by purposely limiting the production of life- saving medications in order to inflate prices. He was found face down in his own swimming pool). Joseph feared that his meddling into the company's affairs, and the eradication of several immoral, yet highly profitable operations, would lead to an attempt on his life.

Frank, as I'm sure you already know, Joseph became overly cautious in the months before his death and he worked mostly from home. That he has now passed away, even despite his caution, suggests there was someone within his own household working against him (one of these 'off the books' employees I uncovered). From several previous conversations I held with Joseph, it is clear that you were one of the few men he trusted, which is why I have broken protocol by divulging the nature of my work for your late boss.

But there is one other reason I have opted to share information with you, Frank, and that is because I believe Joseph's son, Samuel, is in danger. After Joseph's mysterious death, I conducted a further investigation for my own peace of mind. It became very clear to me, once I hacked into the confidential files of several key board members, that Black Remedy Corporation has an unhealthy interest the company's heir. The Raymeady family own 51% of the company, but if Sammie (and Jessica) were to die then the company would become 100% controlled by the Black family and its shareholders. I believe Samuel's death is the number one priority for certain members of Black Remedy. As a man Joseph trusted, I hope you can keep them safe. Don't trust anybody.

Please do not contact me again.

Yours,

George Farley.

Corporate Researcher

"What does the email say?" Mike asked, moving closer to Tim.

Tim clicked delete and sent the email to the recycling bin. With what was said about there being someone in the household working against the Raymeady family, he felt it better that Mike didn't read the email for himself. George Farley seemed to suggest that Joseph was murdered by someone close to him. It could have been Mike.

"It's from an investigation service," Tim explained. "It said Black Remedy Corporation is involved in a lot of bad stuff, and that Joseph's attempts to clean up the company were not being met well by the other board members."

Angela nodded. "From what I've heard about that company, I'm not surprised. They're like Evil Inc."

"Did it say anything else?" Mike asked.

"Not really," Tim lied. "It was just a follow-up email."

Mike came toward him. "Let me take a look."

"Sorry, I deleted it."

"What? You had no right to delete anything on this computer."

"Accident, dude. We should try and use the computer to contact the police. What do you think?"

Mike shoved Tim. "Move aside." He clicked the mouse and Tim knew it would not take the man long to retrieve the email from the bin. The guy was already on edge, and finding out that Farley was spreading suspicions about Joseph Raymeady's death would not help.

"Chill out, Mike," Angela warned.

Tim sensed a presence at the back of the room. Clumsy footsteps. He spun around. "Who's there?"

There was no reply from the stranger, but after a few more clumsy strides, they revealed themselves as Jessica Raymeady. She stood in the centre of the room like a spectre.

"Jessica," Angela said. "Are you okay?"

"Sssssoul." Jessica spoke in a disembodied lisp. "The sssssoul is broken. It cannot be ssssaved. Ssssamuel mussst die."

Jessica fell to her knees and vomited. The noise it made was like custard hitting a fan. She looked up at them with teary eyes, and spoke with a foamy mouth. "W-what is happening to me?"

Tim stood in shock while Angela gathered the woman up off the ground. "Jessica, are you okay? Can you see?"

"I-I... Yes, I can see, but I feel... I feel..."

"Let's get you somewhere comfortable," Mike said. He left the computer and walked over to Jessica, taking her from Angela.

"What's happened to the power?" she asked, looking about in a confused manner.

"It went off several hours ago," Tim told her. "We've been waiting for it to come back on."

"W-who's looking after Sammie?"

"We don't know where he is," Angela admitted.

Jessica straightened up. "What? It's the middle of the night. Why isn't he in bed? What have you people been doing? Mike, take me to Sammie's room now. I need to find him."

"Of course," said Mike, seemingly pleased by the suggestion. He was still the one in the room Jessica trusted.

"No!" said Angela. "We need to stay together."

Jessica strengthened further. "I give the orders around here, Ms Murs. You do not tell me what to do, especially where it concerns my son. I suggest you both retire to your rooms. We'll continue this in the morning and can discuss why my son could go missing in the first place."

Angela went to argue, but Tim put a hand on her shoulder and whispered in her ear. "Leave it, Angela. You won't make her understand until she's regained her senses."

"But we're all in danger," Angela whispered back. "We can't leave the house, Graham is dead, and Jessica herself said Sammie needs to die, plus she sounded like a snake when she said it. None of that makes me want to go to bed and wait things out."

Tim said. "You and I will stick together. We'll survive the night and figure things out in the morning."

Angela sighed. "Okay. In the meantime, perhaps we can try to put some of this together—maybe come up with some answers."

"Yeah," said Tim. "Stranger things have happened."

Chapter 30

Angela invited Tim to hole up in her bedroom and he agreed. It was as safe a place as any. 4AM had arrived, and he was feeling nauseous for lack of sleep, but he didn't expect to get any shut-eye soon. All the same, he slumped himself down in an antique wing chair and tried to get comfy.

The room's double bed lay unmade. Angela's suitcase sat open on top of it. Angela noticed Tim staring at the crumpled sheets and seemed embarrassed. "Housekeeping isn't my strong point," she said.

"Mine either. I live in a van."

"A very neat van, I noted." Angela hopped up on the bed and propped herself up with pillows. A candle on the bedside table lit her face. "We never discussed what happened in your van. I mean, with the Ouija board and everything."

"I know." Tim remembered he'd wanted to discuss it too. "I've done séances before, so I wasn't surprised it worked, but I don't have a clue about the answers we got. Usually, the spirits natter about their families or hidden heirlooms—predictable—but this Chamuel…"

"It was all a little doom and gloom, wasn't it?" Angela said. "Blood… Death… Hell will take you."

"It didn't feel like a threat, though, you know?" Tim said, rubbing at his eyes and leaning forward on his knees. "It seemed more like a warning."

Angela nodded and rubbed at her own eyes. "Chamuel said We're here just as Sammie turned up. It was almost like it was acting like a beacon for him to find us."

"For who to find us? Chamuel or Sammie? Who's in control of that kid?"

"I spoke to Sammie just before we found Graham's body. He seemed scared, just like a kid should be. He said Chamuel wanted to change him, to make him do things he didn't want to."

"Did Sammie say what things?"

Angela sighed. "No. He asked for my help though. He asked me to get rid of Chamuel."

"Then that's what we do."

"How? I get the impression Jessica will kick us out of the house first thing in the morning... or later in the morning as things are."

Tim assumed the same. Jessica had appeared irate at the situation she'd awoken to, but surely in the clear light of day she'd remember what had actually happened. She would remember being blind, or walking into her dead husband's office and giving them a warning in a serpentine hiss? "Maybe she'll feel differently," Tim suggested. "She was confused earlier."

"Are you still going to leave?" Angela asked.

Tim nodded. "I'd be gone already if the place wasn't sealed up."

"Do you know how that's even possible? How are the windows suddenly unbreakable?"

Tim thought the answer was obvious. "Security glass. A house like this, with a family like the Raymeadys, is certain to have tempered glass to stop people breaking in. It might even have been a recent addition if the email I read was anything to go by."

"What did it say?"

Tim shrugged. "It was all a bit weird, but Joseph Raymeady was worried for his life. He had some guy investigating for him. Turns out that Black Remedy is about as ethical as the Mafia—except without the codes of honour. The investigator thinks Joseph's death might not have been an accident."

"He thinks it was murder?"

Tim nodded. "Somebody close to him, he suggested—but not Frank, I don't think. It was Frank who the email was addressed to. Seems like he's been trying to get to the bottom of all of this, too, for his own peace of mind."

Angela's eyes widened. "Then that just leaves Mike."

"Yeah, I guess so, but there used to be a lot more staff here when Joseph died, so it could have been somebody else. Can't say I liked the way he shoved me away from the computer to get a look at that email, though. He seemed eager to see what it said."

"I don't trust him," Angela said. "But I guess you already know that. At first I thought he was a decent guy, but I get the impression he knows more than he's letting on. I think he might be dangerous."

"Yeah," Tim agreed. "Perhaps."

"Which is why I'm begging you to stay."

Tim shifted in his chair. The last thing on Earth he wanted to do was stay at this house a moment longer than he had to, but could he just abandon Angela? He'd only just met the woman. He didn't owe her anything. "I'm sorry," he said. "But I'm out of here."

It looked as if Angela would argue, but she nodded. "That's your choice."

"You should get some sleep," he told her. "I'll watch over you for a few hours."

Angela yawned. "Would you mind?"

"Not at all. If you're going to stay and get to the bottom of things, you'll need the rest."

"Thanks. I feel like I might drop into a coma if I don't sleep soon. Wake me if anything happens."

"Sure thing."

Angela closed her eyes, and within two minutes she was snoring. Tim watched her. What was her deal? The woman was overweight and baggy around the eyes—a drinker and an overeater, both signs of an unhappy soul. Was her misery due to leaving the church, or did she leave the church because she was miserable? Tim could tell that Angela was a caring person, a good person, but her weaknesses were unhidden and clear for all to see. After a certain length of time, depression could become part of a person's personality and the hope of ever shedding it became unattainable. Tim hoped Angela faced herself again one day. That possibility was long gone for himself. He would never be anything except what he already was.

A coward can't change.

Against his better judgement, Tim rested his eyelids for a second. Just a second. Eventually, he had no choice but to let sleep take him.

Angela opened her eyes to darkness. The candle in the room had extinguished. Usually, whenever she woke from a deep slumber, there was a brief moment of confusion while she wondered where she was, but in this case she opened her eyes and knew instantly. Her alert mind was unwilling to let her forget where she was even for a moment. Trapped inside the house.

Raymeady Manor.

She sat up and felt the darkness move around her. Listening out for noises, she worried there might be someone else in the room with, but then she remembered Tim had promised to watch over her.

"Tim, are you there?"

Silence.

"Tim?"

Angela slid her legs off the bed and onto the floor. "Tim?"

Still no answer.

She crept across the room, arms out in front of her as feelers. She bumped against the wing chair Tim had been sitting in. It was empty.

Damn it, Tim! You promised to stay with me.

Angela wondered if he'd gone to get a drink or something to eat. He was exhausted too, so maybe he'd needed something to keep himself from falling asleep. She didn't like the thought of him wandering around on his own. They needed to stick together.

She left the bedroom and sidestepped into the corridor like a secret agent on a stealth mission. If anybody was around, she wanted to make sure she spotted them before they spotted her. As it turned out, the corridor was empty.

She headed downstairs to look for Tim in the kitchen. As she headed for the stairs, moonlight shone in through the windows. She checked her watch. 6AM, yet the moon still hung high in the sky. The sun should have been muscling its way onto the horizon.

She found Tim right in front of her.

"Tim? What are you doing?"

Tim looked down at her from where he balanced atop the staircase railing. His eyes were murky and unfocused. Angela looked over the railing at the three-story drop to the cold marble below. "Tim, get down from there!"

He stared at her vacantly. The antique bannister beneath his feet rocked back and forth. His knees wobbled like loose springs. One false move and he'd fall to his death.

What the hell was he doing up there?

It was like he was sleepwalking, or under some kind of spell. Maybe he'd taken something to help him sleep, something he shouldn't have. He had struck her as a stoner when they'd first met.

Angela crept forwards, one foot placed in front of the other. She didn't want to startle Tim. "Hey, I thought you were going to watch over me while I sleep? You were gone. I was worried."

A strangled moan escaped Tim's lips, like he was a prisoner trying to escape his own body.

Angela took another step.

Tim's moaning continued, grew louder.

She reached out toward him.

Tim flinched. His foot slipped.

He fell.

Angela grabbed a hold of the back of Tim's shirt and yanked frantically. She managed to direct his tumble backwards to the safety of the balcony instead of forwards to his death, and he landed in a crumpled mess on the carpet with Angela lying beside him. "What the hell were you doing?" she shouted in his face.

The milkiness had cleared from Tim's eyes. He seemed confused. "I-I... how did I get out here?"

"You don't remember?"

Tim propped himself up on his elbows and shook his head. "I remember sitting in the bedroom. You were snoring..."

Angela blushed.

"...and I must have fallen asleep. I-I don't know what I was doing."

"Are you a sleepwalker?"

Tim shook his head. "If I am, this is the first time. I wonder how long I've been out here?"

"It's past six."

Tim frowned at her. "What? It's still dark. Shouldn't the sun be rising by now?"

Angela shrugged. She didn't understand it either, but right now she wanted to get out of the open where she felt so exposed. "Come on. I think we should go back to my room. This time you get the bed and I'll keep watch."

Chapter 31

Mike was clueless why the windows were suddenly unbreakable, but it fit well into his plans. Everyone needed to remain inside the house. He didn't know what would happen, but he knew an awakening was at hand—and it would require certain sacrifices. It didn't matter if Angela and Tim suspected him; it was too late for either of them to do anything about it.

Jessica didn't remember a thing about what had happened in her bedroom—about him choking her unconscious. Her voice was croaky from a bruised windpipe, but she was oblivious to the fact Mike had been the one to inflict it on her.

Jessica was sat on Sammie's bed, weeping quietly as she cradled the boy's grimy pillow. Amazing, that the woman still felt maternal over the wretched imp—he was no little boy. Sammie was a monster. Something inside him was manifesting like mould on bread. The boy's soul had putrefied.

"Are you okay, Miss Raymeady?" he asked Jessica.

She looked over with teary eyes. "I feel like I've woken from a coma. Nothing makes sense. Sammie is missing."

"I'm sure he's just playing games, hiding somewhere inside the house. I should get back to looking for him."

Jessica raised her hand. "No! Stay with me, Michael. I don't feel safe without Frank in the house. I don't want to be alone."

"I understand, but we shouldn't leave Sammie alone with those two con artists."

Jessica frowned. "Why do you think they're con artists?"

Mike huffed. "Come on, what have they done since they've been here, other than injuring Sammie and causing trouble? They're the reason Sammie is hiding. They frighten him."

Jessica shook her head. "I believe they're trying to help. Whether that's enough for me to let them to stay, I've not yet decided. What time is it, anyway? I need to decide about them before the new day begins."

Mike checked his watch. "I'm afraid the day's already started. It's a little after eight."

Jessica looked at him like he was mad. "What? It's still pitch-black outside. It can't be morning yet."

Mike hadn't realised it was still dark outside. So much going on in his mind that the familiar surroundings of the house became unnoticed background. Now the prolonged night disconcerted him. The absent sun, the unbreakable windows, it all made Mike uncomfortable. He welcomed events to come, and was there to guide them, but he feared his role was becoming larger than intended.

I'm trapped here like everyone else.

Mike stroked the raised scar-tissue beneath his shirt and hoped the shamanistic flesh carvings would be enough to ensure his safety.

Jessica dropped her son's pillow and moved herself from the bed. "You're right, Michael. We should be looking for Sammie."

Mike opened the door and followed Jessica out into the corridor. She swayed drunkenly, which was ironic, seeing as it was the first time she'd been sober in six months.

She stopped halfway down the corridor and glanced up at the wall. The Edwardian grandfather clock displayed the same time as his digital watch did. Jessica shook her head and frowned. "Impossible..." she muttered something to herself, but then got moving again. Mike followed, and they headed down to the ground floor foyer.

Jessica rattled the handle to the front door. When it wouldn't turn, she looked at Mike with her eyebrows raised. "Why won't this door open?"

"No one has been able to open it since Frank left."

"That makes no sense. What about the other doors? The ones in the piano lounge? The exit in the kitchen?"

"All the same. No one can get out. We were all waiting for daylight to work something out."

"Well, the sun seems to have forgotten itself today. We need to sort this out now."

Mike already knew trying to get the door open would prove fruitless, but Jessica was his boss, and refusing her would raise questions. He stood before her and awaited orders.

"Find something to pry it open, Michael. No point standing around like a monkey without a banana."

"At once, Jessica." He fought the urge to mock-salute the bitch. She was returning to the bossy, unbearable woman she'd been before her husband passed on. That would make killing her easier if it became necessary. "I'll go check the kitchen," he said evenly. "Maybe we can try to pry the door open with a knife or something."

Jessica didn't reply. She continued rattling at the door's handle, growing more and more frustrated.

Mike entered the kitchen and felt a chill. The lack of soft furnishings, and the long metallic surfaces, made the room harsh and cold, but Mike knew the chill biting his bones had nothing to do with the kitchen. More to do with the fact that Sammie was sitting on the centre island, his little legs swinging back and forth beneath him.

"Hello, Michael."

Mike took a step backwards and flinched as his heel struck an empty cardboard box. He looked down to see cookie crumbs, but quickly refocused on the thing before him. "Sammie? We've been looking for you."

"You for different reasons than others, I think, Michael."

"W-what do you mean?"

Sammie hopped off the work counter and planted his dirty, bare feet on the tiled floor. "I get the impression you have an interest in me beyond being my mother's chauffeur."

Mike nodded. "You're a special boy, Sammie. Very special."

"Why, thank you for saying so, Michael. What a lovely compliment."

"My pleasure."

Sammie's smile grew wider. "You seem nervous."

Mike fidgeted with his shirt, tracing the scars on his chest. "It's just tiredness. I've been up all night, as have you, Sammie. You should be in bed."

Sammie took several small steps towards him. "I seem to have less and less need for sleep recently."

"I imagine you have a lot on your mind"

"Because I'm special?" Sammie asked. "I wonder just how special I can be."

"You have no idea," said Mike.

Sammie reached over the nearest work surface and grabbed something long and metallic. "Don't I?"

Mike's breathing increased as Sammie moved towards him with the long chef knife held in his small hand. "What are you doing, Sammie?"

Another step. That knife came closer.

I'm here for you, Sammie. Why are you threatening me?

"Stop what you're doing, Sammie."

"What do you think I'm doing, Michael?"

"I-I don't know."

Sammie thrust out the knife. Mike yelped.

"Calm yourself, Michael." He flipped the knife around and presented it handle-first. "You came in here for a knife, didn't you? To work on the front door? This is the largest we have."

The air rushed from Mike's lungs like a pair of deflating balloon. "Yes! Yes, I did. Thank you, Sammie."

"You best get back to my mother. You know how she can get when the help disobey—such a bitch."

Mike took the knife with trembling hand and felt a spark run through his wrist. He looked into Sammie's coal-black eyes and tried not to panic. "Whatever you require, I am at your service."

Sammie giggled like a child—a normal child—but his voice was that of a far older soul. "Excellent. Then I trust you will not inform my mother of our conversation. This night is endless. I wish to enjoy it a while longer. The moon sings to me, Mike. Oh, what songs it sings."

Mike didn't know what to say, so he laughed nervously.

"I see nothing funny," Sammie said in a voice both soothing and angry. "Leave. Now!"

Michael left the kitchen as quickly as he could, a monster at his back.

Chapter 32

"It's almost nine in the morning," Angela said.

She'd reached the pinnacle of being freaked out now. That she was looking out of the bedroom window at a full moon when there should have been a morning sun was enough to frighten her on a primal level. Nature itself had fled. Human existence relied on certain constants: there would be air to breathe, food to eat, and the sun would bloody well rise each morning. Delete one of those constants and things devolved into chaos.

Tim stood beside her at the window. "This is bad, isn't it?"

Angela nodded. Something evil was at work in this house; something more powerful and malevolent than anything she had ever faced. One man was already dead and Angela feared it was only the start of something bigger. "I need to perform another exorcism," she said, "but this time I need to be more... assertive."

"What do you mean?"

Angela walked over to her suitcase and pulled out her exorcism kit. From inside, she produced a long stiletto-like dagger. "There's something called a Blood Exorcism. It is something the Church condones only in absolute emergencies—no official records even exist, and the ritual hasn't been performed in more than seventy years to my knowledge."

Tim stared at the dagger and swallowed. "But you know how to do one, right? One of these Blood Exorcisms?"

Angela nodded. She remembered the secrecy order she'd signed like it was yesterday. She remembered slicing into the flesh of rabbits and guinea pigs as she practised the sacred ritual. "I learned the Sacrament of Cursed Flesh a long time ago," she said, "but I remember everything. A person doesn't forget a thing like that. There's just one problem, though."

Tim frowned. "What?"

"If I perform the Sacrament, there's a chance Sammie might die. To banish the demon from his soul, I will have to take him to the brink of death. That is the only way to weaken the demon's influence and expel it."

"Helsinki," Tim said, swallowing another lump in his throat.

Angela ran her fingers along the silver spike. "Let's hope the Lord is with us this day. We will need His guidance."

"I think I should probably do some praying of my own."

"You believe in God, Tim?"

Tim placed his palms together. "No, I was thinking about praying to my guardian, Thor."

"That's a joke, isn't it?"

Tim laughed. "Levity is as important as religion at times like this."

"I agree."

"So what can I do? I want to be involved this time. Let me help."

"I want you to. Go to the kitchen and see if you can find any basil."

"Basil?"

Angela nodded. "Where basil is, no evil lives. Sprinkle it in as many rooms as you can, particularly across the thresholds. It will confine the demon's influence and weaken it. If you mix it with black pepper, even better."

"Okay," Tim said. "I'm on it."

He went to move past Angela, but she reached out and grabbed his arm. She looked him in the eye. "Be careful, Tim. I don't want you getting hurt. If this is going to work, I'm going to need your help."

Tim raised his fist at her in a gesture of solidarity, a move better suited to seven-foot basketball players than a skinny white ginger dude, but she appreciated the show of support. He had her back.

SAM

It was time to put a stop to all this.

Angela put on her cassock and smoothed it down with her hands. She looked in the mirror at her tired face and couldn't believe how much it had changed in less than a week. Weariness clung to her cheekbones, but her mind was still strong. Her will was resolute. For the first time in a long time, Angela felt like she was doing God's work. It felt good.

She pulled her crucifix from beneath her clothing and let it hang over the jet-black fabric of her cassock. Her eyes closed in prayer. *May Jesus Christ guide me. May the Lord protect me. May Heaven watch over my soul as it journeys the righteous path.*

She picked up her Bible from the bedside table and held it close against her breast. In her other hand, she clutched the ceremonial dagger—Damascus steel and etched with the verses of Genesis.

Deliver me, I pray thee.

Angela was ready to do what was needed. The only thing left to do was find Sammie. She stepped out of the bedroom and took a candle with her. She felt like Florence Nightingale as she floated down the corridor in her small globe of light. For a moment, she had the strange feeling that the hallway was infinite, stretching on endlessly, but then the stairway appeared on her right and she breathed a sigh of relief. *I'm being paranoid.*

She encountered Mike and Jessica on the ground floor. They were working at getting the front door open. Mike hacked at it with a long knife.

"Still stuck?" Angela asked as she stepped away from the staircase.

Jessica gave her a stern look. "Morning, Angela. If you're looking for Tim, he headed into the kitchen. I take it, from what you're wearing, you intend on staying?"

"If you'll allow me to. Not like I can leave, anyway."

Jessica took in a long breath and let it out in an exasperated sigh. "I'll give you that."

"Can I help at all?"

"No," Mike said. "We have everything under control."

Jessica shrugged. "You can find Sammie."

Angela shook her head. "Afraid I've been in my bedroom. Tim and I can look for him now if you wish."

Jessica nodded, her pointed chin cutting through the air. "Yes, that would be most helpful. I'm a bag of nerves with him out of his room."

"I understand." Angela headed across the foyer towards the kitchen. Tim likely still intended to leave, but at least he had no choice for the moment.

Entering the kitchen, she found it empty. A candle burned on the central work surface and several of the cupboards hung open. It appeared somebody had been there recently, but there was no sign of Tim.

Angela approached the centre work surface and noticed something lying on its surface. She tiptoed towards it, not wanting to risk injury by rushing around in the unlit room. Almost 20% of accidents occur in the kitchen, she remembered. As she got closer, the object revealed itself to be a piece of paper. Angela was just about to pick it up when somebody grabbed her from behind.

She shrieked.

"I'm not sure you want to look at that," Tim said.

Angela punched him in the arm. "You sod! Almost gave me heart attack. Where were you hiding?"

"I wasn't hiding. There's a meat locker back there. I smelt something rotten, so I checked it out. Just a bunch of spoiled fish. Nothing Omen-y or anything."

Angela folded her arms, trying to hide her panicked breaths. "So what is this thing I don't want to look at?"

Tim pointed at the piece of paper on the work surface. "It's another one of Sammie's drawings. Seems like we might have just missed him."

Angela frowned. "What would he have been doing in the kitchen?"

"Dunno, eating a Poptart?"

Angela reached for the piece of paper and slid it towards herself. She looked at it. "Oh, how delightful. Let's hope this isn't a literal interpretation."

"You're telling me," Tim agreed.

Angela rotated the drawing and looked at it from all angles. The four bodies swinging from the charcoal balcony were obviously supposed to represent Mike, Jessica, Tim, and herself. All of them hanged by their broken necks. Their eyes were gouged and bleeding. The detail was immaculate for a child's crayon drawing. It was almost as if the colours were dancing on the page and giving life to the flat, waxy images.

"Should we take it as a threat?" Tim queried.

"Definitely. But it also means something else."

"What?"

"If Chamuel is making threats, it's because he's scared. He knows we're coming for him."

Tim tittered. "Either that, or Sammie is trying to warn us about what will happen if we don't leave this house."

"I guess we'll find out soon enough." Angela said as she tore the drawing to pieces.

Chapter 33

Angela and Tim rejoined Jessica and Mike in the foyer. Angela decided not to waste any time. "I want to perform another exorcism."

Jessica didn't hesitate. "No! Mike told me the last time did nothing. What would be the point of putting Sammie through such an ordeal a second time?"

"There are other rituals I can try."

"Look," Jessica said. "I've had a think about it and, while I appreciate that I was the one who invited you both here, I think our business is finished. I don't believe you can help my son. In fact, I feel ridiculous for having asked for your help in the first place."

"I can still fix this," Angela protested. "You were right to ask for help."

"The only help you can be right now is by finding Sammie and getting him back to his room safe and sound. You'll be paid generously for your time, Ms Murs, but I feel it would be best if you left us. Mike will have to drive you if Frank hasn't returned by then."

Tim stepped forwards, pulling his hair with frustration. "Are you not seeing what we're seeing? There're two concerns I have with what you've just said, Ms Raymeady. Number one is that Frank left the house going on twelve hours ago and hasn't returned from a trip that should have taken him only an hour or two.

Number two is that your request for us to leave at is marred by the fact no one can get the frickin' doors or windows open. I won't even go into the fact that, according to that moon out there, it's still the middle of the night." Tim took a moment to catch his breath and continued. "You tried to commit suicide last night, Jessica, and then you went blind—although only temporarily—and to top it all off, one of your employees is hanging dead out of a hot tub upstairs."

Jessica gawped at him. "What?"

Mike was the one to tell her although he seemed reluctant to do so. He skirted over the more gruesome details about how they had found Graham in the bath tub. "He bled to death."

Jessica put her hands against her face. "Graham is dead? I don't believe it. Take me to him. I need to see for myself. Has anyone called the police?"

"We've tried," Angela told her, "but the phone lines are dead. As for seeing Graham yourself, I wouldn't advise it. There's a lot of blood."

"Try giving birth, Ms Murs. I can handle blood."

Nobody was in the mood to argue with Jessica so they went upstairs. On the second floor, there was a brief flickering of the lights, and it seemed like the power might come back on, but it was not to be. After a brief flash of colour, the bright red carpet returning to existence, darkness resumed.

The door to the spa room was open and the tang of chlorine drifted out from the hot tub. Thankfully, the chemical odour overpowered the smell of Graham's blood.

"He's in there," Mike told Jessica.

Jessica nodded and passed through the door. Almost half a minute passed before she returned to them in the hallway. "Is this supposed to be a joke?"

Angela didn't understand. "What do you mean?"

"Graham is not in that room?"

Angela hurried into the room to take a look for herself.

Graham's body was missing. Puddles covered the tiles and there was a slight pinkish hue to the water, but to a casual observer there were no signs of any murder.

"This makes no sense," Tim said. "Somebody's moved the body?"

"Who?" Mike asked. "I've been with Jessica the whole time. If there's anybody who could have moved Graham's body, it's you and Angela."

"Hey!" Tim protested. "There's no way you'd catch me fondling a naked dead guy. This isn't Weekend at Bernie's."

"We didn't move him," Angela stated. "Somebody is playing games with us."

"This whole thing is a game," Tim said. "We can't be sure we haven't been played since the start."

Jessica folded her arms. "What exactly are you accusing me of, Mr Golding? I'd be very careful. I brought you here in good faith and things have only gotten worse since your arrival. If anyone is to be suspicious of a ruse, it is me. This is my home."

Angela put a hand up in deference. "Tim means no offence, Jessica. We're as confused—and as frightened—by this whole situation as you are. You're right, things have gone from bad to worse since we got here, but I assure you that Tim and I played no part in that."

Jessica softened up a little, let he chin drop. "I want to know my son is safe. Is that too much for a mother to ask? I want to know my Sammie is okay."

Angela looked left and right. "Then let's go find him."

Somewhere nearby, the sound of voices.

Tim's face scrunched up. "Who the hell is that?"

Jessica was the first to get moving. Angela and the others hurried after her. The voices came from a room further along the hallway. Jessica explained the room contained a small, scarcely used lounge.

"Do you think Frank could be back?" Angela asked, but didn't actually believe it was a possibility. Why would he come back and not tell anyone? Besides, she could hear more than a single person's voice. In fact, it sounded like there were several.

Jessica turned around and called back to Mike who had fallen several paces behind. "Michael, open this door."

Mike nodded and strolled forward. He seemed in no rush.

"Hurry up," Jessica shouted.

Mike opened the door and poked his head inside. Angela held her breath. The voices inside the room continued. There were other noises too. It almost sounded like...

"Is that a television?" Tim asked.

"I think so," Angela said, relieved and disappointed at the same time.

"But that's impossible. There's no power."

Angela stepped into the room and examined her surroundings. The room was cloaked in shadow like the rest of the house, but there was a glaring source of light in the far corner. A television mounted to the wall, switched on and working.

Tim placed a hand over his brow like he was looking out to sea. "Isn't that... South Park?"

It was the same crude cartoon Sammie had been watching the day he'd attacked Angela. What is it with that program?

Jessica called out. "Sammie, are you in here?"

No answer. Only the sound of potty-mouthed cartoon children.

Angela rubbed at her shoulders. The room was freezing.

"Sammie must have been here recently," Jessica said. "We need to find him. Mike, switch that television off."

"But I don't even think it's switched on. The power is off."

"Maybe it's a power surge from the weather. I don't know, just turn it off."

Mike scuffled over to the television and reached up to press the power button. He paused, fingers half-an-inch over the button.

"What is it?" Angela asked.

"I... I don't know." He stared into the screen as if mesmerised by. His face moved closer. "I thought I could see a... I don't know... a-"

The television screen shattered.

The panel splintered and exploded in a shower of wicked glass shards. Mike twisted and fell to the floor, releasing a muffled scream.

Jessica ran over to him. "Heavens, Mike. Are you okay?" She wrapped her arm around his shoulders and ushered him away from the litter of broken glass. Tim held a candle in his hands and thrust it out to illuminate the scene.

Mike was in a bad way.

Tim's face wrinkled in horror. "Oh, Helsinki."

Angela had the same reaction. Mike's left eye was a jagged red slit, embedded with shards of glass. Blood ran down his cheek in grisly tears and dripped from his chin. Despite the horrific injury, Mike did not cry out or scream. He was calm.

"Jesus, what do we do?" Tim asked.

"I'm fine," Mike said, trying to open his eyelid. "I don't think it got my eye, just the skin."

Angela took a close look at him. After a short bout of fluttering, his bloody eyelid opened and revealed the watery orb beneath. He'd had a lucky escape. "Thank Heavens. Your eye is okay, but you should get cleaned up. There're still bits of glass."

Jessica told them she'd take Mike to the nearest bathroom. "But you two stay here," she added. "I want no one wandering around."

Angela folded her arms. "Fine."

Tim took a seat on the room's sofa opposite the broken television. Angela was shaken-up so decided to join him.

Tim patted her knee in a friendly manner. "The weird shit just doesn't stop around here, does it?"

"It does not."

"Funny, but that's the third eye injury in this house since we've been here—if you count Jessica's blindness and my experience by the pond. There was one before too, a gardener or something."

"What's your point?"

"Don't know. Guess I'm just wondering if there's any religious significance to eyes."

Angela thought for a moment. "God sees through all of us, so to injure a person's eyes is to reduce God's awareness of our sins. Serial killers sometimes gouge out their victims eyes for the same reason—so that God cannot see their crimes."

"Hmm, interesting. Wonder if we're being sent another message."

There was a shuffling on the carpet in front of them. Angela flinched and pulled her feet up onto the couch.

God help me, I've dealt with a lot of things in the last forty-eight hours, but if that's a mouse...

"Look at the glass," Tim told her.

Angela looked down at the mosaic of littered shards. The moonlight caught their edges and made them glow. They vibrated.

"Be careful," Angela said. "They might fly up at us or something."

Tim shook his head. "No."

The vibrating shards hopped about, slithering across the carpet. They formed into piles, assembling themselves into lines.

Letters?

Are they forming letters?

Angela glanced at Tim then back at the glass. "What's it trying to spell out?"

The shards kept vibrating, hopping about.

H...

...elp me.

Save me.

Kill me.

Angela got down on her hands and knees, close to the glass. "Sammie, is that you? Who is it inside of you? Is it Charles Crippley?"

The glass shards reshuffled. No.

"Then who is it? Chamuel?"

Yes.

"How does Chamuel know me? Jessica sent for me because my name was written in a journal. Does Chamuel know me?"

Yes.

"How?"

Helped you.

Angela didn't understand. "What? Chamuel helped me? How?"

Charles Crippley.

"I don't understand."

Help me.

Angela shook her head, desperate. "I... I don't know how."

Stop the darkness. Bring back the light.

There was a shriek from outside and the glass shards scattered in all directions. The messenger had gone. Angela still understood nothing.

Chapter 34

Tim raced into the hallway to see what the commotion was. He knew enough by now to expect the worst. This was a house where bad things happened.

"No way!" Tim skidded on his heels, tried to make sense of what he was seeing. Jessica was down on her rump, shuffling backwards frantically while Mike tried to pull her back up to her feet. Pursuing them was an abomination—the only way Tim could describe what he saw.

Graham shuffled down the corridor towards, colliding off walls and lumbering like a zombie. In the dim glow of moonlight, the bloody streaks his hands left on the wallpaper appeared as black smudges.

Impossible. Graham is dead. I saw it with my own eyes.

Graham's neck twisted around and faced the wrong way, proof that the man had met his gruesome end, yet his body eschewed the laws of nature and shambled towards them as if fully alive.

Angela came into the hallway and stumbled. She crossed herself and began playing. "Jesus Christ, hallowed be thy name..."

Jessica and Mike screamed.

Tim tried not to piss himself.

Graham continued towards them.

The abomination's body faced away from them, but its head faced forward towards them. It's clumsy, backwards steps thudded on the carpet while a river of blood formed in its wake. The wound on Graham's genitals gaped open like a sucking mouth.

"We're in Hell!" Jessica gasped.

Mike dragged her off the ground and pushed her back. Tim shook his head in despair. For the first time in his life, his anger was equal to his fear, so as much as he wanted to hit the floor, a gibbering mess, he also wanted to turn his face upwards and rage at the Heavens. I am so fucking sick and tired of this. First it was House On Haunted Hill—with a little of The Exorcist thrown in for good measure— but now it's full blown Evil Dead. When will it end?

"Come on," Tim said, grabbing hold of Angela's arm and pulling her down the corridor. Jessica and Mike had already raced ahead. Jessica screamed, once again the emotional mess she'd been when Tim first arrived at the house.

"What happened to him?" Jessica cried. "You told me Graham was dead!"

"He is," Tim cried. "In fact, I'm goddamn certain he is."

"Then how is he walking around?" Mike asked, huffing and puffing as the group scurried down the dark hallway. Graham moaned and hissed from the shadows behind them.

"I have no freaking idea, but I'm guessing he's come back even grumpier than before."

Angela skidded to a stop. "Tim, did you find any basil earlier in the kitchen?"

"What?"

"The basil? I sent you to the kitchen to find some."

"I totally forgot about it," he reached into his pocket, pulled out a spice jar full of basil and held it out. "Yeah, I found some."

Angela snatched the jar.

"Can we think about the ratatouille later?" Mike said. "We have more pressing things to contend with."

Angela sprinkled the basil flakes across the carpet in a line from wall to wall. There was just enough to complete a full length.

"What is that supposed to do?" Mike asked in a tone so mocking that Tim felt like punching him. He probably would have, if the guy weren't capable of beating him to a pulp. Angela seemed to ignore Mike's incredulity though. "Basil has been used for centuries to ward off evil spirits—even the Church uses it. If it works, Graham won't be able to pass."

"You hear that, Balrog?" Tim shouted into the darkness. "YOU CANNOT PASS! I am a servant of the secret fire and stuff."

"Tim, not now." Angela shoved everyone back and stood in front, facing the dark hallway like a sentinel.Tim could hear his own heart beating.

Graham's moans pierced the shadows. The noise got louder, closer.

Eventually, the shadows parted and Graham appeared. His head still twisted around the wrong way but it had gone limp as if the cartilage in his spine had weakened. A viscous meld of fluids dripped from his nose and swung in front of him like a sickening bungee cord. Angela stood her ground, but Tim couldn't help but shrink away. The sight of Graham made his stomach clench in revulsion. "Angela, come on," he urged. "Let's get out of here."

Angela ignored him. She held up her crucifix and quoted the Bible—several passages over and over—so rapidly that she was almost speaking in tongues. Graham kept on shuffling towards them. His blood covered everything. Its stench choked the air.

"I sentence you to Hell," Angela growled. "You will approach no further."

To Tim's surprise, Graham stopped at the line of basil on the carpet. It was almost as if there was a string attached to his waist that had just reached its maximum slack.

Angela's plan is working.

Then Graham reached across the line and grabbed Angela's throat.

Maybe not.

Angela squirmed and tried to break free, but she was caught in a vice. Graham's arms dislocated from their sockets and rose up behind his back at an unnatural angle. His bleeding face grinned.

"Help her," Jessica said.

Tim didn't move. Couldn't move. He stood and watched as Angela struggled with Graham, watched as her face went red and her eyes bulged. In his mind, Tim saw his brother and the old woman, that hotel room. His heart froze in his ribcage. His knees turned to cement.

"I said, somebody help her," Jessica cried.

Reluctantly, Mike rushed forward and barrelled, shoulder-first, into Graham.

He managed to knock his former colleague back down the corridor, and the fact Graham's body faced the wrong way meant his legs tangled up and he fell to the floor. Angela got dragged to the floor with him.

Mike raised his boot and brought it down on Graham's head. There was a vile crack as hard leather met skull bone. The blow was enough to make Graham release his grip on Angela and she scurried away, choking and spluttering. Mike brought his boot up again. And again. Stamping on his former colleague until there nothing left of his head but pulp.

Angela clambered to her feet, cassock twisted and dishevelled. Tim could see the anger in her eyes as she glared at him. "Got my back, huh?"

Tim averted his eyes to the floor. "I'm sorry."

Angela sighed, took a breath, and some of the anger left her face. "No harm done."

"No harm done?" Jessica echoed. "A member of my staff is dead."

"I had no choice," said Mike.

"I know that!" Jessica ground her teeth. "But that doesn't make the situation any better. We need to call the police, or go for help, or... something! Mike, try the phones again."

"Sure thing." Mike took off down the hallway. Tim was uncomfortable seeing him go. He still didn't trust the guy, but he also didn't want Mike gone in case there was another situation in which Tim froze. If Mike hadn't been here to deal with Graham.... Even after all these years, I'm still nothing but a coward.

Angela rubbed at her throat and looked at him. "The dead are walking, the night is eternal. I don't like what's happening here."

"Me either," said Tim.

"No," Angela said. "I mean this is more than just a possessed child. No demon has this kind of power."

"No poltergeist either," Tim added. "So what the hell are we dealing with?"

"I don't know. The Devil? Or one of the other fallen angels? Only the princes of Hell themselves could affect the world in this way."

"You sound like a mad woman," Jessica said, clawing at her own face, oblivious to the fact she herself looked mad. "You're talking utter nonsense."

"I think the time for scepticism is over," Angela said. "It's clear we're dealing with ancient Evil here."

"Ancient Evil, the Devil, poltergeists—I'm stuck in a somebody's paranoid delusion." Jessica rubbed her palms against her eyes and then looked at them both. "So... what do we do?"

Angela touched the woman's cheek reassuringly. "We find Sammie, and you let me perform another exorcism, but this time we go all the way."

Jessica swallowed. "What do you mean, all the way?"

"I mean whatever it takes to end this. We cannot let this Evil remain."

"I won't let you hurt Sammie."

Angela shook her head. "Jessica, sweetheart, your son has already been hurt. The only chance he has left of living a normal life ever again is for me to take this as far as it needs to go."

Tears fell from Jessica's eyes, but despite them she nodded.

Angela stepped back from the woman. "There's one other thing we need to do before we begin."

Jessica wiped the wetness from her cheeks and straightened up. "What?"

"We need to find out what Mike is hiding from us."

Chapter 35

Sitting in the piano lounge, Mike didn't intend on trying the phones as Jessica had demanded. His function at this house was recruitment, and that meant staying around to ensure that his employer's predictions were correct, and that Sammie really was who they were relying on him to be. Sammie was changing. It was Mike's job to ensure the boy knew where his destiny lay.

So why the hell am I being hit in the face by exploding television screens? I'm here to help the little brat.

His wounded eyelid stung, but Mike tolerated it. He'd been cleansed by pain as part of his initiation into the Black Strand—a secret, off-the-books organisation that included the most powerful individuals in the world. Mike was just a cog in a very large machine, but he took his membership very seriously. It was a rare honour bestowed on very few. Even Joseph Raymeady had known nothing of the Black Strand. His father and grandfather had been key figures, but they saw weaknesses in Joseph and kept him in the dark. Joseph's morals only caused the group problems.

With Joseph inheriting controlling interest of Black Remedy, he'd quickly begun an ethical crusade, turning over every one of the company's slimy rocks to see what lurked beneath. It would only have been a matter of time before Joseph discovered the existence of the Black Strand and its purpose—the true purpose of Black Remedy Corporation itself.

Joseph had not seen it coming when Mike strung a rope around his neck and hoisted him over the balcony. The execution had been quick and clean—professional. Mike's employers had been pleased. But where has it got me? I'm beginning to feel like a lamb to slaughter. Sammie was never meant to be any danger to me, but nearly being blinded disproves that. Not to mention the never-ending night, and Graham getting up and walking around like a member of the living dead. None of this was supposed to happen. There's something I don't understand.

What is going on?

Mike poured himself a drink from the nearest bottle, which turned out to be rum. He filled up a low-baller glass halfway and then downed the contents, enjoying the pleasant burn at the back of his throat.

"Drinking is bad for you, Michael. The body is a temple, and it is a sin to defile it."

Mike jolted and dropped the glass. It smashed on the floor. "Sammie, shit, where did you come from?"

Sammie stepped out from the shadows and grinned crookedly. "I've always been here, Michael. Little early for a drink isn't it."

"Usually, yeah, but in case you haven't noticed, the night's gone on a little longer than usual."

"Yes, I did notice that. Beautiful, isn't it? Everything seems so much more intimate in the dark, don't you think?"

"If you say so."

"You seem irritated, Michael."

"You almost blinded me earlier."

Sammie giggled. "Not me. My friend."

Michael poured himself another drink in a new glass. "You know I'm here to help you, right?"

Sammie tilted his head like a confused puppy. "Help me with what?"

"Help you realise who you are—what you are."

Sammie stepped closer. The shadows seemed to flee from his presence. "I don't know what you mean. I'm just a boy, nothing else."

Mike downed his rum and poured a third. He laughed bitterly. "You are far more than that and you know it. A harmless little boy doesn't have the power to raise the dead."

One side of Sammie mouth slid up in a smirk. "Ssshhh, Michael, it's a secret."

"Not from everyone. There are those—a select few—who know exactly what you are. They welcome you with open arms. They are your true family."

Sammie nodded knowingly. "My father's company?"

"No, Sammie, your company. Tonight, you must kill your mother, the Jezebel. Bathing in her blood will be the mortal sin that awakens your destiny."

Sammie continued to speak like an innocent child. Mike found it annoying. "But if I kill my mummy, who will look after me?"

"Your late father's business partner, Vincent Black. He will adopt you. Together you'll change the world. You were born to be great, Sammie. You just have to accept our help."

Sammie looked upwards at the ceiling as if to think about it. Then he looked back at Michael and said, "No, thanks."

Mike froze, glass of rum halfway to his lips. "What?"

"I'll just take control of the company myself," Sammie said. "I don't see what Mr Black could offer me that I can't do for myself. Perhaps, I should kill him instead? Then I would own the entire company."

Mike shook his head and approached Sammie from behind the bar. "No, you don't understand. You won't be in charge until you are eighteen years of age. In the meantime, Mr Black will teach you about the business and about your destiny while you mature. You'll be lost without him."

Sammie put a fingertip against his chin. "Perhaps you're right. I still have one question though." He stepped closer to Mike, only a few feet away now. Mike could feel his skin prickling. "What exactly do I need you for?"

Mike didn't like where this was going. The ungrateful little shit was turning on him. "I have been helping you from the beginning, Sammie. Watching you and keeping you safe. I deserve your loyalty."

"I disagree. I think Frank is the one who has been keeping me safe since your murdered my father. Not that he ever really was my father—we both know the truth of that. Still, I loved the man all the same. He used to sing me lullabies before bed. I think I owe him more loyalty than I owe you, Mike, wouldn't you agree? And what better way to show loyalty than to avenge his death by gutting his killer like a sickly little pig who believes himself to be a wolf?"

Mike had heard enough. The fear was so thick in his veins that his heart threatened to pop. He was trapped inside the house and now Sammie wanted to kill him. There was no choice but to act—and act fast.

He slipped a blade from the holster beneath his belt and thrust it against Sammie's throat. The boy stayed calm, but one false move and Mike was ready to slice his fucking throat. If it's between you and me, oh great Messiah, then I choose me

Sammie started giggling. "Tickles."

"What on earth is going on here? Sammie? Mike?"

Jessica and the others entered the room, stunned by what they were witnessing. Mike didn't blame them. The game was up. No need to keep pretending.

Sammie giggled hysterically.

Chapter 36

"Mike, what the hell are you doing?" Jessica screeched.

Angela's stomach acids crashed against the rocks of her abdomen, making her want to vomit. The sight of a knife against flesh had always set her teeth on edge, ever since the church in Jersey. Seeing a blade against the throat of a child was even worse, but she knew there would be two sides of this story unfolding in front of her.

"Hey, dude," Tim said. "Maybe we should just put the knives away. Things never end well when people start brandishing weapons."

"I'm inclined to agree," Sammie said, extremely calm for a child with a blade against his throat. "Such barbaric actions, Michael. I'm embarrassed for you."

Mike grabbed Sammie by the scruff of his neck and got him in a classic hostage-taking chokehold. He held the malicious-looking combat knife beneath the boy's left eyeball. "You keep your goddamn mouth closed, you little shit. Maybe I should take your eye out like you tried to do to me."

Jessica screamed at Mike. Angela wasn't sure if the man was bluffing or had totally lost it. From the look of his trembling hands and darting glances, it didn't seem like Mike was in full control of himself. His usually cool demeanour had slipped away like a satin sheet from an unveiled painting. All that that remained was a frantic shell of a man.

"Let's not do anything hasty," Angela said. "You must be upset about Graham's death. He was your colleague. Is that what this is about? Do you hold Sammie responsible?"

Mike laughed at them. "He is responsible. What the fuck do you think's been going on around here? Open your eyes, idiots."

"What do you mean?" Angela asked.

"Wake up!" Mike yelled. "This is all because of Sammie. He's not a boy. He is his father's son—and his father is a great and powerful man."

Tim frowned. "You mean Joseph?"

"No, I do not mean Joseph. Tell them, Jessica. Tell them what a whore you are."

Whether it was due to Mike's accusations or because her son was in peril. Jessica was distraught. "How do you know about that, Mike? How do you know?"

Sammie titled her head at her. "Mummy? What is the nasty man talking about?"

"I'm sorry, Sammie." Jessica visibly shattered as she began to explain. "When I met Joseph, I was a young woman, and he was always away at his father's beck and call. I was often lonely."

"I think I see where this is going," Tim commented.

"I used to go to bars," Jessica admitted. "Sometimes I... I used to pick up men and bring them home." She wiped a tear from her eye. "But it was hardly ever. Once in a blue moon."

"It was often enough for you to get pregnant by another man," Mike said spitefully.

"Who was it?" Angela asked. "Who is Sammie's real father?"

Jessica took a breath and tried to compose herself. "Joseph was Sammie's real father. He raised my son. If you mean who was the biological father, then I'm ashamed to admit it was a stranger. I met the man only once. Some charmer with an Irish accent, but I couldn't resist. I forget his name now, but he seduced me in minutes and had me in bed before the hour was through. I fell pregnant, and that was the last time I ever cheated on Joseph. The shame has never left me."

Angela patted her on the back. "We all commit sin, Jessica. It's whether we repent that matters. Let go of the guilt because it is not God's plan for you."

Mike sniggered. "Oh, I don't think you'd be so forgiving if you knew the full story."

"Let my son go!" Jessica demanded. She took a step forward and pointed her finger. "You're finished, Mike. By the time I'm through with you, you won't be able to show your face in public ever again. You're lucky I don't have you killed."

Mike chuckled. "Now that sounds more like the Jessica I know. Black Remedy would be ecstatic to hear you talking like that."

Jessica stared daggers at him. "Those days are over. My husband was dedicated to cleaning up the company, and I will finish what he started."

"Think you might find opposition there, love, like from your precious son for starters. The company will be his one day, and you can trust me when I tell you Sammie's methods will differ from Joseph's."

"I don't know what you're talking about, Mike, but you have three seconds to let go of my son before I come over there and rip your goddamn face off." She screamed the last words.

Mike wrapped his arm tighter around Sammie's throat and pointed the knife at Jessica. "You stay back, bitch!"

"What did you call me?"

"I called you a bitch. The only reason you're anything is because you sucked off a rich guy so good he married you."

"How dare you!" Jessica ran at Mike with her fingernails outstretched like claws. Mike threw Sammie against the bar—his head cracked against the thick wooden top. Then Mike readied himself for Jessica's attack, legs apart, shoulders wide, knife pointed out in front of him. Their bodies collided in a flurry of limbs. Jessica's nails swiped furiously at Mike's face, drawing blood. Mike snarled angrily. "You're the one who's finished, bitch!"

Jessica's ferocity diminished. Her attack faltered. Both flailing arms fell to her sides, and she stumbled against the bar beside her son. Blood mushroomed through her blouse, emanating from a spot mere inches above her heart.

Mike still clutched the combat knife in his hands, but now it was dripping with Jessica's blood.

Jessica reached out a hand to Angela despite being several feet away. Angela didn't know why, but she couldn't help herself from reaching back to the woman, as if they could somehow stretch her limbs and hold one another.

Jessica slumped to the ground, a pool of her own blood spreading out.

Angela stared at Jessica's body in disbelief. "Mike, what have you done?"

"What I needed to. Now I will end this whole fucking mess. Screw the Black Strand, screw this house, and most of all, screw this kid." He wiped the combat knife on his clothing and looked down at Sammie. The boy was unconscious from hitting his head on the bar. Mike held the knife over his chest, the tip pointing downwards. "Time to die, bastard."

Angela screamed, but it was too late. She would never make it over to Mike in time to keep him from delving the knife into Sammie's soft chest. He would kill the boy.

Mike plunged the knife downwards.

An explosion rang out behind Angela, funnelling through her ears and occupying her skull. It left her unable to hear anything but ringing.

Mike's knife clattered to the ground. The look on his face was one of stunned surprise. A small well of blood formed in the centre of his chest.

Another explosion sounded and part of Mike's skull disappeared. His lifeless body tumbled to the floor.

Frank pushed past Angela and made his way across the piano lounge until he was stood right over Mike's body. He fired the gun once more, finishing off what was left of the dead man's skull.

After a few more seconds passed, during which time Frank stared silently at the remains of the man he'd killed. Eventually, he turned around, but before he said anything, he slumped against the nearest table and fell onto his knees.

Frank was hurt.

"Can't leave you people alone for a minute," he grunted, and then collapsed onto the ground.

Chapter 37

Angela and Tim propped Frank up on a chair. The man was woozy but conscious. Angela placed a hand against his cheek and it was like a block of ice. "Frank, what happened to you?"

His eyelids fluttered. "Car crash. Flipped into a ditch. Got out before the whole thing went up in flames."

Tim poured him a scotch from a bottle on the table. "It's a miracle you're alive. How did you get back here?"

He took the scotch and sipped it. "Walked."

"You walked?" Tim asked. "You got up and walked home after flipping your car into a ditch?"

Frank nodded weakly. "I was... seeing things. I walked. Didn't even know where I was going, but somehow I ended up back here."

"Good thing too," Tim said, looking down at Mike's bloodied corpse and then over at the piano, which they had place Sammie next to. "You saved the day."

"What the hell was Mike doing? Why was he trying to hurt Samuel?"

"I don't know," Angela admitted. "He just lost it. Stabbed Jessica and was going to do the same to her son."

Frank's bloodshot eyes went wide. "He stabbed Jessica?" He leapt up from the chair and staggered forwards. When his gaze fell on Jessica's body beside the bar, he flung himself down beside her and cradled her limp form. "Jessica! Jessica, wake up."

Angela stepped over Mike's body and crouched down beside Frank. "She's gone. I'm sorry."

"No, she's not," Frank growled. "We need to get help."

Angela put a hand on his shoulder and tried to ease him away, but he was having none of it. He swatted at her like a pestering fly.

Jessica's eyes opened.

Angela grabbed the bar to keep from falling. "Jesus Christ."

Jessica coughed and spluttered. Flecks of blood spewed out of her mouth. Frank shuddered with relief. "Jessica! We're going to get you help. Everything will be fine."

Jessica's eyes were unfocused, and it was hard to tell exactly where she was looking—or if she were seeing anything at all. "Frank," she muttered. "Is that you?"

"Yes, Jessica. It's me."

"I can't feel anything."

"It will be okay. We're going to get help. Try not to talk."

Angela knew there was no help that could get there quick enough. Jessica might be awake, but the seconds were ticking down on her existence. Her pupils were pinpricks as they looked up at Frank. "F-Frank, listen to me. Promise me you will look after Sammie. Promise me...."

Frank blinked away tears. The emotion seemed out of place on his strong, angular face. "I promise, Jessica. I swear to always keep him safe."

Silence as they waited for Jessica's next words, but they never came. Angela placed her hand back on Frank's shoulder and this time he allowed himself to be pulled away.

"I'm sorry, Frank. She's in a better place now."

Frank said nothing.

Angela looked down at Jessica and thought the woman finally seemed at peace. Her troubles were over.

"Hey," Tim said, breaking the silence. "How did you get inside the house, Frank?"

Frank shrugged, as if the question was stupid. "How do you think? I came in through the front door."

Angela and Tim looked at one another.

"Come on," Tim said. "We can get out of here."

Angela didn't argue. She and Tim hurried out of the piano lounge and into the foyer. Frank stayed behind with Jessica and Sammie—and Mike's dead body.

In the foyer, Angela faced an amazing sight—the front door hanging wide open. They were finally free of this wretched house.

Tim grabbed Angela's arm. "Come on."

They sprinted towards the door, the fresh air outside a simple yet irresistible goal. She would return to help Sammie, but right now she needed to get the hell out of Raymeady Manor. They needed to regroup. Too many people had died. She picked up speed, feet hammering against the marble floor, each step taking her closer to freedom. In just a few seconds, she would be outside and breathing fresh air. Outside, daylight had returned. The sun resurrected. Just a few more steps.

The front door slammed shut. Angela hurtled right into it, bashing one elbow and both her knees against the thick wood. She bounced back and skidded along the marble on her back. Tim went over the top of her and they ended up in a heap. For a moment, the two of them lay there, stunned and horrified.

"What the fuck?" Tim shouted as he struggled back to his feet. "What the motherfucking fuck?"

"It's sealed again." Angela said, knowing it to be true.

Tim tried the door handle, rattled it, shook it. Kicked it, begged it. He turned around and looked at Angela, his skin ghostly pale in the returning moonlight. "Yeah, it's locked. Looks like we're still stuck here."

"What did Mike know about what is going on?" Angela asked.

Tim slumped back against the sealed door. "Who cares, he's dead. He seemed pretty sure that Sammie was involved, but I guess that's not really a stretch."

"He mentioned Joseph not being Sammie's real father. You think maybe it has something to do with Black Remedy? Maybe they killed Joseph and had Mike kill Jessica so that Sammie would inherit the company. Then they could prove he was illegitimate and take the shares away from him."

Tim frowned. "You think this whole thing is a corporate power play?"

"Maybe. The whole house could be rigged up. Mike might have been controlling everything that's happened. Maybe there's a giant cinema screen outside convincing us it's night."

"Thought I was the nerd. It's a nice idea though. Would much rather be up against some arseholes in suits then the Devil. Yeah, maybe the front door is on electronically controlled hinges. I bet Graham is in on the whole thing, too. Don't ask me where he got the whole backwards man costume from, but enough money can buy you anything. No, wait... It doesn't explain the Ouija board or the glass shards making messages in the TV room. Also, what part are we supposed to play in all this? Why do we need to be here if the plan was just to eliminate Sammie's parents?"

"That wasn't part of the plan. Jessica called us because she didn't know what was going on, and now we're just stuck in the middle. Or maybe we're here as witnesses for a cover story."

"So you think this Chamuel is just a fabrication?"

"Maybe."

"I don't know what nonsense you two are talking about," Frank said as he entered the foyer, "but you're forgetting one thing."

"Oh," Tim said. "What is that?"

"What's wrong with Sammie? If you're suggesting that a ten-year-old boy is part of a conspiracy to kill his parents then you're both crazier than I thought. I know this family. Joseph offered me a job when I was at a low point, just about ready to throw in the towel. I have dedicated my life to this family since then. Whatever made Sammie ill, made him change like he has, is not down to a conspiracy. You were brought here to help Jessica's son, and that is what you are going to do. I promised I would look after him, to keep him safe. I intend to do that."

Angela was as confused as ever. Is there evil in this house, or is it merely the machinations of evil men? The only thing she held confidence in was that Sammie was an innocent boy. An innocent boy who needs rescuing.

"Okay," she said, adjusting her dog collar. "Let's figure this thing out once and for all. It's time for another exorcism."

Chapter 38

"What are you intending to do?" Frank asked Angela. They stood in the piano lounge. Tim had carried a still unconscious Sammie into the foyer. "Haven't you already tried this?"

"No," Angela said. "In fact, I have never tried this. A Blood Exorcism is very dangerous, but it's the only option left. If we are all in agreement that Sammie is—I'm just going to say it—possessed, then this is what I have to do. The entity inside of him—this Chamuel—is too powerful to expel with the ordinary Rite of Exorcism. We have to go harder."

Frank crossed his arms. "Harder? I don't like the sound of that. I won't allow you to harm Samuel."

"Please understand," Angela said, "that my only intention is to help Sammie."

"Intentions don't always match the end results, Ms Murs."

Angela studied the man and felt pity for him. Despite his strength and ability, the man's job to protect the Raymeady family had been a failure. The burden obviously weighed on his soul.

"Look, Frank. I want to see Sammie healthy again, a normal little boy. I want the same as you, so let me do what I need to, okay?"

Frank swallowed a lump in his throat and looked down at the floor. "Please help him. I can't take much more of this."

Angela went over to Frank and took his hand in hers. "We will sort this, Frank, I promise. Let's get Sammie back to his room and we'll get set up."

Frank nodded.

Angela re-joined Tim in the foyer. He looked relieved to see her, probably glad to no longer be left alone with the child with a demon inside.

"Everything okay out here, Tim?"

Tim glanced sideways at Sammie, who had awakened and was now stood staring out of a nearby window, humming a quiet tune. Tim leaned in towards Angela conspiratorially. "Kid's just been standing there gazing up at the moon. Hasn't said a single word, just humming that creepy song."

"Twinkle Twinkle Little Star," Angela said. "It's what was playing on the piano before we found Graham."

"Joseph used to sing it to the Samuel," Frank explained. "I've heard him humming it many times before."

"Think it means anything?" Tim asked.

"Probably that the boy misses his father. Come on. Let's get him back to his bed."

Angela stepped over to Sammie at the window and placed a hand on the clammy flesh of his bare shoulder. She looked out the window with him and saw what the boy saw: a black and featureless night broken only by the ethereal glow of the moon and stars that shouldn't be there this late in the morning.

Twinkle twinkle little star...

Sammie broke from his staring and turned to Angela. "You know, some people say the stars are angels in Heaven and that a shooting star is an angel falling from grace."

"You mean like Lucifer?" Angela asked.

Sammie frowned, all innocence. "Who is that?"

Angela expected the boy knew full well who Lucifer was, but she played along with his ignorance. "According to the Bible, Lucifer is the Devil. He waged war against Heaven and was cast out for his sins."

"Why didn't God forgive him?"

"Would you forgive someone who tried to destroy everything?"

"I'm not God," Sammie explained. "I thought God was supposed to forgive?"

"He forgives, Sammie. He forgives all the time."

"When it suits him, it would appear. Sounds like your God is a hypocrite, Angela."

"No one is perfect, Sammie. It is overcoming our flaws that makes our existence worthwhile."

"Do you think God forgives you?"

Angela swallowed. "Forgive me for what?"

"For licking cunt. You're no better than the catamites; a perversion of God's creation."

Sammie's mind games would not affect her anymore. She was beyond them. "I don't think you understand the things you're saying, Sammie. One day, when you're grown up, you'll see that the world is diverse and wonderful. We all follow our own paths and worship God in our own ways. You don't have to judge anyone."

"Don't worry," Sammie said. "I'm not judging you, that is not my place. You'll be judged in the next life."

Angela felt a chill down her spine but tried to ignore it. "Let's get you back to bed, Sammie. You must be tired."

Sammie allowed Angela to take his hand, and along with Tim and Frank, they made their way upstairs. Sammie continued humming and swung his hand back and forth childishly. Angela had to fight to hold on to him.

Hanging back, Tim asked a question as they traversed the staircase. "Frank? Did you have any idea that Mike was working against the Raymeady family this whole time?"

Frank growled like an antagonised pit bull, but kept his voice low. "What do you think? It's obvious to me now that Joseph knew there was a traitor in his midst, but he never found out quick enough to save his own life. I never found out quick enough either,"

"Joseph trusted you, Frank," Tim said. "There was an email on his computer from some investigation agency. Apparently, the only member of staff Joseph trusted was you."

Frank's eyes flickered for a moment and his head lowered to the ground. "That only makes it all the worse I failed to protect him."

"Don't beat yourself up, Frank," Sammie chimed in, apparently having heard. "I'm sure if father forgives you. You took care of mom after he died, didn't you?"

Frank's scowled at the boy. It was the first time Angela had seen the man show anything but concern towards Sammie. He said nothing though and eventually looked away.

"You okay, Frank?" Angela asked.

Frank nodded.

They reached Sammie's room and Tim stepped forward to open the door. The sweaty stink hit them as soon as they entered the room and Angela felt the walls close in. She hated this room. It was a lair, not a bedroom.

"Could you get into bed for me, please, Sammie?" she asked. "The adults need to talk alone for a moment."

Sammie did as he was asked, but had a sly grin on his face while he did it. Angela took Tim and Frank aside and held a whispered conversation with them. "I need to get some of my things and prepare," she said. "Are you two okay to stay here with Sammie while I go get them?"

Frank nodded, but Tim seemed less sure.

"Everything will be all right, Tim," she assured him. "I'll just be a few minutes."

"Five minutes is all it takes for things to go Amityville around here," he said. "But you do what you got to do. If I could get my ass out of here, I would, but seeing as that isn't an option, I'd rather be here with Harrison Ford's grumpy brother than anybody else."

Frank grumbled.

"Okay," Angela patted his elbow. "If I'm not back in ten minutes..." she trailed off. "Well, I would say call the police, but I guess the only thing you can do is pray."

Angela left the room and went to get what she needed.

Chapter 39

Tim lit as many candles as he could. Frank helped light several too. The strong, grey-haired man now seemed weak and weary, standing over Sammie with fatherly concern.

"How you holding up?" Tim asked Frank.

"I won't kid myself any longer. I've failed to protect Joseph's family, and I think it's time somebody else took over. Whatever Ms Murs is planning must be for the best. I've seen enough death to last me a thousand lifetimes—my days in the army were bad enough—but this whole experience has rocked me to the core."

"You were a soldier?" Tim asked. "That figures."

"What figures?"

"Why you're so intimidating. You've killed men, haven't you? I can tell. It clings to a man—colours his soul. Not everyone can sense it, but I can; you reek of death, Frank. Sorry."

Frank seemed far off for a moment as if his mind were some place else. "You're right, Mr Golding, I have killed men—women and children too. I was a soldier. It was my job."

"Still. Job or no job, it's never easy to know people are dead because of you."

"What would you know about it," Frank snapped.

"More than you'd think. At least when you took lives, you were a hero and not a coward."

Frank softened, but then shook his head and resumed his anger. "If you're looking for a therapist, I can recommend several, but please spare me your need for catharsis."

Tim put his hands up. "Just trying to pass the time. I blabber when I'm nervous, and right now I'm so nervous I could shit my pants."

"Well, I try to restrain yourself," Frank said.

"So..." Tim continued, deciding to change the subject. "What really happened to you on the road? You were gone a long time, hombre."

Frank sighed. "To be honest, I don't know what happened on the road. I do know one thing though—something wanted me dead, and it used Joseph Raymeady's memory to make it happen."

"And let me guess," Tim said. "That was a BIG mistake?"

Frank sneered, but it wasn't aimed at Tim. "The biggest."

Tim ran his hand over the top of a nearby candle and let the kiss of heat against his palm remind him he was awake and not dreaming. He scratched at the ginger stubble on his chin and whispered something to Frank so that Sammie could not hear. "What are you going to do when all this is over?"

"I don't really care. I expect I'll be arrested for killing Michael."

"Probably," Tim admitted. "But Angela and I will tell the police what happened. You saved Sammie's life from the crazy mamajama who just killed his mother. You've done nothing wrong."

"I doubt they'll take much pity on me. Britain's richest woman is dead and her son is now an orphan. They'll want to send someone down, and a dead killer won't be enough for them."

Tim had a thought—an unanswered question. "Hey, do you know who Sammie's real father is?"

Frank shook his head. "Jessica confided in me once that Joseph wasn't Sammie's biological father, but that was after Joseph's death. She felt guilty and wanted to confess, I think."

"Makes you wonder though," Tim mused. "Maybe Sammie's real father was more than just some stranger."

"I'm not sure I know what you mean," Frank said. "But let's not discuss a dead lady's secrets. It's disrespectful."

Tim understood and left it. The more he learned about Frank, the more he realised the guy was just another confused victim in all this. There wasn't anything the man was hiding. At least nothing that was any of Tim's business. The man was straight as an arrow—perhaps the only person who was.

Tim took a seat at Sammie's drawing desk and swivelled around so he was directly facing the boy in his bed. The last thing he was willing to do was sit with his back to Sammie. Angela seemed to have faith that she could save the kid from whatever ancient demon Chamuel represented—if that was in fact the dealio—but Tim wasn't expecting things to end well. Whether or not Sammie was possessed, one thing was for the sure:

This kid is dangerous.

Chapter 40

A ngela lied when she'd said she needed to get some things. She had all the things she needed: her Bible, her faith, and the ceremonial dagger to be used in the Blood Exorcism. The real reason she had left Tim and Frank alone with Sammie was because she needed a few moments to mentally prepare herself. Angela's resolve had wavered. She was afraid. Could God's protection penetrate the malevolence afflicting the Raymeady estate? Or was she a naïve mouse standing in a snake pit?

When she had left Sammie's room, she had headed back down the staircase to where she now stood inside the piano lounge, trying to ignore the stench of blood. Jessica still lay on the floor, her body twisted, expressionless face staring up at the ceiling. Angela reached down and moved the woman's legs so they pointed straight. Then she positioned Jessica's arms over her chest and closed her eyes. Safe journey, Ms Raymeady.

Angela clasped her hands together in prayer.

"May the road rise up to meet you.

May the wind be always at your back.

May the sun shine warm upon your face;

the rains fall soft upon your fields and until we meet again,

may God hold you in the palm of His hand."

The old Gaelic blessing she'd learned as a child was not the typical way to bless a soul's passing, but it seemed like something Jessica would have liked. It made Angela feel better knowing that something had been said to mark the woman's passing. *Now I just need to say a prayer for myself.*

Bon Jovi said it best:

We've got to hold on ready or not.

You live for the fight when it's all that you've got.

She sang the next line out loud like a war cry. "Wooah, living on a prayer."

She was ready, she was pumped, but once she took a few steps, she stopped. Mike lay face up on the ground where they'd left him. Angela looked down at him and wondered what had led him down the path he'd chosen. Mike had killed Jessica, yes, but he had seemed afraid, even panicked. Whatever his sins, he was a human being and had had his own reasons for whatever he'd done. Angela knelt down beside Mike and blessed his passing. "I am the resurrection and the life. He who believes in me will live, even though he dies; says the Lord."

Mike's eyes snapped open. "Angela!"

Angela fell backwards onto her hands. A jolt of agony shot up her wrist. Mike lifted his crooked face and glared at her. He was alive. *No. No, he's dead.*

Mike's swollen eyes rolled back in his head, showing only the bloodshot whites. His ruined mouth worked silently as if it were being operated by gears and cogs. Angela knew without a doubt he was definitely dead, yet he was sitting up and talking to her.

In a raspy voice, Mike whispered, "Time is running out. His power is growing. You must slay the beast."

Angela stared at Mike's body, sickened to see his human flesh being manipulated like a puppet. "The beast? How do I slay the beast?"

Mike's eye sockets bled and his lips twitched and contorted. "You mussst separate the beassst from the purity."

Angela nodded. "I know. I will perform the exorcism right now." She couldn't believe she was having a conversation with a dead man, but she knew it wasn't Mike inside. "Who are you?"

Mike's teeth fell from his mouth, one at a time, plinking on the tiles like notes on a xylophone. His entire face was gradually crumbling to pieces. "You mussst ssslay the beassst. Exorcisssm... not enough...."

Mike's lower jaw hung and then dislocated from his skull. It fell to the floor with a clunk! His body collapsed face down on the floor.

Angela sighed. Guess that's the end of the conversation.

What had the message meant, and who had given it to her? Was it Sammie, Chamuel, or somebody else? The conversation had given Angela more questions than answers, but one part gave her cause for concern: Exorcism... not enough. It indicated there were more trials ahead. The only instruction she'd heard was to 'separate the beast from the innocent.' That sounded like an exorcism as far as she was concerned, so that was what she would do.

But it wouldn't be enough.

Angela clutched the ceremonial dagger beneath her cassock and dragged herself up off the floor.

Chapter 41

Tim jumped out of his skin when Angela arrived back at Sammie's room, not because she'd opened the door so forcefully, but because his nerves were so taut that a fly on a windowpane would be enough to make him flinch.

"Everything okay in here?" Angela asked as she strode into the room.

"Yeah, nobody died if that's what you mean?"

Angela gave him a reassuring smile. Something about her current manner gave him hope things might just work out okay. As much as Tim expected the worst, Angela looked ready to expect the best.

"Did you get everything you needed?"

"Yes. We should begin."

Tim swallowed a lump in his throat and nodded. "Ready when you are. Just let me know what you need."

"I need you to be vigilant," she said. "Do not touch Sammie, do not speak to Sammie, and whatever happens you must not interfere." She looked at Frank specifically when she gave the last order.

Frank sighed, but gave a nod of compliance.

"Okay then. Let's begin. I'll start by talking to Sammie. I need to learn as much about the entity inside of him as I can. Knowledge will be power if a battle of wills ensues."

Tim wanted to get himself into the habit of remaining silent so he made no reply. He simply smiled, a gesture of solidarity for Angela that he was there if she needed him. Frank stood there too, but gave no such gesture himself.

Angela pulled the chair away from the drawing desk and dragged it up beside Sammie's bed. She plonked herself down and leant forward. "Sammie? What is your favourite thing?"

Sammie looked at her and immediately said, "South Park."

"Why? Why do you like South Park?"

"Because it shows me what the world is like."

Angela frowned. "I don't think so. South Park is a cartoon. It's not real life."

"I disagree. It is real life. Prejudice, sex, drugs, violence, it is all happening behind every closed door, yet I am stuck here unable to experience anything of life. South Park is all I have."

"Does that make you angry, Sammie? That you don't get to leave the house? Do you enjoy seeing the worst in people on your program?"

"No, Angela, I am not angry. My time to see things first hand will come. Until then, it appears I am not the only one who cannot leave this house."

"Is it you that's keeping us trapped inside, Sammie?"

"No."

Angela continued. "Okay, then. You know, if we could get out of here, we could go get help. Your mother has been hurt."

"My mother has been killed," Sammie corrected her dispassionately.

"How do you feel about that?"

"Sad, of course. She was my mother, and I loved her."

Tim couldn't believe how much the boy's voice lacked conviction. It was as if he were reading the words from a script. How To Behave Like A Ten-Year-Old Boy. "What do you want Sammie, or Chamuel, or whoever we're speaking to? Everyone around you is dead, and it sounds like you don't even care. What is it you're trying to achieve?"

Sammie smirked. "I'm just trying to grow up."

Angela shot a scowl at Tim before returning her focus back to Sammie. "Why do you want to grow up, Sammie? You're just a boy."

"But I will be so much more than that."

"What do you mean?"

Sammie shrugged his bony shoulders. "Haven't you heard? I now control Black Remedy Corporation. I even own this house you're standing in."

Tim couldn't help himself again. "Sammie, you mother isn't even cold yet and you're talking about your inheritance."

Angela shot him a chastising look, but he didn't care. He was tired acting like the kid in front of him wasn't responsible for everything that had happened—all the death.

Sammie pouted. "Why are you so angry with me, Tim? Is it because you're a coward and taking out your rage on a young boy is all you're capable of?"

"You know nothing about me." Tim felt himself spit the word. "Nothing!"

"We'll see," Sammie said. "I'm sure there'll be more opportunities to prove your lack of courage."

Tim stepped forward but Frank placed a hand against his chest.

"Enough of this," Angela scolded. "I told you to be quiet, Tim. So be quiet!"

Sammie grinned. "Yes, Tim. Do as the lesbian tells you."

Tim bit his lip. He was doing exactly what he meant not to do. He was letting Sammie get to him, get inside his head. Take a breath. Calm down. Keep your eye on the ball.

He stepped back up against the wall. "Just get on with it," he said to Angela. "I'm getting bored."

Angela sighed and turned back to the boy in his bed. "Sammie? I'm going to ask you something, and you will not like it, but if you agree to it, then everything will be a lot safer for everybody."

Sammie raised an eyebrow and seemed concerned. "What?"

"I want to tie you down to the bed. It will be for your own good."

"No."

"Sammie...."

"I said no. Nobody is touching me."

Angela looked at Frank who was staring right back at her. Tim could see the man did not approve.

"What are you playing at?" Frank asked.

"I need to make sure Sammie is secure before I get started. It may get very physical and I don't want him hurting himself, or us."

"Nobody is touching me," Sammie said again.

"Frank, we need to do this. I can't do it without your help."

Frank shook his head and rubbed at his eyes with his palms. "Damn it. Okay," he said. "Hold him down."

Angela looked at Tim and he cursed under his breath. "Let's get it over with."

Tim took the left side of Sammie's bed while Angela took the right. In unison, they grabbed Sammie's arms. The boy screamed and thrashed like a beached shark.

"Keep hold of him," Frank said. He ran to the windows and yanked at the curtain ties.

"Hurry," Tim huffed and puffed, dodging at a kick to his face. "This kid is stronger than he looks."

Sammie screeched. Thick wads of spittle flew from his gnashing teeth. Tim struggled to hold onto his sweat-drenched arm, and it seemed like Angela, too, was close to losing her grip.

Frank rushed over with the curtain ties and wrapped one around the arm that Angela was wrestling with. He yanked Sammie's left arm towards the bed post and tied a double knot. Just as he got the one arm secured, Tim's grip gave out and Sammie broke free.

Sammie twisted his body at Tim and lashed out with his teeth. His jaws clamped down.

"Fuck! Get him off me!" The crushing force on Tim's hand was like a tightening vice. He felt the bones threaten to crack and splinter beneath his tearing flesh.

Frank leapt up onto the bed and straddled Sammie's waist. He clutched the boy's shoulder and tried to pull him away from Tim, but the small teeth hung on like fish hooks. The agony in Tim's hand continued. "He's a fucking bloody pitbull. Jesus Christ!"

Sammie opened his mouth and spat blood into Tim's face. "Blasphemer!"

Frank took advantage of the opportunity and got the remaining curtain tie around Sammie's right wrist. Tim joined in by holding the boy's wrist down against the bedpost. Between them they got Sammie secured to the bed, albeit with his untethered legs kicking and pumping like pistons.

Tim staggered backwards, clutching his hand. The skin was shorn from his knuckles. Blood dripped onto the carpet like the ticking of a clock.

Sammie glowered at Frank, who had climbed down off his bed. Blood coated the boy's teeth and shone in the darkness, making his lips shimmer dull red. He struggled against his bonds, but it did no good. The curtain ties held him. "How could you, Frank? My father trusted you. You're supposed to look after me. That's your job."

Frank was panting. "It's more than just my job, Samuel. I'm trying to help you. You're a sick boy."

"The only sicko around here is you. How long have you been fucking my mother? Was my father still fresh in the ground?"

Frank looked pained. "I loved your father, Sammie, and I loved your mother. I did nothing but look out for the both of them."

Sammie cackled. "Good job."

The comment seemed to be all Frank could take, and he turned away. Tim knew how he felt. Sammie had a knack of getting inside people's heads. Somehow, hearing your truths laid bare by a child was worse than admitting them yourself.

Angela tried to regain control. "Sammie, it's important that you listen to me until this is over, okay?"

"Choke and die, cunt!" he spat phlegm at her. The thick brown wad shimmered against the jet fabric of her cassock.

"Nobody else is dying," Angela commanded, ignoring the mess on her clothing. "The evil in this house is impotent. Nobody else will be harmed. Do you understand me?"

Sammie cackled. "You fools. You weak, pathetic fools. All will die tonight at my merest whim. You will expire last, priest, so you can see what you have reaped upon these poor souls. The blood will be on your hands. My rebirth will be christened by your flesh. Your guts will spill, your soul will burn-"

"Quiet!" Angela demanded. "I demand you leave this child, or suffer the consequences."

Sammie's voice dropped several octaves. It boomed at them like a drum. "I mock your consequences. I shall be judged by no one, for I am above judgment. You will all cower. You will all obey. You will kneel. Or you will die. Those are your consequences, priest."

"I do not fear you," Angela said. "You are weak. I pity your weakness in the shadow of my almighty Lord. It is you who shall kneel before Him."

Sammie laughed, a great, booming heckle.

Angela chose that moment to slip something out from under her cassock. Tim saw it glint in the candlelight as it appeared. It was the ceremonial dagger, long and slender. Sammie's eyes went wide at the sight of it.

"Whoa!" Tim said, wishing he'd asked more questions earlier. "Is it a good time to get all knifey?"

Angela didn't look at Tim but answered his question, anyway. "We must draw blood. It is the only way to weaken the hold the evil has on the boy."

Tim didn't like the tone of her voice. It was flat and emotionless, as if she'd cleared her mind of all compassion, to do what was necessary.

"I can't allow that," Frank said. "It's... it's not right."

"This has to happen, Frank. We go all the way, or we lose."

Frank seemed in two minds. "What do you plan on doing?"

"She should shove it up her twat!" Sammie bellowed, still struggling to get free from his bonds. It was then that Tim realised the boy was urinating on his sheets, letting loose a steady stream that mushroomed through the fabric.

Angela held the dagger out in front of her. "For the boy's soul to be cleansed, he must suffer the wounds of Christ. His suffering will bring him closer to Heaven, to a place where evil cannot follow. His mind will return to us, free of the corruption that has been threatening to destroy it."

"We could go to prison for this," Tim said. He was thinking more and more about retrying the front door to the house and escaping. He wanted out of there so bad, before things went too far.

"We're already on our way there," Frank said. "God help me! Just do it, Angela."

Tim was shocked. Something in Frank had snapped. He clearly now believed in what Angela was doing and had lost the rationality to see the danger. Cutting a ten-year-old boy with an antique dagger was insane. Why did he agree to any of this?

As it turned out, Angela didn't wait for anybody's permission. She approached Sammie with the knife.

"Get away from me, dyke!"

Angela hopped up onto the bed and straddled Sammie's waist in the same way Frank had earlier. She held the dagger above her head as if she were about to plunge it deep into the boy's chest. Tim held his breath .

Sammie bucked and twisted beneath Angela's weight, trying to escape her.

"The Lord demands you repent your sins," she screamed. "Demon, do you repent?"

"Fuck you!" Sammie spat what looked like two bloody molars at her face. Mucus shot forth from his lips and spattered her chest. It did not deter her.

Angela plunged the knife and drew it across Sammie's forehead with a vicious flick of her wrist. The blood flowed, covering Sammie's face in a gushing wave.

"Do you repent?" Angela repeated. "Demon, do you repent?"

Sammie's dark eyes scowled at her through the veil of blood. "I... repent... nothing."

"Then you will suffer."

Angela drove the dagger down into Sammie's left hand, plunging all the way through and out the other side. The boy's screams were animalistic, inhuman, and also that of a ten-year-old boy. The noise was sickening.

"Stop!" Tim shouted, unable to take any more.

Angela ignored his pleas and also those of the screaming child beneath her. She pulled free the dagger from Sammie's hand, blood spitting into the air, and drove it down again. This time the blade pierced Sammie's right hand.

Tim had seen enough. He rushed forward and grabbed Angela around the waist, threw her off the bed to the floor. She looked up at him in anger and surprise. The bloody dagger dripped in her hand.

"This has to stop!"

Before Angela could get back up, he grabbed one of Sammie's wrists and untied the bond. He was about to reach over and untie the other one, but Frank stopped him. "Calm down!"

"Calm down? Calm down? This is insane."

"How can you deny what you've seen?" Angela demanded of Tim as she dusted herself off. "Have you forgotten the pain in your hand where he bit into you like an animal? Have you forgotten the death and destruction you have seen in this house?"

Tim clutched at his hair. "Mike and Jessica were both killed by other people. There was no evil involved. This is madness."

"So you deny that there is anything happening here?" Angela's expression was one of disbelief.

Tim cursed at the ceiling. "Shitballs, mother-fucking dog piss. I know there is something going on here. Christ, of course I know that. I just don't think this is right at all. Whatever is going on, Sammie is just a child. We can't torture him like this."

Something moved in the shadows.

Sammie leapt from his bed and ploughed into Angela. She fell backwards into

Frank and the two of them hit the floor with a thump. Tim stood there, stunned. Sammie crouched on the floor like a feral beast, glaring up at him with baleful eyes. The wounds on his hands and forehead were no longer bleeding, yet were puckered like the sliced flesh of frozen poultry.

"You should have stuck me like a pig while you had the chance." Sammie sneered at them all. "Now you will die."

Sammie struck at Tim, tearing a thick strip of skin from his cheek. Then he sprinted away, yanking open the bedroom door and disappearing into the darkness of the hallway.

Chapter 42

"Sammie, you come back here!" Frank shouted into the darkness of the hallway. Angela placed a hand on his shoulder to get his attention. The last thing she needed was Frank disappearing into the shadows.

"He won't come back on his own," she said. "We need to go find him."

Tim groaned. "Before he finds us."

Angela liked Tim, but he was no good under pressure. Some people saw problems while others saw solutions. Tim was the former, and it made him difficult to rely on. You'd think a professional ghost hunter would be braver.

"So what's the plan?" Frank asked, fidgeting and acting like he might take off at any moment.

"We go after him. But we stay together. Sammie is more dangerous now than ever."

"Might have something to do with the fact you keep wanting to stab him," Tim commented.

Angela faced Tim down. "It is because the Blood Exorcism is almost complete. Whatever is inside of Sammie has nothing to lose."

Tim's eyes narrowed. "Almost complete? What else is left?"

"There are two more stigmata to perform, two more wounds of Christ to bestow upon Sammie's body."

Tim's eyes narrowed further. "You need to pierce his feet?"

Angela nodded.

"You're insane."

"Piercing the feet should be enough to banish the demon, because if I am forced to perform the final stigmata it would banish the demon to Limbo for all eternity. The final stigmata is piercing Sammie's side and kill him. Just the threat of it should be enough to drive Chamuel out."

Tim swallowed. "And if it's not enough?"

"Then we have to decide if sacrificing Sammie is something we should do for the greater good." Angela couldn't believe the words coming out of her mouth, but she was without any doubt that something terrible lurked in the boy. Ever since the death and destruction she witnessed in Jersey at the hands of Charles Crippley, Angela understood the importance of defeating evil before it had time to bloom.

"We're not killing a kid," Tim objected. "Frank, you're with me, aren't you?"

To Angela's dismay, Frank agreed nodded. He had seemed with her until that point. "I have to draw the line somewhere, Ms Murs."

She was outvoted. But they might change their minds before this was through. "Okay. Let's just find Sammie. We can figure things out later."

Tim folded his arms. "Fine."

"Frank, you lead the way. You know the house better than we do."

Frank nodded and took the lead. They filed into the hallway and padded down the corridor silently like bedraggled commandos. Darkness bathed the entire house, every corner a potential hiding place for unseen horrors.

Frank opened a door on the left and stuck his head inside, then closed it again. "Just a storage room," he said. "No sign of Sammie inside. There's a bathroom over there. Go check it out."

Angela nodded. Sure enough she found a bathroom. White and black tiles. Smell of bleach hanging heavily in the air. The room was empty. There were no hiding places.

Except one place.

A freestanding bathtub occupied the far corner of the bathroom. A modern affair with a wraparound shower curtain from end to end. It would be easy for a ten-year-old boy to hide inside.

Angela crept, yet the sound of her feet on tile seemed loud. If Sammie was hiding in the bathtub, he had heard her coming. Should she call out to him? No, it would be pointless. A hiding child does not respond to their name being called. She closed the final few steps, stood within arm's reach of the shower curtain, and placed her fingers against the plastic sheet.

Here goes.

She let out a breath.

Pulled back the curtain.

The bathtub was empty.

Somebody grabbed Angela from behind. She spun around, ready to scream.

"Any sign?" Frank asked her.

"Bloody hell, Frank. You almost gave me a heart attack."

"Sorry. Tim said he heard something down below. I heard nothing myself, but I lost twenty-per cent of my hearing during my days in the forces, so I tend to doubt myself."

Angela nodded. "Okay, let's go check it out then. You shouldn't have left Tim alone. It's not safe."

"He insisted. Said he'd be fine."

"I hope so."

When they went back out into the hallway, Tim was gone.

Frank looked left and right. "Where did he go?"

"He's afraid," Angela said, understanding what had happened. "I imagine he's trying to find a way out."

Frank's nostrils flared, and he snorted like a bull? "Coward."

"There's nothing we can do about it now. If Tim wants out of here, then he'll be of no use to us, anyway. We need to find Sammie. Do you think Tim was at least telling the truth about hearing a noise downstairs?"

Frank shrugged. "Probably not. In fact, I doubt it entirely. Perhaps we should work from the top down. Go to the top floor first?"

"Sounds like a plan. You still got that gun?"

"Huh? Yes, it's tucked under my shirt. Why?"

"No reason. Just nice to know you have it."

As they walked, Angela filled the time with questions. "So now that Jessica has..." she struggled for the right words, "passed on, what'll happen to the family's shares in Black Remedy? Will they all belong to Sammie?"

"Yes, but they'll be overseen by his legal guardian until he's eighteen."

"Who's his guardian?"

Frank shook his head. "I'm not sure. Vincent Black was the boy's godfather, so perhaps him."

Angela stopped walking. "Isn't he the other owner of the company?"

"Forty-nine per cent, yes. The Black family provided most of the funding the Raymeady family required to build the company."

"Mike was working against the Raymeadys. Do you think he was working for the Black family? Are they trying to take control of the company?"

"I'd imagine so," Frank said, sounding resigned to the fact. "With Sammie so young, the Blacks will likely raise him as their own."

"Doesn't that bother you? Jessica, Joseph, they could be dead because of some greedy American businessman."

"It bothers me immensely, but what would you have me do? My job was to protect this family. I've failed. Time for me to move on."

"Move on?" Angela couldn't believe what she was hearing. "You can't move on. You failed this family, so you owe Sammie."

Frank sighed. "It's already too late. If the Black family is behind everything that's happened, then they've achieved everything they needed to."

Angela clenched her fists. "It's not over yet, Frank. You will do everything you can to protect that boy once this is over. Do you hear me?"

Frank sighed. "Yes. Yes, I hear you."

"Then come on. Let's go make this right."

Chapter 43

Tim hated himself. It didn't matter how hard he tried, he could never bring himself to jeopardise his own safety for anyone else's. He was a natural coward, and it made him sick, but that was just who he was.

It was Angela's sick God that made me this way.

The house made Tim so anxious that his spine was in a constant state of rigour. He tiptoed across the thick marble floor in the foyer. Trying to get the front door open would be a fool's errand, but what else could he do. One way or the other he was getting out of this fucking house.

The thick wooden doors loomed as he approached them. It seemed as if they were in on the whole conspiracy too. Tim still felt the victim of some elaborate hoax, but was quickly becoming more open to the possibility of something else. Something worse. He couldn't deny Evil existed. He had witnessed it.

I have to get out of here.

Fruitlessly, he placed a hand around the doorknob and took a deep breath. He twisted his wrist and yanked.

The lock turned.

Tim almost choked. The door opened.

Tim's hands fell to his sides. He stood staring at the door, but did not move. The house was allowing him to leave. Daylight beckoned outside. His van sat invitingly on the pebble driveway.

Tim stepped forwards, hands shaking.

"I suppose this is goodbye?" someone said behind him.

Tim froze. No confusion in his mind about who stood behind him. Ahead, lay the exhilarating freedom of the English countryside. Behind, lay the icy wickedness of a creature.

"I have no need of you," Sammie said. "You are insignificant."

Something about the word irritated Tim. Insignificant. He turned around. "What is all this, Sammie? What's it about?"

Sammie examined him with jet black eyes, tilted his head and smiled. "What is anything about in this decaying crust of existence? It is about power. Power to mould existence."

"And what do you want to mould it into?"

Sammie opened his arms wide like a bat unfurling its wings. "An existence without fear or suffering, a world of order and consistency."

Tim backed away towards the open door. He could feel the breeze on his back. "That sounds very much like a world without free will. You plan on enslaving humanity, Sammie?"

"Slavery, freedom. Mere semantics. The only thing you need to realise is that God's world is a failed experiment. It is time for new management, wouldn't you agree?"

"You're the Devil," Tim spat. "Angela will stop you."

Sammie sighed. "I am not the Devil. The Devil is weak, perverted by spending millennia among the seductive filth of humanity. I am beyond God, beyond the Devil. I am the wolf amongst the lambs. Your cleric will kneel before me and her death will be sublime."

Tim took another step backwards. "You say I am insignificant. So what do you want with Angela? Why did you summon her here?"

"I did not summon her here."

"Then who did? Who scribbled her name in your sketch pad?"

Sammie took a deep, whistling breath and let it out in a gust that stunk up the air with festering meat. "There are more forces at work in this house than you realise, Mr Golding. There is another. He who shares history with your priest. Angela's presence defiles this place. I will take exquisite pleasure in claiming her soul."

"You won't-"

"ENOUGH!" Sammie's voice was like a hive of bees, buzzing inside Tim's head. "Leave this place. Leave before this house becomes your tomb. The door is open, but my clemency is not without end."

Tim turned to face the door. He cleared his throat and stepped outside.

Chapter 44

After checking the top floor and finding it empty, Angela and Frank checked the third floor. It too was deserted. What was Sammie planning? Would he jump out at them any moment, or was he planning to flee the house? She still didn't understand what he wanted, but she was confident about one thing: the Blood Exorcism was the solution—if it wasn't, Sammie wouldn't have fled. The demon feared her. *I need to drive the dagger through Sammie's feet and all this will finally be over.*

Angela considered what she'd done, and what she was yet to do. Once, she'd been a servant of the Lord. She had lost her way, but now felt closer to God than ever before. Her renewed faith would allow her to do what she needed to do.

God help me.

Frank returned from one of the bedrooms. Angela smiled at him as he approached. "Find anything?"

"Empty like all the rest. The next room is yours. Did you want to check it out?"

Angela nodded. She headed up to the door on her left that led to the Freidkin Suite where she'd been staying. Inside, things were just as she'd left them. Suitcase on the floor beside the bed, contents spilling onto the floor. The bed was still unmade. Tiredness pulsed through Angela's skull and licked at the back of her eyelids with a dry tongue. Her watch said it was almost four in the afternoon, yet the moon was still out as if it were midnight.

A man can no more diminish God's glory by refusing to worship Him than a lunatic can put out the sun by scribbling the word 'darkness' on the walls of his cell.

The C.S. Lewis quote had popped into Angela's head unbidden as she turned a full circle of the room, scrutinising every nook and cranny. She even knelt down to inspect under the bed. All was clear—no little boys hiding or evil beasts lurking. The last thing that caught Angela's eye was the painting above the bed of the two cherubs fighting. She didn't know why the picture kept catching her eye, but she was convinced she was missing something. Or maybe I just think it's ugly.

She exited the room and re-entered the hallway. Frank was not where she'd left him, now further along the corridor by the grand staircase. "Frank, are you okay?"

Frank remained silent, but he heard her. He raised one hand beside his head that made it clear he'd acknowledged her but wished not to speak. Angela crept forward, stomach full of dread. It took more than a dozen steps to catch up to Frank. Once she did, it was clear what had rooted the man to the spot.

Sammie climbed the stairs, coming towards them. He took each step slowly, ascending like a spirit. A smile graced his lips, contorting his face almost into a grimace.

Angela moved beside Frank and whispered. "Do you think Tim is okay?"

"Tim made his own bed," Frank muttered.

Sammie continue up the stairs. Angela couldn't help but shout out to him. "Sammie, what are you doing?"

Sammie didn't acknowledge her, only continued his slow, gliding ascent up the staircase. His smile grew wider, crooked teeth taking up more and more of his face, leaving him more shark than boy.

"Sammie? Where is Tim?"

Sammie glanced up and finally acknowledged her. "Tim has abandoned you, priest."

"So we were right," Frank said. "Tim ran out on us. Coward."

Angela raised a hand. "You cannot blame a man for being frightened. None of us have power over bravery. Courage chooses us only when it is needed. Tim is not important."

Sammie reached the top of the stairs and stood six feet away from Angela and Frank. The knife wounds on his hands had blackened and sealed as if they were days old.

"I need to finish this, Frank," Angela whispered.

Frank stepped forward. "Sammie, are you willing to come back to your room?"

Sammie laughed. "What do you think?"

Frank sighed. "Hard way it is then." He made a snatch for the boy but was nowhere near quick enough. Sammie leapt up onto the balcony's bannister, bare feet and filthy toenails gripping the wood like a vulture's talons.

Angela made her own grab for the boy.

Sammie kicked her in the face from his elevated perch and sent her reeling backwards into the wall. She tasted blood at the back of her nose and tears blinded her. Blearily, she saw Sammie glaring down at her with sunken eyes. The smell wafting from him was foul.

Frank made another snatch at Sammie, but again the boy was too quick. He sprung off the banister and cleared Frank's head by several feet, landing behind him in a crouch and hissing like a feral cat.

"He's not even human," Frank said, steadying himself against the railing. "More like an animal."

Angela used the back of her hand to wipe away the blood that was filling up her nostrils. "The Evil has twisted him, Frank—activated his primal instincts. We need to finish this now or Sammie will be lost forever."

Her words seemed to spur Frank on, and he bellowed in defiance. He made a lunging tackle for Sammie, thick arms wrapping around the boy's legs and tripping him to the ground. Sammie squealed with childish laughter, unconcerned by his capture. It was just a game to him.

"I need you to hold his legs," Angela said. "I must pierce his feet together. Then it will be done. It will be over."

Frank straddled Sammie and wrestled to put the boy's ankles together. Sammie kicked his legs and giggled. "Give it up, Frank," he said in the voice of a child. "You will never be the hero. You couldn't save my parents and you never saved Conway, Nichols, or Albright. They died on your watch, Sergeant! Right after you shot a pregnant woman in the stomach. So much death at your hands. You'll never wash the stink off."

Frank reacted as if he'd been kicked in the ribs. His grip on Sammie loosened. The boy shuffled free.

Angela yelled, trying to be the only voice Frank heard. "Frank, don't listen. Whatever he is talking about doesn't matter. We all have pasts. It is what we do now that matters."

"Tell that to those men's families," Sammie said. "Tell that to Conway's son. Tell him how you sent his father into a village you said was friendly, and how you left him to die on the lonely sands of Iraq. I thought the Parachute Regiment never left a man behind. Well, you left three behind to save yourself."

Frank staggered to his feet and backed away from Sammie. "They... they were pinned down, wounded. The entire village was armed—even the pregnant woman. If I stayed behind, we would all have died. I needed to bring in support before the rebels dug in somewhere else and killed more of us. Someone needed to get back alive."

Angela shouted. "Frank! Frank, it doesn't matter. He's just trying to break you. You need to get a hold of him so we can finish this."

Frank shook his head. "Things were finished for me a long time ago. Protecting this family was supposed to be my salvation. Instead it's my condemnation." He spun and grabbed Angela, shoved her against the balcony railing and winded her. "I'm sorry," he said as he snatched the ceremonial dagger from her fingertips and rushed towards Sammie. He let out a wail of anguish like an ancient warrior.

Sammie swatted Frank aside with inhuman force. The blow sent the large man clean off his feet and into Angela. The sudden impact took her by surprise and rocked back against the balcony railing. Her momentum carried her over the top. She fell.

The marble floor waited two stories below.

A hand grabbed her wrist.

Angela flipped over in the air, legs dangling from wrenched sockets. She hung by her left arm, but began to rise slowly back towards the balcony. Somebody had saved her at the last second.

Thank you God.

"You ought to be more careful," said a voice that was not Frank's.

Angela looked up and saw Sammie clutching her wrist. He was lifting her upwards as if she weighed no more than a bag of flour. The look on his face was like that of a cat toying with a mouse. Angela knew Sammie's intention was not to save her. He was only prolonging the moment for his own amusement.

Sammie raised her high enough that they were face to face and she could feel his fetid breath on her cheeks. He held her there, suspended, and it was then that Angela saw Frank writhing on the floor. The ceremonial dagger jutted out of his thigh. He must've fallen on it when Sammie flung him across the balcony. There was no chance of him saving her.

Angela was doomed.

"Where is your God now?" Sammie purred. "Has he abandoned you? Are you forsaken? Perhaps, he doesn't even know you exist."

"Let her go," someone demanded. That person stepped forward out of the shadows.

Sammie raised an eyebrow and smirked. "Mr Golding? I thought you'd left. How very stupid of you to not have."

Tim glared at Sammie. "I said let her go."

"Yes, I heard you, but considering her current predicament, I don't think that's wise, do you?"

Tim stepped forward. "Pull her up and then let her go."

Angela felt Sammie's icy fingers tighten around her wrist. For a moment she thought he might actually lift her to safety as Tim demanded, but then he said otherwise. "How about I let the bitch fall, Mr Golding, and then twist your head off like a wart from a pig's back? I could even send you to join your wretched brother in his eternal torment. All that guilt inside of you, Tim. I could end it all so easily. Let me help you, Tim. Let me make it all go away."

Tim's confidence seemed to waver—Angela noticed him trembling—but he remained resolute. "Pull. Her. Back. Up. Now. Arsehole."

"Oh Tim. Silly, silly Tim. I thought you were the smart one. The only one who realised their own weakness. You were right in wanting to leave. Your mistake was coming back."

Tim took another step forward.

Sammie let Angela drop.

She screamed.

But he still held her. He'd just let her drop a few inches. It was all it took to make her cry out in despair. Tim stopped moving and put his hands up in front of him. "Take it easy, Sammie. I just want to take Angela and get the hell out of here. Leave, just like you said."

Sammie sniggered. "Oh, she isn't going anywhere, I'm afraid. I'll tell you what though—let's see if you can make it over here before I have time to let her fall and rip out your throat with my teeth. Or I could give you one last chance to leave on your own. Your choice—do you want to live or do you want to die?"

Angela saw the fear in Tim's eyes. Coming back to help her now was an erroneous blip in an otherwise faultless career of cowardice. Angela looked down at the marble floor thirty-feet below her ankles and knew it would be her grave. She watched with weary resignation as Tim turned away and started towards the staircase. He was leaving. Somehow, she still couldn't bring herself to blame him.

Sammie turned to Angela and chuckled. "Do you see, priest? Do you see what this world is made of? Cowardice and fear. Selfishness and hatred. Mankind is a cesspool."

Angela strained, tried to pull herself up. "Who... who are you, Chamuel?"

Sammie looked at her, shaking her head with pity. "You don't understand a thing, do you? I am the new beginning. I am what comes next. Unfortunately, you will not live long enough to bare witness."

Angela closed her eyes and prepared to die. But before she did... "Someone needs to spank you, you annoying little shit."

Sammie's grip fell away. Her body plummeted.

The her fall ended. Another hand around her wrist.

Was Sammie still playing with her.

Angela looked up.

Tim squinted down at her with locked jaws, effort of holding her summoning great beads of sweat from his forehead. "How about a little help here, Angela," he groaned as a vein pulsed in his forehead.

With the final dregs of strength she had left, Angela heaved herself upwards. Pain ripped through her back as rarely used muscles awakened. Tim's wiry biceps looked like they might detach from the bone, yet somehow he got her up. Angela's free hand reached the banister and her fingertips clawed to get hold. She swung her leg and, with one desperate effort, she climbed onto the railing. She through herself over and landed hard on top of Tim. Both of them lay there moaning.

There was no time to recuperate.

"Get up," Angela said, panting. "Sammie!"

Tim staggered to his feet and looked around for the boy.

"You came back," Angela commented.

Tim shrugged like it was nothing. It was not nothing. "Guess I'd rather die with a clear conscience than live with any more guilt."

"Nobody else is dying tonight," she promised him.

Frank was still writhing nearby. He sat upright, staring down at the long blade sticking up from his thigh muscle. In the supernatural moonlight, he looked ghostly pale.

"Are you okay?" Angela asked him. A stupid question.

Frank groaned. "You need the dagger?"

Angela nodded. Ripping the blade free could nick an artery, and as an ex-Army man, Frank would know it too. The sensible thing would be to keep the stiletto in place and get help—but that wasn't an option.

"Just take it," he said, voice high and nervous.

Angela thanked him with a node and wrapped her fingers around the dagger's hilt. She needed to get it out with one pull—quick and clean. Failing to do so would cause more damage to Frank's leg.

She yanked before he had a chance to take a breath.

The blade came free with a grim sucking sound and Frank hissed in agony. A jet of blood spurted into the air, but thankfully didn't persist. The dagger had missed the major blood vessels.

Angela held the dagger and winced at the blood on its shaft. The sight of it turned her stomach, but she had to fight against her revulsion. A cry of pain called her into action. Sammie reappeared and through himself around Tim's neck, like a normal ten-year-old boy wanting a piggyback ride. Tim screeched as Sammie bit into his neck and tore away a strip of stringy flesh.

Angela raced forward to help him.

Sammie's eyes caught sight of her sprinting towards him with the dagger in her hand. He released Tim from his clutches and hopped away like a giant bug. Tim staggered, clutching his bleeding neck. "Jesus Christ, that hurts."

Angela put a hand on his shoulder and gave him a quick shake. His wound looked sore, but they would not kill him. No time to indulge aching bodies and torn flesh. She pointed the dagger at Sammie who snarled at her. "It's time to end this," she said. "I'm tired and I haven't had a drink in hours."

Sammie scuttled across the carpet like a spider and surprised them all by scurrying up the wall. He sprung sideways at Angela and caught her on the shoulder. She fell sideways, once again striking the balcony's railing. Sammie was right on her, intending to tackle her over the ledge again.

But Tim shoved Angela aside and met Sammie head on. The boy's unnatural strength presented itself again and sent Tim crashing clear through the ancient bannister that gave way like termite-infested balsa-wood.

Angela tumbled to the floor, helpless as Tim disappeared over the balcony. She scurried over to the edge, and what she saw below brought tears to her eyes. Tim's body lay sprawled on the marble floor like a pretzel. One leg twisted beneath his body at a sickening angle. The fall had snapped his bones like chalk.

God bless you, my friend. May Heaven welcome you with open arms.

Angela spun around, just in time to catch Sammie launching another attack. He leapt at her, intending to send her right after Tim, but she dodged aside and avoided the blow. So Sammie rushed her again, this time too fast to avoid, and knocked her to the ground. Angela rolled onto her rump, ready to face the next attack, and sure enough Sammie swung a claw-like foot toward her face. She dodged and rolled sideways onto her belly.

The next kick caught her square in the ribs. Something broke inside of her and suddenly she couldn't breathe. Sammie pranced around giggling with childish glee. Angela clawed at the carpet and tried to drag herself away, but the hot coals inside her lungs made moving impossible. No way could she get away. She was defenceless.

But she still held the ceremonial dagger.

Sammie stood over her, eyes swirling with malevolent darkness. "I'm bored with you now," he said. "I think you should die."

Sammie raised a foot as if to stomp on her skull, but his ankle returned to the floor benignly. He tried lifting his foot again, but the same thing happened. It soon became clear that something was impeding Sammie's movement.

Angela rolled onto her side and lifted her head. Frank lay on the floor behind Sammie with his arms wrapped around the boy's shins, forcing them together. "You need to pierce his feet, right? So bloody do it."

Angela clawed her way forwards on her belly, dagger out in front of her.

Frank squeezed Sammie's legs tighter so that his dirty feet overlapped. Angela raised the dagger, tip pointing down.

"I'll send you to suck Charles Crippley's cock, you self-righteous bitch," Sammie snarled.

"I'm a lesbian!" Angela spat and then brought it down with every last ounce of energy she had. The dagger pierced through the small bones and pliant flesh of Sammie's feet so forcefully that the tip embedded in the floorboards beneath the carpet. Sammie bellowed.

The floor and walls shook.

For a brief moment, Angela thought the volume of Sammie's voice would reduce her brain to mush and the house to ashes. Black smoke billowed off Sammie's flesh—his entire body was soot and a hurricane had come to disperse it.

Still on the ground, Angela watched in awe as the ceremonial dagger shifted upwards and slid out of the boy's pierced feet like pus from a zit. The steel blade popped out and pinwheeled across the carpet. With one last, final bellow, Sammie flew backwards through the air and hit the floor with a resounding thud!

His tiny body went still.

Angela shook, unable to take a full breath. Her vision blurred. She wondered if she would pass out, but managed to slowly climb back to her feet. Frank too got himself standing although he favoured his left leg. He limped towards her, looking up at one of the house's many windows. "Look," he said, pointing. "The sun is out."

The moon outside retreated as the sun rolled up to take its rightful place. Before they knew it, the day had arrived and the endless night was defeated. The house felt different. The malignant veil which had seemed to hang over everything, was finally lifted.

Angela got herself together and hurried over to Sammie. His tiny body had been through a terrible ordeal. She wasn't certain he would survive this, but she knelt down beside him and saw immediately that things were different. The boy's pallid skin had already begun to fill with colour. His crooked teeth were straighter. His dark, sunken eyes were now a pleasant green. The boy had been cleansed, body once more his own.

Frank moved beside Angela and placed a hand on her shoulder. "Is he...?"

"Sammie's alive," she assured him. "The Blood Exorcism worked. The demon has retreated. Sammie will be all right. Whatever that means."

"Thank God," Frank said, tears in his eyes.

"Yes," Angela agreed, smiling. There was a warmth inside her chest that had been absent for far too long. "Thank God."

Epilogue

A ngela lay tucked up in the luxurious four-poster bed of the Freidkin Suite. For the first time since she'd arrived, she actually enjoyed being at Raymeady Manor. Although a year of rest won't be enough to get over this week.

Angela had decided to stay for a few days to help Frank put everything in order. A thorough police investigation was under way, and both Angela and Frank had a lot of explaining to do. That was beyond her concern for now though. God had never stopped watching over her and whatever was meant to be would be. *I may have given up on him, but he never gave up on me. I'm sorry, Lord.*

The best news to have come out of the last couple of days was that Tim would pull through. His awkward landing took the biggest toll on his right leg and pelvis, snapping them like kindling, but his other injuries were far less severe—two broken ribs and a nasty concussion. He would live, albeit it consigned to a wheelchair. Tim's body might be injured, but she knew his bravery would do a massive amount to repair his damaged soul. He would have no regrets about coming back to save her, she was sure.

Sammie was also doing well. It turned out he was a very shy boy at heart, with a kind and playful personality. He'd stopped talking like an adult and now exercised the vocabulary one would expect from a ten-year-old. He looked infinitely healthier too—at least a stone heavier with his rosy skin filling out to become smooth and plump. His near-nakedness ceased and shorts and t-shirts became the norm. All in all, Samuel Raymeady seemed like quite a normal little boy. Considering what he'd been through, and that both his parents were dead, that was a miracle in and of itself.

Frank confided to Angela that he intended to fight for custody of the boy and raise him as best he could. Angela intended to help him with the cause in whatever way she could. Part of her even considered of re-joining the clergy, but it was something requiring more thought. For now, all I plan on doing is relaxing. I feel like my bones are filled with soup. And not nice soup like chicken or Oxtail, I'm talking vegetable broth and minestrone.

Despite it being early evening, Angela had decided she would turn in for the night. Frank was looking after Sammie so there was little to worry about. She got up from the bed and went into the bathroom, wanting to brush her teeth before having a long sleep. When she entered, the room was steamy, the shower in the en suite turned on. Angela frowned.

She padded over to the shower and reached inside to turn the knob. The water stopped with a splutter.

Then she turned back around and—

"Jesus!"

The sudden fright sent Angela reeling backwards, landing ass-first in the wet shower cubicle. The steam in the room was swirling and shifting, collecting around the contours of what looked like a human shape. An entity occupied the room with her and it was taking shape.

"Who-who are you?" she asked the steam cloud.

The vapour swirled and twisted, making up the curves of a round, humanoid head. The figure's voice was like dry leaves crackling. "I helped you once beforrre. Now you have helped meee."

"What? Who are you?"

"Chamuel. I am Chamuel. It was my power that helped you expel the demon inside Charles Crippley. I was there that day, at the church. I heeded your prayer. I helped you. And then I summoned you to help meeeee. And you have done sooooo. Thank you."

Angela shook her head and blinked the moisture from her eyes. "How did I help you, Chamuel?"

"You freed meee. The father Joseph brought me here, praying for an angel to watch over his son. I came to protect the boy, but found him fouled. I tried to cleanse the boy's soul, to save him from evil, but once inside I found no soul to save. I became trapped in the void where the boy's soul should have existed. A dark place. A wretched place. Devoid of any hope or joy. That boy is a place of emptiness."

Angela shook her head, trying to understand.

"The child made me his servant, abused my power and used it for himself. I tried to rot him from within, to sicken him, but he only used my influence to grow stronger. My torment inside of the boy was endless until you emancipated me. Thank youuu."

Angela's thought about the painting above the bed and the statue outside of Sammie's door—cherubs. Finally, she remembered what she had been trying to recall for the last several days. "Chamuel! I know you! You're the angel who expelled Adam from the Garden of Eden. One of the seven Archangels?"

"I am the Loving One; Archangel of Love and leader of the Cherubim. You freed me from Hell and returned me to Heaven, but your work is not yet done. Angela, the boy is malignant. He lacks a human soul."

"Sammie? He's... he's evil? He was never possessed."

The steam wisped and curled around Chamuel's spirit, bringing him more into shape. He looked like a rain-drenched statue as he continued speaking. "He is the purest evil. The Devil's own spawn. Damnation itself."

"God help me," Angela said, not wanting to believe it. "Sammie's the antichrist?"

"His nature was unknown to me until it was too late. I was imprisoned and helpless. Now I am free, but still unable to act. I can take no hand in this. It is mankind's burden. You must finish what you started, Angela Murs. Finish the Blood Exorcism."

"But I already finished it."

"No."

"The final stigmata? I need to pierce Sammie's side and kill him?"

There was no answer from Chamuel. The steam was again just steam. Angela dragged herself up from the shower floor and sprinted into the bedroom. She reached into her luggage and pulled out the cloth bundle containing the ceremonial dagger, but when she pulled opened the bundle, the dagger was gone. Only a dried bloodstain remained.

"No, no, no. Sammie has the dagger." Angela shuffled her feet into her shoes and crossed the room in three urgent strides. She ran out and headed for the staircase. She needed to warn Frank before it was too late.

She thanked the Lord when she found him on the floor below. He was taping up the broken railing that Tim had smashed through and fallen to the marble below.

He smiled when he saw her coming. "Ms Murs. Just trying to make this place safe again. Last thing we need is Samuel taking a fall after all we've been through to keep him from harm."

Angela ignored Frank's words. "Sammie wasn't possessed—I mean, he was, but not in the way we thought. It was an angel inside him, trying to help, not a demon. Sammie is the demon. The evil came from him. He has no soul, Frank. No soul."

Frank looked at her with concern. "Whoa, whoa, what are you talking about?"

"Sammie is... God, I can hardly say it. Sammie is the antichrist. It all makes sense. If he takes over Black Remedy one day, he'll be powerful enough to rule the world. All the signs were there, I just missed them. He's the bastard son of a stranger, destined to take on great power and responsibility."

Frank laughed. "Are you really saying Samuel is the Devil?"

"Yes!"

"But he's been fine since the exorcism. Everything worked out."

Angela shook her head in frustration. "The Devil deceives. He's pretending. It was Chamuel who was making Sammie ill, to try to warn us, or kill Sammie before he could grow into the man he's destined to be."

Frank still sounded incredulous. "So what are you suggesting?"

"We need to find the dagger and kill Sammie, but the dagger is gone. I think he's done something with it."

"Samuel has done nothing with the dagger," Frank said matter-of-factly.

"Frank, you're not listening to me."

"I hear you well enough." He produced the dagger from beneath his jacket and drove it deep into Angela's chest. "I know Sammie didn't take the dagger, because I took it."

Angela tried to speak but found her throat filled with blood. Frank shoved her through the gap in the railing and the ground went out from under her. The last thing she saw before the ground met her and her vision went black was the sight of Frank leaning over the balcony two floors above and mouthing the words, "I'm sorry."

* * *

Frank headed for Samuel's room at once, feeling sick at what he'd just done. Unfortunate, that Angela had insisted on staying behind. It had always been a matter of time until she figured it all out. She was smart. It only made Frank more aware of his own stupidity. Insane to think he hadn't seen what was right in front of his face the whole time.

Sammie was not just a little boy.

Samuel had confessed his true nature the evening after the Blood Exorcism. Frank had been stunned, but somewhere deep in his heart he knew Samuel Raymeady was the Devil's spawn. Yet, when he contemplated killing the boy and putting an end to his evil intentions, he found himself unable to. He loved the Raymeady family, and he loved Sammie. He had failed the boy so much already and there was nothing else that mattered. He had promised Jessica he would protect her son. Besides, there was already Hell on Earth; he'd seen it from his days in the army and every day since. Frank's eyes had been opened years ago, and he was not against the changes Sammie's eventual reign would bring. Things could not be any worse.

When Samuel had asked Frank to be his guardian until he was old enough to take the reins of the vehicle that would steer him towards world domination—Black Remedy Corporation—Frank had hesitantly agreed. He knew it would be an unsavoury job with questionable responsibilities—killing Angela had proved it—but he made his decision. Protecting Samuel Raymeady would be the last job he ever took, but he would see it through to the end. Frank had murdered for his country, so why not for a young boy he loved? Perhaps he could even manage to steer him away from the dark path before him.

Frank entered Samuel's room with a melancholy sigh. The boy—his soon to be adopted son—was watching South Park, but pressed pause when he saw Frank entering. Frank understood now why the boy loved that particular show so much. It highlighted all the darker parts of humanity, but also gave clever insight into politics and the public's unspoken view of things. It was reading between the lines and understanding the underbelly of society that would help Samuel gain control over the world.

"Everything okay, Frank?" Samuel asked with a polite smile.

"There was a slight issue, but I dealt with it."

Sammie nodded. "Shame, I'll surely miss our resident priest. Still, there will be little need for preachers, in time. The world will have a new God to worship and will need to heed only one voice—mine."

Frank swallowed a lump in his throat and sat down on a chair beside the boy who would one day become head of the world's largest corporation, and perhaps even mankind itself. The world would not know what hit it.

But oh how he loved the boy.

END

Iain Rob Wright is one of the UK's most successful horror and suspense writers, with novels including the critically acclaimed, THE FINAL WINTER; the disturbing bestseller, ASBO; and the wicked screamfest, THE HOUSEMATES.

His work is currently being adapted for graphic novels, audio books, and foreign audiences. He is an active member of the Horror Writer Association and a massive animal lover.

www.iainrobwright.com
FEAR ON EVERY PAGE

Made in the USA
Middletown, DE
25 April 2019